I0760667

# THE PERFECT GETAWAY

KIERSTEN MODGLIN

Copyright © 2020 by Kiersten Modglin
All rights reserved.
No part of this book may be reproduced in any form or by any electronic or mechanical means, including information storage and retrieval systems, without written permission from the author, except for the use of brief quotations in a book review.
This is a work of fiction. Names, characters, places, and incidents are either the product of the author's imagination or are used fictitiously. Any resemblance to locales, events, business establishments, or actual persons—living or dead—is entirely coincidental.

www.kierstenmodglinauthor.com
Cover Design: Tadpole Designs
Editing: Three Owls Editing
Proofreading: My Brother's Editor
Formatting: Tadpole Designs
First Print Edition: 2020
First Electronic Edition: 2020

*This book is dedicated to hope—*
*may we have it, may we give it, may we fight for it with everything we have.*

# CHAPTER ONE

## LAURA

The envelope was white, our names and address scrawled across the top in messy handwriting. I stopped when I reached it in the stack of mail. Who wrote letters by hand anymore?

I tried to think back to the last time we'd received anything handwritten—utterly baffled that I couldn't even remember—as I tore the envelope open, laying the stack of mail on the table. Brad looked up from his coffee and laptop, noticing what I assumed was a worried look on my face.

"What's that?" he asked, setting the mug down to give me his full attention. I chewed my lip, tearing the envelope the rest of the way.

"I don't kn—ah, just junk mail." Relief and disappointment filled me, but I tried to keep it hidden. What had I expected anyway? The picture of a tropical island—the couple on the front dressed all in white, her blonde hair blowing in the wind as she kissed him, and her hand on his stubbled chin—taunted me. "Apparently we just *have* to get away," I teased, winking at him as I tossed it back into the stack and lifted the electric bill, grimacing. "The electric's nearly a hundred more this month. We're going to have to turn the air up."

I laid the bill back into the stack and walked away, back toward the sink where I'd been loading the dishwasher a moment before the mail had arrived. Just before I turned on the water, I heard my husband say, "Now, hang on a second. This is actually addressed to us."

I looked over my shoulder, narrowing my eyes at him. "What is—*oh,* the resort thing? Yeah, so? Most of the junk in there is addressed to us. Doesn't make it any less junk."

He shook his head, turning the back of the brochure around to face me. "It's addressed to us. The offer. It says," he turned it back around to read, "there's a new resort opening up in the Caribbean, and they're looking for new couples to try it out, completely free, all expenses paid, in exchange for a review before they officially open."

I shook my head. "Yeah, right. All they need is our credit card numbers, socials, eighteen small payments of one hundred thirty-nine ninety-five." I snorted. "It's a scam, Brad. No one *gives* you a free vacation."

Before we could say anything else, we were interrupted by the sound of tiny footsteps hurrying down the stairs of our townhome. I looked up, watching as our children descended the stairs, hurrying through the open-concept living room and into the kitchen.

"Elena, sweetheart, what have you gotten all over your face?" I asked, giving up on dishes for the time being as I bent over to swipe at my daughter's purple cheek.

"It's marker," she admitted. "I didn't do it."

I gave her a skeptical look, then glanced toward Britta. "Well?"

Her older sister pressed her lips together. "We wanted to be kittens. I told her we shouldn't do it."

I giggled, looking across the room at Brad, who was already

lost in his computer, and lifted our daughter toward the counter, grabbing a paper towel and wetting it to clean her cheeks.

"I think this might be legit, Laura," I heard Brad say again.

"What?" I asked, already forgetting what we were talking about before the interruption.

"The resort. When I look them up, *Isla del Amor,* it just brings up a landing page where you can enter an email to be notified when they're open and ready for booking. It says they'll open next summer."

I put Elena back on the ground, looking over at my husband, who'd taken a break from his work to show me the screen. The image was nearly identical to the brochure—a happy couple, surrounded by sun and sand. I looked around at the kitchen I desperately needed to clean and sighed, walking toward the computer for a closer look.

"I want to go on vacation!" Britta yelled. "Are we going to visit Gramma and Gramp?"

I shook my head. "No."

At the same time, Brad said, "Maybe."

I looked at him, hands on my hips and lips pressed together as Britta squealed with delight. Seeing my expression, he closed the computer and addressed her. "Maybe, sweetheart, but maybe not. Mommy and I were just talking, okay?"

Her shoulders slumped. "But why can't we? We haven't seen them since Christmas."

"Your mom and I are going to talk about it, okay?" He grinned. "Now, what do you say to Dad's famous grilled cheese for lunch?"

The girls climbed up in their chairs at the table while Brad slid his laptop into his bag, the conversation momentarily dropped. I picked up the mail from the table and moved it to the counter as he made his way across the room to start lunch.

I stared down at the brochure on top, reading the side I hadn't paid any attention to before.

***Isla del Amor —***
***Where your paradise is our destination***

**Brad and Laura,**
**You have been nominated to take part in an exclusive, all-expenses-paid trip to the brand-new Isla del Amor on June 10th through the 16th.**
**At our island of love, you will enjoy a six-night stay in one of our private paradise huts, just steps away from the ocean. During the day, spend your time getting pampered, enjoying lavish cuisine crafted by our world-renowned chef, relaxing on the beach, and much more!**

**This trip is all-inclusive and 100% free.**
**The only thing we will ask is that you provide a review detailing your time on our island for future guests when we are open to the public.**
**Prepare to disconnect from your everyday life, reconnect with your partner, and enjoy yourselves like you never have before.**
**We request your response by June 3rd, so that we may fill your spots should you choose not to attend.**

**We hope to see you soon!**

**Amor,**
**Your Isla del Amor Team**

At the bottom, there was an email address and phone number where you could reserve your spot. I read through the message again. Brad was right; it did sound like there wouldn't be a catch...but there had to be, right? It wasn't like we couldn't have used a vacation. Between work and the kids, the chance to reconnect with my husband was incredibly tempting, but could we afford the time off from our busy schedules? And what would we do with the girls? There was also a very big part of me that still worried this was a scam of some sort. It just didn't make sense. Who ever heard of a completely free vacation?

Besides that, I read the first line again... Even if it was real, *who had nominated us?*

# CHAPTER TWO

## NICK

"Good morning, handsome." I felt her hands snake around me, rousing me from sleep. I inhaled sharply, stretching my arms as I looked over my shoulder.

"Good morning," I said through a stretch, reaching up to kiss her lips. She remained on top of me as I rolled over, her blonde hair hanging down over my chest. "What are you doing up so early?"

She grinned, but it fell short of her eyes. "I've been up for a while. I wanted to get my meditation in before we left. Did you forget?"

"Forget?" I rubbed an eye with my fist. She was most beautiful like this, in the few quiet moments we shared each morning—no makeup, fresh skin, messy hair. I took in the sight of her before shaking my head. "Of course I didn't forget."

"Do you even know what I'm talking about?"

"If I said I did, would you believe me?"

She groaned, sitting up. "We're supposed to have cake tasting at Le Crème."

I glanced over at the clock, grasping her hand where it rested on my chest. "I thought that was Monday?"

"You asked me to reschedule for today so you didn't have to miss work," she said, twisting a piece of her hair around her finger.

I sighed. She was right, of course, and it had only just slipped my mind. "You're right. I'm sorry." I pushed myself up so I was propped on my stack of pillows. "I didn't forget, I swear. I was just half asleep."

She looked unconvinced but didn't argue. "I'm going to take Winston out for his walk," she said, shaking her head playfully. "I want you up and getting ready."

I mock-saluted her. "As you wish."

With that, she was up off the bed. She pulled on her black bike shorts and a loose-fitting pink T-shirt before tossing her hair up into a sleek ponytail. I watched her cross the room toward our bathroom and heard the water running as she brushed her teeth and spritzed perfume—she was the only woman I knew who wore perfume to work out.

She reentered the room, staring me down. "You should be up..."

I sat up, throwing the covers off my legs. "I'm going to get a shower now. Give me twenty minutes, and I'm all yours."

Her smile warmed. "I'm counting on it."

With that, she grabbed the rhinestone leash off the top of her tall, white dresser and marched out the door, the small, white fuzzball of a dog at her feet.

As I climbed in the shower, letting the hot water wake me up, I tried to focus on the task at hand. We needed to pick out a cake, I still needed to name a best man—it wasn't easy when your best friend was a woman.

At that, I thought of Laura. If I asked her, I knew she'd do it for me. Like I'd done for her. She'd be my best *woman*—I'd have to come up with a better name—like I'd been her *man* of honor if I asked, but I desperately didn't want to ask.

I'd been avoiding it for weeks now, trying to convince myself that asking one of my brothers to do it would be easier. *Not likely.* One was deployed, and there was no guarantee he'd make it back for the big day at all, let alone for the tux fittings or whatever else was required of my best man. The other, Danny, was an ass who I'd just as soon not invite at all. The fact that we hadn't spoken in over ten years and he lived just a few miles away did little to assure me he'd be up for the job.

Twenty minutes later, I'd stepped out of the shower, drying my face and hair, when I heard quick footsteps rushing my way. I opened the bathroom door, worried something was wrong, and stared as Megan rushed in, Winston in one hand, his pink leash hanging on the ground, and a white envelope in the other. Her grin was unbearably chipper.

"What—"

"I can't believe you did this!" she cried, interrupting me.

"What did I do?" I asked, taking the envelope from her as I tried to understand what was happening. There was a postcard inside, a couple on an island on one side with a fancy script: ***Isla del Amor.***

"You entered us to win a honeymoon, didn't you?" she squealed, squeezing my arm with her free hand. "An island in the Caribbean. Oh Nicky, it's amazing!"

"H-hold on…" *Shit.* Now I was going to have to actually do something like that. "I haven't—" I flipped the card over, reading it carefully. "We were *nominated?* Hang on a second, Megan, I didn't do this. I don't even know what it's talking about. I've never heard of this place."

Her face fell, but only slightly as she pulled the envelope back to her and read over it, her green eyes darting back and forth across each line of text. My mind swirled with possibilities.

"Then how did we win? *I* didn't do it."

"I don't know," I said skeptically, moving around beside her as I wrapped the towel around my waist. We read the invitation together again. "Could this be one of those timeshare things? They get us on an island, and we have to listen to sales pitches for days?"

She shook her head. "I don't think so. What good would that do? Are you sure you didn't do this? Maybe you've forgotten."

I scoffed. "I would've remembered something like this. Besides, the trip's in less than a month. We won't even be married by then. It wouldn't make for a very good honeymoon."

She twisted her lips. "Well, I think we should go either way, don't you? We can't say no to a free vacation."

I couldn't believe she was serious. It sounded ridiculous. People didn't just give you a free vacation without there being some sort of catch. *Beautiful, naïve, Megan.* "I don't know, sweetheart. It could be a scam. I'll have to do some research."

She kissed my cheek. "You will, though, won't you? We have a few days to respond. If it's real, we're going, right? It'll be the *perfect* way to get away and de-stress before the wedding. We *need* this, Nicky." She purred my name, leaning in to kiss my lips, though my eyes were still trained on the paper in her hands.

"I'll look into it, but no promises, okay?"

She pushed her lips into a pout. "Sometimes good things just happen, okay? We shouldn't look a gift horse in the mouth." She reached down, pulling my towel from my waist and placing Winston on the ground. "Now, why don't you finish getting ready. We're going to be late!" She squealed again and handed the envelope to me, pulling out her phone. "I need a new bathing suit… Do you want one? You didn't get a new one last year, did you?"

I murmured something, not even sure what answer I gave her as I flipped the paper over in my hands, looking for the catch. It couldn't be real. It just couldn't. But how was I going to prove it? And why had we been chosen in the first place?

# CHAPTER THREE

## NATASHA

The front door slammed, and I recoiled, my body tensing at the sound from the kitchen.

"Nolan!" I screamed, shutting off the faucet so he could hear me.

"Huh?" came the response, passive and barely listening if I knew him at all.

"How many times have I told you not to slam that door? You're going to break the glass." I turned around, drying my hands on a towel as my son entered the room. "And take off your shoes when you come into my house." I groaned. "If I hadn't done it myself, I'd swear you were raised by farm animals."

He watched me, his expression turning from apathy to irritation. "You act like I just do it to annoy you."

"Sometimes I think you do," I snapped. "And pull up your pants unless you want me to buy you a belt."

He jerked his sagging jeans up with one angry fist, a wrinkle forming on his forehead. "What's for dinner?"

I scoffed, turning back to the dishes as I scrubbed the plate caked with ketchup harder than necessary. "Whatever you want to fix yourself, I guess."

"What's the matter with you?"

I sighed because the problem really wasn't with him and he knew it, but I wasn't about to admit it right then. "What's the matter is that my son can't seem to treat this beautiful house I pay for him to live in with respect," I said, my upper lip curled.

"*Beautiful's* a bit of an exaggeration—"

*"Excuse me?"* I slammed the plate down. This boy was going to be the death of me. "What the hell do you know about—"

"What is going on in here?" Jaren demanded, walking into the room dressed in a sweat-stained white T-shirt and jeans. His forehead gleamed with sweat as he laid his toolbox on the kitchen table. "I can hear you two arguing from outside."

"We weren't arguing. I was informing *your* son that he needs to take his shoes off before he goes traipsing across my floors. I just shampooed the carpets last week, and between the two of you," I glanced at my husband's grease covered shoes, "I'm already going to need to do it again."

Jaren looked at me, then at Nolan, his lips pressed together with a sigh. "Just take your shoes off, son. Do as your mother says. Don't make it more difficult than it has to be."

"Dad, I just walked in. If she'd just asked—"

"Why should I have to ask? You're seventeen years old! I've been telling you your whole—"

"Enough," Jaren said, holding out a hand to stop me mid-sentence. "Do what you're told, Nolan."

Nolan's head leaned back with an irritated sigh. "Whatever, man, this is bullsh—"

*"Language!"* I chided, cutting him off.

He disappeared from the room and, when he was far enough away, Jaren sank down in a chair, untying his boots and plopping them on the floor. I watched the dried mud fall onto my freshly swept tile. "You know, if you actually made an effort to do it, he might, too."

"For God's sake, Natasha, I just walked in the damn door. I sided with you, okay? Isn't that enough for this exact moment?" I shook my head but didn't say anything else. "What's gotten into you anyway? You still mad about this morning?"

I hmphed. "Nope."

He stood, walking across the room and pulling open the fridge. He grabbed a canned beer from the top shelf and popped it open. "You know we can't afford to take the time off."

"I know."

"We'd do it if we could."

"If you say so."

He rested a hand on the open refrigerator door. "Don't be like that."

I turned off the water again, drying my hands and spinning around to face him. "I'm not being like anything, Jaren. We both know what this is..." I lowered my voice. "We both know we're just counting down the days until he turns eighteen. It was a stupid suggestion anyway."

His jaw tensed. It wasn't unspoken—we'd said it aloud many times to each other during a fight, but it may have been the first time it had been said calmly. Either way, it was true, and we *did* both know it.

"Don't be like that. It's not that simple. We can't afford the time off," he said, shaking his head slowly, his voice soft. "And, even if we could, do you trust leaving him here for a week by himself while we're out of the country?"

I looked in the direction our son had just headed, my chest tight. The very idea terrified me. We'd raised a good boy, though I felt like I didn't recognize who he'd become in the past year, but he was a teenager. With teenage ideas and teenage plans. I knew what would happen if we left him alone—and dirt on my carpets would be the least of my concerns. "Like I said, it was a dumb idea." Truth was, the very idea of getting away from the day-to-day was enough to push me to do it. Even with a husband who drove me insane. Even with a teenage son who was sure to cause problems for me to fix upon our return. The last vacation we'd taken was so far back, I could hardly remember it. I deserved the chance to get away, but no one would ever see that. It wouldn't be mentioned. Jaren wouldn't work it out as a treat for me. I knew that like I knew it would be me cooking dinner in an hour when Nolan still hadn't resurfaced from his room to do it and my husband still sat on the couch waiting. It was always me.

I walked across the room, lifting the white envelope—our names scrawled across the front—from its place. "I just thought it would be like...I don't know." I inhaled sharply. "We never had a honeymoon of our own. We haven't been on a vacation since Nolan was a toddler. We deserve it, don't we? A chance to enjoy ourselves for once?"

Jaren laughed under his breath. "That's for sure."

I stared at him hopefully, watching his expression for any variation that would show he was considering it.

He wasn't. I tossed the envelope into the trash. "Just forget it." With that, I walked out of the room, leaving my husband with the refrigerator door still standing open, his gaze locked on the trash can.

*It was a dumb idea in the first place.*

# CHAPTER FOUR

## ANDY

I rushed into the house, the white envelope in my hand, nearly exploding from joy.

"Guess what?" I asked before I'd even made it into my bedroom. She was sitting on the edge of my bed, typing on her phone—posting something on her Instagram, most likely. "Guess what?" I repeated, drawing her attention to me finally. She looked up, her dark hair tied back in a tight bun. *God, she is so beautiful.* She always looked like a ballerina like that, though she hated for me to mention it. "This was in the mail when I got home from work." I couldn't stop my eyes from traveling to where the fabric of her dress stretched too tight across her chest.

"What?" she asked, placing her phone on the edge of the bed. Her gaze traveled to the envelope in my hand, her eyes widening as she stood. "Oh my God. Is that what I think it is?"

She took the envelope from my hands, and I ruined the surprise before she could see the brochure. *"They chose us!"*

She grinned, a melancholy look filling her face as she ran her fingers across the front of the brochure, over the couple and the script of the resort's name.

*Isla del Amor*—Spanish, maybe? Or French?

Either way, I didn't care because we'd gotten it! We'd been chosen. Or, rather, *she'd* been chosen. I was just lucky enough to be her plus one. She flipped it over, reading the instructions for RSVPing.

"It sounds perfect. I can't believe they chose us."

She looked up, blinking slowly behind thick, dark lashes. I could get lost in her eyes so easily. "It's super exciting."

"Are you okay?" I asked, shocked to see her smile fading so quickly.

"No, of course I am. It's just...I'm shocked, I guess. I mean, I get trips like this all the time, but I'm feeling really grateful to be able to bring you and your friends along. It's going to be magical." She pressed up on her tiptoes, leaning in until our lips met, enveloping me with her honey scent.

When we broke apart, she smiled again, her eyes closed as if she were soaking in the moment.

"Do you think they got their invitations yet? I should've warned them they might be coming."

She shook her head, placing a hand on mine. "We didn't want to get their hopes up, right? Trips like these only go to the biggest bloggers and influencers—"

"Which you *are*," I insisted.

Her cheeks pinkened. "Well, I don't like to get ahead of myself."

"So, should I call them? They're going to be so excited! When is it again?"

"We'll need to head out on June ninth, and that'll put us getting to the island on the tenth," she said, without looking at the invitation. "Maybe you should invite them out to dinner again? We could discuss everything in person. Besides, you're still taking me to dinner tonight, right? I didn't get all dressed up for nothing."

I kissed her lips again, almost interrupting the sentence. My hands wrapped around her waist. When she pulled away, I grinned, resting my forehead on hers. "Yes, duh. You look hot, babe. And dinner is a great idea." I kissed her again. "You're brilliant, you know that?"

Her smile was stiff. "You're just saying that because I get you free stuff." It was a joke, but a poor one. I'd never felt the way I felt about Emily, about anyone else—at least not in years. There was something so fascinating about her. Aside from being easily the most beautiful woman I'd ever been with, she was so free and fun it was contagious. She made life more interesting, made *me* more interesting.

I gripped her shoulders. "You know that isn't true, right?" She had to. "I'd still think you're amazing even without all of… this." I gestured toward the phone and invitation in her hand. I'd dated so many women in my life—so many—but no one had ever pushed me the way Emily did. Made me work for their attention. Made me appreciate the chase. I wanted her to know how serious I was about her, and the island was a big step for me. I hadn't spent the night with a woman since college—I'd refused. So agreeing to stay nearly a week with this woman was a big deal. Didn't she realize that? God, even my thoughts were irritating. *Who am I becoming? What is she doing to me?*

"Yes, I know," she teased, nudging me with her shoulder. Her phone chimed, and she glanced down, her eyes growing wide. "My Insta was just tagged by Chenise Taylor." She squealed, hugging her phone and walking away from me. "Oh my *God!*"

She didn't elaborate on who she was talking about, but she didn't need to. With Emily's ever-growing career in travel blogging, she was a huge social media influencer, constantly being tagged or spotlighted by any number of huge names in the industry. I tried my best to keep up and stay supportive of her dream—even when I didn't fully understand it. She was young—still full of hopes and desires most people my age had long since given up on. Every time I saw her eyes light up, I promised myself I'd never let her give up. She deserved to have everything.

She was across the room by the time I looked at the envelope she'd placed back in my hand.

This was going to be the trip of a lifetime…

My friends would owe me big time.

# CHAPTER FIVE

## LAURA

Brad was chattering away on his phone to a client when we arrived at the restaurant. I walked behind him, lost to my own thoughts. He'd been arguing heatedly with a coworker most of the way over, so I was grateful to hear his voice calming now that we were in public. We enjoyed our regular nights out with friends, and I was so thankful we'd all made them a priority. Despite everyone's busy schedules and lives, we never missed a chance to get together. It was nice that a group with so little in common could enjoy each other's company so much.

We picked our usual spot as Brad ended his call, sliding around the empty, oversized booth to take the usual place at the far end. If I knew my friends like I thought I did, Nick and Megan would be next, just a few minutes behind us. Natasha and Jaren would follow behind—probably fighting as they walked in the door. Last would, of course, be Andy and whatever girl he was bringing with him this time.

Without asking, the waitress spotted us, bringing over drinks for everyone without having to ask.

"Hello, Lila," I said as she placed my white wine in front of me. "You've gotten your hair cut since we saw you last."

The girl put a hand to her short, auburn hair self-consciously. "Yes, I did. I wanted a bit of a change, you know?"

"It looks lovely."

"Thank you," she said, sliding Brad his mug of beer. She put out an ale for Natasha and a pitcher of beer, placing two empty glasses in front of Jaren and Andy's seats for them to split. As she set down a glass of Jack and Coke for Nick and the red wine for Megan, I heard their voices.

"Hey, Lila," Nick said, sliding into the seat next to me as he greeted the waitress. She smiled at him shyly, then lifted the tray.

"Hey, guys. I'll be back to take your food orders when everyone gets here."

"Thank you," we all said at once then laughed.

Nick leaned over me, shaking Brad's hand and giving me a one armed hug. "Hey, y'all, sorry we're late."

I glanced at my watch as I hugged him back before waving at Megan. "You aren't."

Megan shook her head. "It was my fault. I had a cake in the oven, and I didn't time it right. I have a baby shower tomorrow, and it's come down to baking it at the last minute."

"Aww," I cooed. "That's so sweet. Anyone you know? Or a customer?"

"A customer," she confirmed. "The store's been so busy, we're hardly able to keep enough baked for our customers that shop during the day. Custom orders have started having to be pushed back, and I'm doing them at home quite often." She grimaced, taking a sip of her wine. "It's looking like I'm going to have to shell out for an extra oven, but I just keep waiting for the other shoe to drop and business to slow down."

"Which it's not going to," Nick told her, nuzzling his nose into her cheek.

I smiled, looking down. "Well, that's great. That...you're having so many orders. Not a bad problem to have, right?"

She chuckled. "Not at all."

"How did cake tasting go? Did you guys decide on a flavor?" I asked. It shocked me that Nick had convinced his fiancée, the baker, to let someone else make their wedding cake, but if she was so busy, it made sense. Not everyone was as obsessive about control as I was, I guessed.

Megan looked at Nick, her cheeks flushing pink. "We're torn between two, I think. Lemon and carrot. But I also really loved the double fudge." She laughed. "Or the red velvet."

"Well, you have time to think it over, right?"

"Definitely. A few weeks, at least, before they need our decision," she said, taking a sip of her wine.

"How's business, Brad? Glad tax season's over?" Nick asked, glancing across the table at my husband.

Brad nodded, sliding his phone into his pocket as he lifted his beer from the table, a slick ring of condensation in its place. "You have no idea, man," he said with a hearty laugh. "Starting to get back to business as usual…but next year will be here before I know it."

Nick laughed. "I tell you what, your business slows down, and then we pick up. Isn't that right, Laura? People get that income tax and come straight in for whatever dental work they've been putting off all year." He shook his head.

I nodded in agreement. "We can't seem to keep any slots for walk-ins over the summer, that's for sure. It's just a shame, you know? Dental insurance really isn't that costly."

"But it doesn't cover much, does it?" Megan asked, then covered her mouth. "Sorry, was that rude?" She patted Nick's cheek. "Speaking as someone with quite a sweet tooth, I've always heard such horror stories about it. I've paid out of pocket my whole life."

Nick inhaled sharply. "Well, some of it's better than—" The schpiel I'd heard him give to our patients over and over was interrupted as Natasha's voice pierced through the crowded restaurant. I could always pick out her tones in a crowded room. I think at that point, we all could've.

"That's not the point, Jaren," she grumbled. "The point is that he needs to be home when we tell him to be home. If you keep letting him get away with breaking curfew, it's just going to get worse."

"The boy's nearly eighteen, Natasha. What do you want me to do? Ground him? We can't do that."

"Like hell we can't. He's nearly eighteen living under our roof, is he not? I don't care if he's forty. Rules are rules, and I won't have my son running around all hours of the day and night."

"I just don't think there's a lot we can do. You know Marcus already said he could move in. You enforce too many rules, and that's exactly—"

"That boy ain't movin' in with his broke friends, and you know it. It's a threat because he knows you don't want that to happen. If you keep giving in—"

"What am I supposed to—" Jaren stopped talking, rubbing his forehead with exhaustion, as he seemed to realize we were all watching them get closer to our table.

"Hey, everybody, sorry we're late," Natasha said. She was still dressed in her jeans and black polo, with the logo from the restaurant where she worked sewn into the upper shoulder.

"It's okay, love," I said, as Jaren slid in next to Brad and Natasha took the outside seat. I reached up, squeezing her hand across the table. "Good to see you."

Her nose crinkled at me as she smiled back. "You too, doll." She sighed, and I watched the calm wash over her as she fell into place in our group. Raised by a single military father, Natasha came across tough and unbending, but I'd seen her break. I knew the softness with which she held her son during the first few days of his life; I'd watched her cry on the day we put her father in the ground. She was my best friend, aside from

Nick, and my closest confidant. It was just necessary to get past the hard outer shell to appreciate her the most.

"Work's good?" Nick asked Jaren, who was pouring some of the beer from the pitcher into his glass.

"Hm? Oh, yeah. Busy as always," he said, setting the pitcher down and taking a drink. "You guys?"

Brad and Nick nodded, mumbling about their busy schedules. Megan reached in her purse, pulling out a pink baggie, and I tensed. *Not again.*

"Jaren, I brought you a few more of those cowboy cookies you liked so much. We had a few extra at the shop." She smiled sweetly, sliding the bag across the table. Jaren's eyes shot toward Natasha, but their exchanged glance was interrupted by Megan again.

"Oh, and Natasha, I just love your earrings. Where did you get them?"

Natasha's answer came hesitantly as Jaren pulled the pink bag of cookies toward him awkwardly. "Thanks. They're from Target."

"They're adorable. I love the simplicity."

Natasha nodded, her hand moving instinctively toward her earrings. "Thanks." As sickeningly sweet as Megan was, there wasn't an ounce of ill-will in her words. She was just *that nice.* When Nick introduced her to our group a year ago, we'd thought it was a put-on because she was the newbie and she wanted to impress us, but a year later, she was still doing all that she'd done before. She always brought Jaren, who had an unmatched sweet tooth, new desserts to try, she sent baskets of flowers and goodies to Natasha and me at work, she donated constantly to the charity Brad ran, and she sent all her friends and customers to Andy's garage whenever they needed repairs. Some of her gestures were big, some were small, but she was kind as if it were an instinct and that was very clearly just who she was.

"So," Brad said, interrupting the awkwardness with a hint of humor in his tone, "who do we think Andy will show up with tonight?"

We all exchanged knowing glances. As much as we loved Andy, there was no denying his playboy ways.

"I'm going blonde," Natasha said, taking the first sip of her ale. "He had the brunette last time."

"I thought last time was the redhead?" Nick asked, folding his hands in front of him at the table.

"Amber?" Megan offered, though the rest of us had given up remembering names long ago. There were too many to even attempt it anymore. Once, he'd brought one girl to a brunch and then another to an evening barbecue—two in one day. I had no idea how he managed to keep it straight.

"No," Jaren said quickly, "I mean, yes, probably, but no, the redhead wasn't last. She was before the one with really short hair. Remember, he dated the one with red hair on Valentine's Day."

"Where did the British one fit in?" Brad asked.

"Wasn't she with us when we went to the lake?" Jaren asked.

"Ahh, yeah," Nick said, stroking his chin as he thought back, and I knew he was picturing the tiny bikini our men had all appreciated with way too much enthusiasm, much to our annoyance.

"Well, don't give yourselves strokes thinking too hard," Natasha said. "We don't have to wait very long to find out." She pointed toward the window, where Andy's head could be seen just above the dark strip of tint from the restaurant's logo.

He pulled the door open, stepping back so his date could walk in—always the serial dating gentlemen—and I sucked in a breath.

"Is that—"

"No way," Nick said, shaking his head.

"Holy hell," Natasha whispered.

"Emily!" Megan cried out, reaching out for a hug as the familiar face came into view.

I met Natasha's eyes, returning her dubious glance. *What the hell?* In the twenty-two years I'd known Andy, I'd *never* seen him date the same girl twice. He was a non-committal dater, who changed women the way he changed his clothes. So to see him returning with not only a familiar face, but the face we'd seen the last time we all got together, was such a shock.

Emily slid into the booth next to Megan, leaving Andy at the end. "What's wrong? You all look like you've seen a ghost," she said when she broke out of Megan's hug.

I forced myself to breathe, laughing along with the rest of the group.

"It's so good to see you," Nick said.

"How're things, Andy?" Brad asked from across the table.

"Things are good." He gave a happy nod. "You guys? How're the girls?"

"They're great. Growing like little weeds," Brad said.

"Emily, how are you?" I asked her.

She beamed from her seat, her black hair slicked back in a high ponytail, thick eyeliner and a dark, maroon lip I couldn't have pulled off if I tried. Then again, she was almost literally half my age and stunningly gorgeous. Even more beautiful than most of the women Andy usually dated, and that was saying something.

"I'm great, thanks, Laura. How are you? Oh my gosh, you look so pretty."

I felt heat rush to my face, though I knew she was only being polite. "Thank you. I'm doing well."

As they settled into their seats, Lila was back to our table in a flash.

"Um," Emily pointed to the empty place in front of her. "I'm the only one who didn't get a drink."

"Right," Lila said, looking at Andy uncomfortably. "I wasn't sure who, er, I mean what, um—sorry, what can I get you?"

"I'll take a cosmo please," Emily said, clicking her painted black nails on the table.

Lila nodded, without writing it down. "I'll get that put in and be right back to take your orders."

When she disappeared, Andy looked at Emily, his eyes bright. "So...can we get to the elephant in the room."

She pressed her lips into a tight smile. "I know you're ready. Go ahead. Tell them."

*Oh my God, she's pregnant.* Natasha's shocked gaze met mine again, and I could practically hear her screaming internally.

"So, as you all know, Emily is a pretty big deal in the travel blogging scene," Andy said, clasping his hands in front of him. He looked as if he were going to explode, his cheeks flushed red. His eyes traveled around the circle, waiting for us to acknowledge it.

"Right."

"Yes."

"Go on," we all chimed in, realizing he was waiting.

"Well, a few months ago, she got word that a new, private resort was opening up in the Caribbean, and she was one of the first bloggers to get to sign up for it. But, the thing is, they're doing twelve weeks of trial runs before it opens and they're only inviting select groups on the island for a week each, so it was a major long shot." He looked at her, just as it hit me what they were saying. "But we just found out she got accepted! And, well, of course, they want groups, right? So, we thought, what better group than this one?" He held his arms out, waiting for a reaction.

We hesitated as a group, and I saw the eyes traveling around—Jaren and Nick, Brad and I...

"Wait, what?" I asked.

At the same time, Natasha said, "So that was you?"

"The invitations?" Megan asked, looking up at Nick.

Andy's face fell. "You already got them?"

"You're the ones who invited us?" Jaren asked, pointing at them.

"Yeah!" Andy said, his excitement back. "I thought we'd hear back before you, but…isn't that great? Guys, it's an all-expenses-paid trip to a private island! Why aren't you more excited?"

"Andy, we," I looked at Brad, who looked as uncomfortable as I felt, "look, it's a sweet offer, Emily. Honestly. We just, we can't really afford to take the time off—"

"Oh, come on," Andy scoffed. "You guys are your own bosses. If you can't get the time off, who could?"

"Yeah, man," Brad said, "but we're crazy busy at work right now. Even if we wanted to take the time off—"

"What, you couldn't?" Andy's brow furrowed. "You're seriously telling me you are going to pass up a free week on a *private island*? A free trip to paradise, and we have no takers?"

"We have the kids," Brad said. "We'd have to get a sitter, and that's not going to be easy for a full week."

"And Laura and I are swamped at work. Plus, Megan's been baking at home because she's so behind…"

Andy looked at Jaren. "What about you, man? You guys are always talking about how you want to take vacations but something's always coming up so you can't afford them. Everything's included! Food, stay, flight over, everything. And Nolan doesn't need a sitter." His eyes lit up. "Hey, maybe Nolan could watch your kids!" He looked toward us again, and my stomach tensed at the thought.

Jaren twisted his mouth. "Yeah, I mean, it'd be great, but can we afford to take the time off work? If I'm not working, I'm not getting paid."

"And we're short-staffed as it is," Natasha pointed out. "Until Erica gets back from maternity leave, I don't know if I can ask for any time off."

"You're the manager," Andy argued.

"Yes, but I don't get to say when I come and go if we're short-staffed. Being there is my job," she said quickly, shaking her head. "I'm sorry, Andy."

I watched Jaren, watching her with an incredulous expression. Andy dropped his hands to the table, his jaw dropping open. "Okay, so...so, *none* of you want to go?"

He looked to his right, past Emily, to Megan, then Nick, then me, then Brad, then Jaren, then Natasha. At first, no one spoke. Feeling incredibly guilty, I leaned forward.

"It's not that we," I moved a hand between Brad and me to show I was only speaking for us, "don't *want* to go, it's just that it seems like we won't be able to make it work."

"But have you even tried?" he asked, obviously disappointed. "Come on, the Brad and Laura I knew in college wouldn't have turned this down. Is this what becoming adults has done to us? Come on, guys, life is short, right? It's so short, and we can't just sit around saying no to things that aren't convenient. This trip," he laughed dryly, "this trip is an opportunity of a lifetime."

"All right, we'll go," I heard Nick say, causing me to dart my gaze in his direction.

Andy's face lit up as Megan's did. "You will?"

Nick threw an arm over Megan's shoulders. "Yeah, why not? We could use a practice honeymoon, don't you think?"

She leaned her head onto his shoulder. "Oh, Nicky! Yes, it will be perfect." She sat back up, resting her hands on Emily's shoulder. "Thank you so much for thinking of us, honestly. I'm just over the moon about this experience."

Emily smiled at her, nodding gently. "Of course. It was my pleasure. It'll be good to travel with some familiar faces."

"Okay, so who else is in? We've got two on board," Andy said, patting the table excitedly as Lila reappeared with Emily's bright pink cocktail.

"Sorry, guys. I'll be right back to take your orders," she said, dashing to the table across from us with the rest of the drinks on her full tray.

When she walked away, Natasha looked at Jaren, who cocked his head to the side. "I mean, if you trust Nolan, I guess I'm good with it," he said. "We'll have to save up to cover the week without work."

"Oh, so now you're good with it? Nick jumps on board, and suddenly you're good?" She rolled her eyes playfully, turning back to Andy. "I'll have to talk to my team at work, see about moving some shifts around to make sure we have coverage."

"But you'll go?" Andy asked.

She pursed her lips, dragging out a long inhale. When she met Jaren's eyes, he gave a dubious nod, and she copied it. "We'll go."

All eyes fell on me, waiting for what we'd say. At that point, we were incredibly outnumbered. On one hand, I could desperately use a vacation, but on the other, it was such short notice. And I hated the thought of being away from the girls for that amount of time.

"Come on now," Nick teased, bumping my arm with his. "You don't need my permission, but I'm giving you the week off, too. We'll go half capacity, let Heather and Kelsea fill the schedules with cleanings for the week."

"Can we even afford to do that?"

"We can do whatever we want. We're the bosses," he said with a wink. I looked away, then glanced at Brad.

"What do you think?"

Brad seemed conflicted. "What about the girls?"

I chewed my lip in thought. "We could take them down to my parents, I suppose. Depending on where the flight leaves from, I mean. Maybe we could drive to Florida and fly from there?"

He nodded. "I'm fine with it if you are," he lowered his voice, "but we don't have to go if you aren't comfortable with it."

I closed my eyes, picturing the sand, sun, and sea already, despite the growing lump of worry in my belly. "Okay," I said, opening my eyes and looking at Andy. "We'll do it."

"All right," he said, a little too loudly, pounding a palm on the table and lifting it up for high fives.

We all laughed, because as with so much else in our lives, we were all in it together. Andy tossed around awkward high fives, though we were all seemingly lost in our own thoughts as Lila came back to take our orders.

I should've been more excited than I was—and maybe I should've taken that as a sign.

I thought the worst that could happen was that I'd miss the girls too much. Or get a bad sunburn. Maybe the budget would be a little shorter that month when all was said and done, but all in all, it would be the trip of our lives. A vacation to remember.

It was a vacation I'd remember, that's for sure.

But I had no idea that what I thought would be the worst wouldn't even scratch the surface of the nightmare that was about to unfold.

# CHAPTER SIX

## LAURA

I spent the plane ride to the first island worrying about my children, who were staying with my parents at their beach home in Florida. A whole continent away. Would my parents abide by my wishes not to overload them with sugar? Would they watch them closely during their time at the beach? Would they remember to apply extra sunscreen to Elena's sensitive skin? Worries and regrets plagued me, a heavy pit in my stomach as I stared out the window watching the clouds with intent. Was this selfish? Going on a vacation, just the two of us? What did the girls think of us? They'd been all too willing to stay with their grandparents, it was true, but deep down, did they resent us for leaving?

Brad seemed to share exactly none of my reservations. He insisted that they loved my parents, and my parents loved them —which was true—and that everything would be fine.

Brad always assumed everything would be fine, and though he was usually right, it did little to settle my frantic nerves. We were the perfect yin and yang—always on opposite sides of every spectrum. I was hot, he was cold. I was worried, he was calm. He had a temper, I kept my cool. I was a drinker, he was done after a beer. We held opposite ends of each and every argument, and yet somehow, as his hand slid into mine, it just worked.

From the airport, we were chartered to a large catamaran, which would see us safely to the island. It was a long, eight-hour journey, but the boat was loaded down with food and drinks, and the captain and crew had been playing music all day. Everything was in place and everyone was having fun. It was the most seamless transition I'd ever experienced. Everyone we dealt with was kind and courteous, and everyone knew what was happening and where we would need to be sent next.

We rode atop the catamaran, the warm sun beating down on my face, wind whipping through my hair. Despite the sunscreen I'd applied at the beginning of our journey, I knew I was beginning to burn already. Brad's forehead was bright pink, and I knew he was trying his hardest not to get sea sick. I could practically taste the salt in the air.

"We made it, guys! There it is!" Andy called, standing up from his seat and pointing straight ahead. Emily sat beside him, one long leg crossed over the other, wearing her signature ponytail and a black bathing suit underneath a see-through white dress. I followed Andy's finger, to where we could make out the shape of an island in the distance—a golden lump in the vast blue.

As we grew nearer, it began to take shape. The island was largely forest, green palm trees as far as the eye could see. Toward the edge of the water, just where the sand changed from dark and wet to light and dry, there were eight white, reclining chairs, no legs, just flat on the sand. Behind those, there were dozens of hammocks placed sporadically around the trees.

"Holy cow," I said, sucking in a breath.

"Woohoo!" Andy screamed, cupping his hands on either side

of his mouth. "Look at that!" He pulled Emily to stand up next to him, kissing her lips.

"It's incredible," Brad whispered in my ear, and incredible it was.

There were small, shaded huts with beds and chairs, open and waiting for us. Off to the left, there was a round, enclosed pergola, with a handful of white dots of employees moving inside them. And behind that, further down the shore, there was a large structure with lights shining from it, despite the bright sun, and I could make out tables and chairs sitting in front of the building, scattered among the sand under an oversized awning hanging from the building.

Far to our right, I saw tiny cabin-like structures. All wood, the front half on short stilts, the back half on the sand. The sunlight glinted across the large windows on the front of each one. The cabins were in groups of four, scattered across the entire right-hand side of the island, clusters of palm trees separating them as if they'd been planted for that purpose. The cabins stretched out as far as the eye could see. In short, it was pure paradise—everything you'd expect a tropical getaway to be, from the airy feel to the salt in the air. Suddenly, my sunburn didn't bother me so much.

Across from me, Megan was snuggled into the crook of Nick's arm, a warm and carefree smile on her face.

Beside me, Natasha and Jaren sat. They hadn't spoken a word to each other most of the flight, nor since we'd boarded the boat. Natasha had an open book on her lap, fighting the wind and flipping the pages tirelessly, while Jaren wore dark sunglasses, his head bobbing against the railing so much that I wasn't entirely sure he hadn't fallen asleep.

"Nice," Brad said quietly, bobbing his head with joy.

Nick sat up straighter, keeping an arm around Megan as he stared out, one hand over his brow to block the sun. "There it is, ladies and gents. Paradise." He grinned broadly at me, and I smiled back, unable to take my eyes off of the way his arm looped around Megan. Brad and I hadn't touched in such a way in years. *Young love.* Though they were our age, the relationship was young, and I supposed that was what mattered.

As we neared the shore, the energy seemed to switch. We'd all been excited before, but it was nothing compared to the excitement we felt as the boat began to near the long dock. Natasha closed her book, and Jaren lifted his head. All eyes were on the island. This was really happening.

"This is it, you guys!" Andy cried, one hand in the air as the boat came to a stop.

"Wow," Natasha said softly. "It really does look just like the postcard."

Within a few moments, the captain appeared, taking off his hat to bow to us. "As you may have noticed, we have arrived at our destination. You may now disembark."

In a single-file line, we climbed down the stairs, saying goodbye to the crew as we made our way across the ramp onto the wooden dock while they unloaded our luggage. One by one, we collected our bags and began wheeling them toward the end of the dock, where a man dressed in all white was waiting for us. He had thick brown hair, an even thicker mustache, and suntanned skin, and as we grew nearer to him, he took a step forward, meeting us directly where the sand met the wood of the dock.

"Greetings, friends. The island has blessed us with a beautiful day, and we are so thankful for newcomers to share it with. I am the resort owner, Manu, and I will be here for you every step of the way during this beautiful week on my Isla del Amor." He gave a small bow and walked backward, gesturing that we should follow him onto the sand. We did, and once we were all on the island, he extended his hand toward Brad first. Brad took it, though once clasped, Manu enveloped both hands around

Brad's, keeping them completely immobile, a smile on his face as Brad introduced himself.

"I'm Brad Walker, this is my wife—"

"Brad," Manu repeated slowly, then moved his hands from Brad's to mine. "And you are his wife?"

I nodded, swallowing. "Yes. Yes, I'm Laura Walker."

"Laura," he repeated, his voice a low, steady rumble. It was oddly soothing. "Pleasure." He took a step in between us, making his way to the next couple in line. "And you are?"

"Natasha Clemmons," she answered, her tone clipped, and when he released her hand to take Jaren's, she widened her eyes at me. I grinned, trying to tame it down as Jaren introduced himself.

He continued the ritual, holding each of our hands clasped in his and repeating our names back until he reached the last couple—Andy and Emily. When Emily introduced herself, she mimicked his actions, gripping both of his hands in hers, her tone suddenly filled with warmth.

"Emily," he repeated, standing up straight as he released her hand. "You are the beautiful soul who has invited your friends to my paradise."

"Yes," she agreed. "Thank you for accepting us, Manu. We are all so excited."

He chuckled patronizingly. "It is *I* who should be thanking *you*." He spun around so he could see us all again, his back now to the water as we watched our boat start up and begin sailing away. I suddenly felt nostalgic for the crew we'd spent the day with, wishing they were staying, too. "I should be thanking all of you for coming to my island. This has been a longstanding dream of mine, to open a resort beyond the normal expectations. My dream is to see others living theirs." He held out his arms. "And, alas, it has happened. Of course, there will be kinks to work out. Mistakes will be made. But I truly believe I have hired the best staff there is, to take care of my guests." He pointed at us, before continuing on.

"Over the course of this week, you will be pampered, you will be able to relax, to play, to get active, to stay lazy, to eat five-star food, to connect with your partner, to connect with your friends." He paused, letting it all sink in.

"We have every amenity I could squeeze onto the island here. A spa for the ladies, a gym for the men. Kayaks, canoes, beach chairs, hammocks, massages...anything you can think of for a perfect beach vacation—it is all here. My waiters will be at your beck and call, making sure you never get thirsty or hungry and, of course, everything is one hundred percent free to you. We will dine oceanside under the pavilion every night, and you will sleep in your own luxury huts, just steps away from the ocean. If anything, and I do mean *anything*, is not to your satisfaction, or if you have any suggestions for improvement, I am all ears. All I ask is that you be honest in your reviews and, of course, the most important thing...enjoy yourselves."

My chest swelled with pride and excitement. For the first time, I was so happy we'd decided to take this trip. It was everything I could've hoped for, and any feelings of worry were washed away like the water across the sand.

"Now, if you will all turn around, your stewards await you to take you to your new homes for the week. Get unpacked, relax for a moment, freshen up, and then I will ask you to join us for dinner at six. Welcome again, and I look forward to getting to know you more this week."

We turned around, and I jolted at the fact that our stewards were literally *right behind us.* Half a step away, stood a group of four employees, all dressed in identical garb to Manu. Two men, two women.

"Andy and Emily?" called one of the men.

They stepped forward happily, and the man grabbed their bags. I watched them walk away, their deep footprints trailing in the sand as they lost themselves in conversation with the man.

"Brad and Laura?" the second man called. He was tall and bald, with a friendly smile. His white pants and flowy, relaxed shirt that matched the other employees blew in the breeze. When we raised our hands, he moved toward us, taking our bags at once. "I'm Malik. Right this way. I'll take you to your hut."

We followed Malik across the hot sand; I eventually gave up and kicked my sandals off as they kept filling with every step, making it harder and harder to keep up.

"Welcome to Isla del Amor," he said, slowing down when he noticed we were so far behind. "Is this your first time at a resort?"

"For me, yes," Brad said, "but Laura went to a few resorts with her parents as a child."

"Yes, and we've planned to bring our own kids to some, but they're just now getting to an age where I think they'd finally start to enjoy them."

"Oh, you have kids? How old?" Malik asked.

"We do, two daughters. Britta is six and Elena is four."

"So precious," Malik said, nodding. "I have a sixteen-year-old, Oliana."

"That's beautiful…" I told him, trailing off as our hut came into view. Andy and Emily were just ahead of us, saying goodbye to their steward from the doorway of the third hut as Malik stopped at the second.

The huts were gorgeous, walls consisting of large windows, with a structure of mostly bamboo and a ceiling covered in straw. The fronts were set up on stilts so they were just a few feet off the sand. Like the brochure promised, they sat just a few yards away from the ocean, and several feet from each other. There were four in total, and I could see another group of them off in the distance, past a thick set of palm trees.

"This is yours," he said, gesturing to the open door of the second hut. We climbed the steps to the front porch and stepped inside the open sliding glass door. There was a bed in the center of the room, white canopy sheets draped down over it. To the left, was a set of stairs, which led to a second floor. On the right, was a built-in, cushioned area for seating. Another seat sat across from it. The walls directly across from the bed were solid glass, giving a perfect view of the ocean, though there were curtains tied back that could be closed for privacy.

"Second floor," Malik said, pointing up, "is your private bathroom and shower. No windows up there."

"This is beautiful," I said in awe, and I truly meant it. Everywhere I looked, there were new intricate details to appreciate. The place must've been just less than five hundred square feet of space, but they'd utilized every square inch of it. It felt luxurious.

"I'll leave you now, and let you get settled. I've placed a bucket of ice and a bottle of wine on your counter." He pointed to the small bit of counter space next to the bed. "Is there anything else I can get you right now?"

"No, I don't think so," I said.

"There's a button here," he said, pointing to a red button near the door. "If you need me, you press it. I'll get paged and be here within minutes."

"Thank you so much, Malik," Brad said, reaching out a hand to shake his.

Malik shook his hand kindly then bowed to me. "I will make sure you enjoy your stay. See you at dinner."

As he backed away, I wondered if there was something more than genuineness in his voice. I pulled out my phone, walking toward the bed to sit down and call my parents.

"Any updates?" Brad asked, doing the same.

I shook my head, staring at the blank screen. "No... That's strange."

"What is it?" he asked, leaning over to get a look at my screen.

I put the phone to my ear, hoping my suspicions were wrong, but when the call disconnected instantly, I put a hand to my lips, the feeling of worry back with a vengeance. "Brad, our cell phones don't work here."

# CHAPTER SEVEN

## NICK

When our steward, Nani, left us alone, Megan approached me, her arms sliding around my waist as she leaned up, pressing her lips to mine. I kissed her back, distracted by the breeze from the open sliding glass door. Through our windows, I could faintly see into Laura and Brad's next door.

"What are you looking at?" Megan asked, resting her head on my shoulder.

"Checking to make sure they didn't get a better setup than we did," I teased, looking away quickly.

"This place is gorgeous," she said, inhaling deeply. "You can smell the salty air from here, Nicky. I can't wait to dip my toes in the water… I've never seen anything so blue."

Sometimes she was so irritatingly perfect, it was as if everything she said came straight from an advertisement. "It's great."

"Aren't you glad we came?"

I wrapped an arm around her stiffly. "So glad. Have you checked on Winston?"

"Not recently." She pulled away from me, walking to the bed and sitting down on the edge, digging through her bag.

"Melanie texted me just before we boarded the plane and said she'd just taken him for his walk. He's doing well under the circumstances… I've never been away from him for more than a day." She poked out her bottom lip, though I hardly noticed as my eyes traveled back to the window, where Laura and Brad appeared to be arguing about something. She looked tense. *What's wrong?*

"Nick?"

I jolted to look at Megan, my eyes wide and breathing labored as if I'd been caught red-handed doing something atrocious. "Yeah?" I asked, turning my back to the window and taking in her worried expression.

"Everything alright?"

"Yep," I said, taking a seat next to her. "How's Winston?" Had she already told me? I couldn't remember.

She didn't look at the bag she was still digging in, keeping her eyes on me. "What were you looking at?" Her usually warm expression cooled.

"What?" I feigned ignorance. "I was just looking around. Outside. We're in paradise, in case you hadn't noticed."

She sighed. Not angry, just disappointed. I knew what she was thinking, but she wouldn't say it. She wouldn't accuse me of lying because that wasn't the relationship we had. We'd built a foundation of honesty. Of trust. "Are you sure everything's okay?" she whispered, resting a hand on my arm.

I leaned in, pressing my forehead to hers. There wasn't a day that went by that I wasn't grateful for the patient and understanding woman I'd been given. If only I could stop pining for the one I could never have.

"I wasn't watching her," I swore, heading off her thoughts. I closed my eyes for fear she'd see the lie in them. "I was watching a boat that drove past."

Her expression remained stiff and unyielding. "Across the sand and straight through Laura's hut?"

"Across the water." I lowered my lips to hers, letting the kiss linger. "It's *you* I love. It's *you* I'm going to marry. You know that, don't you?"

Her lips grew thin with a grim expression as she gave a stilted nod. "I love you, too."

"I've actually been thinking." I lifted my hand to hers, sliding my palm under her fingers. "What do you think about me asking Laura to work three days a week and then I could work the opposite three?"

Her eyes lit up. "Could you do that?"

"Of course I can."

"Nick, I don't want you to do that for me. I trust you, you know that."

"I do," I confirmed, rubbing my nose against hers. "But I don't want you to have to worry. Laura is my best friend, but you are going to be my wife." She was unable to conceal her smile then. "And I'm going to ask Andy to be my best man, I think."

She raised a brow. "You are?"

"I've been thinking about it, and…I can't *not* invite Laura—"

"I'd never ask you to do that—"

I put up a hand to interrupt her. "I know. Because you're perfect." I kissed her again, unable to stop. "You're perfect, and you deserve for that day to be everything you have dreamed, so I understand why given my feelings *in the past* you wouldn't feel comfortable with her being in the wedding. Plus, Andy will throw me a killer bachelor party." I winked.

She groaned, slapping my chest playfully. "Are you sure about all of this? I promised you that I wouldn't cause issues with you and Laura. I love her. I love you. I don't want you to lose your best friend."

I squeezed her thigh. "You're my best friend now. It's time I started proving it." She tucked a piece of hair behind her ear, looking up at me with hopeful eyes.

"I love you, Nick London."

"I love you, too, Megan Graham. More than you know." I kissed her nose, then her lips, ending the conversation.

It was a conversation we'd had before, but one that I never grew comfortable with. Megan came from a family of talkers, of lovers, people who flourished under good communication and soft tones. I was raised in a family of chaos, three older brothers, cats and dogs running around, a mother who was a teacher and worked at the local grocery store three nights a week to help make ends meet. My father was a dentist, too, starting the practice I eventually took over, but in those days, the profit was less and the hours were longer. There was love in my house, sure, but we expressed it differently. We didn't talk much, unless it was an argument, and everyone had a short temper. Blame it on our fiery Greek blood.

When we broke apart, the worry was all but gone from her face. "Are you serious about splitting up days with Laura?"

I nodded, though I hadn't thought of it until that exact moment. "It wouldn't hurt the business, and it would give me more time with you. Maybe I could even help you with the bakery."

"As long as you don't go near the ovens." She laughed. "Lord knows you burn water."

"I'm not *that* bad." I ran a hand over my forehead, relieved the argument had been avoided.

When she spoke again, her voice was soft. Hesitant. "I never want you to do anything you aren't comfortable with. I trust you, Nicky. You don't have to prove anything to me."

It felt as if my heart squeezed in my chest at her words. Physical pain radiated through me at her trusting, hopeful expression. How in the world had I gotten so lucky? Why hadn't the angel in front of me kicked me to the curb already, to be with someone much more deserving than I? "I know I don't have to, but I want to. I had feelings for Laura once, like I've admitted to you, but Brad's a great guy. They're my friends. I'd never do anything to jeopardize that, or this." I rested my hands on her hips. "I love you, Megan. More than anything or anyone else." She leaned forward to kiss my lips, and I saw a glint of tears in her eyes.

"I love you, too," she whispered, her voice holding no power. When we broke apart, she lifted the bag back to her lap, digging inside. As she discovered her phone, she pulled it up and turned it on. I ran a hand through her wavy blonde hair and tucked it behind her ear. She smelled of warm sunscreen and coconuts, her skin glowing from the tanning oil she'd applied. I ran a hand over the bathing suit cover she was wearing, white with purple, pink, and blue flowers across it. It was see-through, just enough that I could see the bright orange bikini top and black shorts underneath.

"There may be a problem..." Megan said, looking up at me. I glanced at her phone screen as she hit the button to place the call, a call we'd paid the phone company fifty extra dollars this month to be able to make without roaming charges. A black box filled the screen.

**No Service.**

**Call Disconnected.**

# CHAPTER EIGHT

## ANDY

I jogged up the stairs to the top floor of the hut as soon as our steward left us. "Babe, you've got to see it up here!" I looked out the window in front of me, checking out the awesome view of the ocean. It was like paradise here, straight out of a movie. I'd never seen anything so perfect.

Below me, Emily was taking advantage of the scenery by placing her camera on the shelf, propped up on her favorite of her phone holders. She was always so inventive with ways to use the self-timer on her phone and creative with her photo ideas. It was what made her rocket to success the way she had, and I never failed to be impressed by her. I leaned over the rail, watching her stretch out on the bed, one leg bent up, her elbows holding her body up, a half laugh on her face. She held still for a few seconds, then jumped off the bed and rushed across the room to check it. I watched as she twisted her mouth, already sure that she wasn't happy with the way she looked.

There was something to be said for staying with someone long enough to know them. To know the subtle intricacies within the way they moved, the way they carried themselves, the way the crinkle formed between their eyes when they were frustrated. It was true that I hadn't always been the most serious about the women I'd dated, and my friends liked to joke about how many there'd been, but with Emily it was different. She made me want to be different, and I was determined to show her that.

She moved back to the bed, this time sitting on the edge with one leg draped over the other, the back of one of her hands pressed to her forehead. She closed her eyes, turning the side of her face toward the camera. After a second, she jumped down again, her face still contorted with displeasure.

"Want me to take it?" I offered, hurrying back down the stairs. In the weeks that we'd been dating, Emily had taught me so much about posing and camera angles. Most of the time, I still got it wrong, but I was always happy to try.

"That's okay, baby," she said, giving me a lopsided grin and patting my cheek before glancing back down to scroll through her phone. "I'm just not loving the lighting in here. It's going to be much better outside, anyway. Maybe I'll have you take one of me in front of the hut."

"Maybe we could have someone take a picture of the two of us," I offered.

Her eyes lit up. "That's great! We could ask Laura. I think they put her next door."

"Do you want me to go ask her?" I pointed next door with my thumb.

"No worries. I want to change before dinner, and we can get one before we head out. I won't be able to post anything until we leave, anyway. I just want to be sure I have a ton of material to post." She grinned, her cheeks turning pink with a familiar pleasure. "My followers aren't used to me going so quiet."

I smiled, but it was weak at best. It was pathetic to be jealous of three hundred thousand people who lived a world away, most of whom Emily didn't know anything about, but I was anyway. I couldn't help it. She'd warned me on our first date that her followers came first, always. They were the ones paying her bills, the reason she was able to live the life she did, and now that that life included me, I supposed I should've been grateful, and I was—truly. But that didn't stop a small amount of bitterness from filling my chest every time she smiled brighter for a new comment than anything I did.

"Wait," I said, letting her words sink in finally. "What do you mean? Are you going to be off your phone while we're here?" Was I finally going to get her full attention?

She dropped her arm to her side, phone in hand, and scoffed. "Well, I won't really have much choice, will I? There's no service on the island. It's part of their branding—they want couples to reconnect, without everyday distractions." She held up her phone again. "Hello, distraction number one."

I smiled, filled with an emotion I couldn't quite register. "So, we can't use our phones at all?"

"I mean, I'm sure they have one for emergencies somewhere, but there's no cell service or Wi-Fi anywhere on the island." She cocked her head to the side. "I mentioned that, didn't I?"

I shook my head, my throat dry as I watched her slide her phone into the side of her bikini top and turn to her bag.

*Finally.* Finally I'd have her all to myself. For one whole week, I wouldn't be sharing her with three hundred thousand strangers.

If it were up to me, we'd never leave the island.

# CHAPTER NINE

## NATASHA

Our steward, Lei, led us to the last hut, next to Andy and Emily, and disappeared quickly after. I walked to the desk, where she'd left a bottle of wine chilling in a bucket of ice and two glasses.

"This is nice," I said, turning to face Jaren, who was moving the bags from the floor to the bed.

"Yeah," he said simply, only partially listening. "Where'd you put my other sunglasses?"

"I didn't pack them," I said. "I thought you did."

To my relief, the wine was a screw top, so I opened it quickly, pouring myself a glass. I took a sip, holding the soft notes of peach in my mouth. It had been so long since we'd gotten to relax at all, let alone on a beach with free drinks. It was exactly what I needed, and I could feel the tension leaving my shoulders the moment my feet touched the sand.

"What do you mean you didn't pack them?"

I snapped back to reality, watching Jaren sit down on the edge of the bed, sliding his shoes off. Apparently he hadn't gotten the memo that we were relaxing. "You packed your own bag. Why would I have specifically packed any of your sunglasses?"

He jerked his head to face me, his eyes wide with indignation. "I didn't pack my own bag."

My heart dropped. "What?"

"*You* packed it."

I shook my head, my lips pressed together. "No, I didn't," I said slowly.

"You had them on the bed…you washed our bathing suits." He turned around, tearing his suitcase open. I watched in horror as he opened it, revealing only his swimming trunks, a pair of sandals, Sperrys, and his water shoes. "No. No. No. No. No. You've got to be kidding me." He slammed the suitcase closed.

"I packed your bathing suit because I had to wash it, and I went ahead and put your shoes in there when I did mine, but I told you to make sure you packed your stuff. Your suitcase was sitting out for a week!"

He groaned, hands over his face. "I know that, but I hadn't gotten around to it! And then you had it zipped up, so I just assumed you packed it."

It took all I had not to laugh at the ridiculousness of it all. "I zipped it up because I was cleaning the windows and it had been laying in the window seat for a week. You mean you didn't notice it wasn't full when you loaded the bags in the car?"

He shook his head. "I didn't pay any attention. I had four bags in my hands, and you were already in there, playing on your phone. Excuse me if I didn't have time to look through each one."

"Well, excuse me if I didn't think I had to pack my forty-five-year-old husband's bag for him. I told you to pack it, so don't blame me. You should've checked it. What do you have in your carry-on? I'll bet they have places here where you can buy some shirts and maybe some extra swim trunks. You can wear that most of the time, I'm sure, anyway. And, for the record, I wasn't *playing on my phone,* I was texting your mom to let her know we were leaving and to keep an eye on Nolan. And then I was checking the weather to make sure we weren't driving into a storm."

That didn't seem to impress His Highness. His lips quivered with anger. "So, when we go to dinner tonight, you're wearing a dress and I'm wearing swim trunks? I don't have any damn underwear, Natasha."

"Well, whose fault is that? What do you want me to do, call the boat back to get you some clean drawers?"

His expression fell flat, and he shook his head. "Whatever, make a joke about it. Fine. I'm going to take a shower."

"Go on," I told him, watching him storm up the stairs. "Maybe they have a towel up there you can fashion into a diaper." He slammed the door, and I took another drink of my wine, walking out onto the deck of our hut. I took a seat in the wooden rocking chair.

*Just another day in paradise.*

# CHAPTER TEN

## NICK

We stood outside our hut, waiting for the rest of our group to join us. Slowly, they trickled out of their front doors. Natasha first, several paces ahead of Jaren, Laura and Brad next, then Emily and Andy, who flagged down Laura to have her take a picture of them in front of their hut. We were all dressed up—suits, blazers, and dresses seemed to be the agreed upon attire, despite the heat and the fact that we hadn't discussed it. I looked down the line, thinking about how good we all looked, and stopped squarely on Jaren, who'd taken a more casual approach. *Much* more casual— he was dressed in just his T-shirt and swim trunks.

I smiled, then glanced at Laura, who grinned at me when she noticed my staring, and I looked away back to Megan, who, to my relief, wasn't paying attention this time.

"You look so pretty, Natasha," Megan said, waiting for her to catch up with us before we kept walking, the rest trailing just a few feet behind.

"Yeah, well, I have a feeling I'll be looking like Cinderella compared to my date all week," Natasha snipped. "Jaren forgot his clothes."

My jaw dropped, and I looked back. Embarrassment washed over his face.

"Dude, *forgot?*" Andy asked.

"All of them?" I asked.

"You mean the airport lost them?" Brad asked.

Jaren shook his head. "There was a mix-up. Long story. I didn't ever pack anything."

"Do you need to borrow anything?" Brad asked. "Laura packed us both extra clothes, so I have some I can spare."

Jaren cast an ice-cold glance at Natasha. "That'd be great, man. Thanks."

"Yeah, don't mention it. Or, actually *do,* I guess," Brad joked. "I'll need you to remind me when we get back to the huts later."

"I've got some extras, too," I offered. "Between the three of us, surely we can get you covered."

"'Preciate it," Jaren said, nodding stiffly. I could tell how badly he wanted to talk about anything else.

"Hey, guys?" Laura asked.

"Yeah?" Megan looked back at her.

"Did you notice there's no service on the island? Malik said it's part of the experience..." She trailed off, and I knew she'd be chewing on her bottom lip from nerves, though I couldn't see her. "I was hoping maybe it was just our carrier."

"I'm sorry, Laura," I heard Emily say. "It's an all-immersive experience. I thought Andy explained it before we left, but I'm pretty sure it was in the brochure, too. They want you to be solely focused on your partner and relaxation while you're here, so there'll be no phone service or Wi-Fi."

"Oh," Laura said stiffly. "I hadn't realized. Well, it's just...our kids... What if something happens and my parents need to get a hold of me?"

"Are your parents listed as your emergency contact? Or someone else?"

"My parents, and Brad's."

"Well, there you go, then. When they sent them a confirmation, there was a number for the resort on the email. The island takes safety very seriously, so they've confirmed that they have a way to get a hold of your emergency contacts. If your parents can't reach you, they can call the resort, and someone will get word to you."

"You sure know a lot about this..." Natasha said, and I glanced back at Laura, who looked incredibly uneasy.

"It's my job to know, and rate, the finer details," Emily pointed out.

"It's—" I started to offer Laura comfort, but Brad beat me to it.

"It's going to be fine, darling." *Darling.* I curled my upper lip at the pretentiousness of it all. "Your parents will take great care of them, and it's just a week. Nothing can be solved by worrying about it." When I looked back again, he had his hand locked with hers, and she was smiling at him.

I averted my gaze back ahead as we passed the white lounge chairs on the sand, the tide coming dangerously close to touching them as it rose. The round pergola to our right had employees inside that waved as we walked past. I didn't recognize any of them.

As we grew nearer to the building at the end of the stretch of beach, I could smell food cooking, the savory smells of chilis and spices. Manu, dressed this time in bright white pants and what could best be described as a thick, white dress draped over the pants, stood at the head of the largest table under the pavilion. There were place settings for nine, so I assumed he planned to join us for dinner.

He laughed before we'd made it to him. "Welcome, welcome! Come on, do not be shy. Take a seat!" He gestured to the empty chairs as we arrived, looking at each other awkwardly. I made a move for a chair as quickly as Emily did, smirking at her before giving up the seat. I pulled the one next to her out, allowing

Megan to sit, and taking the place next to her. Jaren, Natasha, Brad, and Laura took their places across from us.

"Well," Manu said, once we'd settled in. "I take it your huts are all to your liking, then? You have found everything you need? Was everything to your satisfaction?"

We nodded in unison, but it was Emily who spoke. "Everything's so lovely here, Manu. You've done a beautiful job preparing for our stay."

If it were possible, his smile grew even more endearing at her words. "Thank you, Emily. It brings me great joy to hear you say that." He looked around the table, waiting for someone else to speak.

"Manu," Laura said, "Malik told us there's no cell phone service on the island... Is there a way for our families to reach us here? My parents have our daughters, and I'm very worried that something will happen and I won't be able to get in touch with them, or vice versa." She cleared her throat, speaking so quickly she lost her breath when she reached the end of the sentence.

Manu chuckled under his breath. "Laura," he said, expelling a sigh with her name. "The worrier...as mothers do." His smile was small. "Yes, of course. We do have a phone on the island in case of emergencies, and I have personally seen to it that each of your emergency contacts have that number." He glanced up, apparently thinking. "Mona, correct?" *Her mother.* "Your mother?"

She nodded, and I saw the shock on her face.

"Yes, lovely woman. She knows how to contact you if she needs you, but the beauty of the island is in the fact that you do not feel pressured to keep electronics on you at all times. If you want to jump in the ocean, you are free to do it. No more spending your days handicapped by the fact that your most valuable possession is in your pocket, or your hand. While you are on Isla del Amor, you are free. Free to do what you want.

Free from the pressures of society and social norms. You are free to focus on your partner and on your friends, without feeling like you should be doing something else. No distractions." He smiled. "And, of course, if you hate it, it *is* only six nights, seven days. Though we will do everything in our power to make sure you are begging to stay longer once your time to leave has come. I know it must seem scary in the beginning, but from the feedback we have been receiving, our couples are really finding it an amazing chance to disconnect from their phones and reconnect with each other." He gestured toward Brad. "This beautiful man next to you wants your attention, my dear. This is your chance to give it to him."

She looked back toward Brad and shrugged one shoulder, nodding at Manu, but not responding.

"Do you have any stores here?" Jaren asked. "Like for T-shirts?"

Manu shook his head. "Ah, I am afraid we do not. We want everything here at Isla del Amor to be all-inclusive, so a store does not quite fit that narrative. But, if you would like to suggest it, I am very happy to consider one in the future. It does not help us now, though. I am sorry."

"Okay, cool," Jaren said. "No big deal."

"All right, then. I'm sure you are all starving...and I hope you are because our chef, Alon Valencia, is world-renowned and highly coveted, and he has prepared a few delicious meals for you to choose from." He gestured toward the menus lying on the white tablecloth in front of us. After a few moments, a waiter approached the table, taking our orders. I chose Caribbean fish stew with a '96 Fevre Chablis.

"So, tell me about yourselves," Manu said when the orders were taken and our waiter had disappeared. "What do you do for fun?"

"This," Emily said gleefully, sinking back in her chair with a laugh.

"Yes, yes," Manu said, smiling joyfully. "And what about your partner there? Andy?"

Andy looked up, apparently distracted by something. "Sorry, what?"

"What is it you do for fun, Andy?"

"I...I like to work on cars. I'm obsessed with 'em."

"Very nice," Manu said. "And you, Megan?"

Megan smiled, her hand wrapping around my arm. "Well, I love to bake. I own a bakery, so it's basically what I do all the time, but Nicky and I are planning our wedding, so that's especially fun for me right now."

"A wedding. Oh, how marvelous." He clasped his hands together in front of his chest. "Congratulations," Manu said, glancing at me.

"Thank you," Megan said with a sigh.

"And what do you like to do for fun, Nick?"

I patted Megan's hand. "Anything I can do with Megan."

He smiled, but there was something in his expression that made me think he didn't believe me. Maybe I was just paranoid. Either way, he moved on. "And you, Natasha?"

Natasha twisted her lips in thought, a wrinkle forming on her forehead. "I like to read, but I haven't done it in years. And I like..." She paused, giving herself time to think. "I don't really know. Netflix, I guess. I don't ever have time for fun, honestly."

"Oh, everybody has time for fun," he chided playfully. "Perhaps you can put our library to good use while you are here. It is just inside our relaxation center." He pointed to the building our waiters had exited from moments ago. "Inside, you will find our state-of-the-art spa, gym, a library, a movie theater, the kitchen, and a small indoor eating space for when we have bad weather. Oh, there is also a pool on the other side. I know it sounds a bit crazy, but some of our guests have found it quite useful. You would be surprised how many people come to an island resort and dislike the ocean. There is also a restroom straight inside those doors, as well as one down by the kayak rental booth."

"Thank you, Manu. This all sounds so awesome. I'll have to check the library out."

"Yes, you must. There are a great many classics, as well as modern literature that I think you would quite enjoy," he said, moving on. "And you, Jaren?" He said his name, overenunciating the a and n.

Jaren twisted his empty wine glass. The quietest of our group, he was the type to rarely talk unless asked a direct question, and even then, it wasn't something he enjoyed. "I'm a sports guy," he said. "Mostly football… And mostly watching. I haven't played in years."

"Well, I am afraid we do not have football here, but we do have a small basketball court inside in our gym. Perhaps you would enjoy yourself in there."

Jaren nodded, looking relieved to have had the attention taken away from him as Manu directed his gaze to Brad. "And you, Brad? What do you like to do for fun?"

Brad cleared his throat, as he so often did before speaking. I couldn't deny the way it drove me crazy. He looked at Laura, who was looking at Manu. "I'm like Natasha, I guess. I haven't had time for fun in years. I'm a dad to two amazing little girls and I run my own accounting firm, and I also work with a company that's bringing clean drinking water to developing countries." *Saint Brad.*

"Perhaps, then, relaxing is something you should be doing for fun," Manu joked, and Brad's eyebrows bounced up as he gave an agreeable laugh. "And you are last, Mrs. Laura. What do you enjoy doing?"

"Oh," she said softly, her eyes bouncing to Brad, then me, then Natasha, and back to Manu. "I don't know. I'm a mom to two little girls, like Brad mentioned, so that takes up the majority of my time. But, when I'm not doing that, or when I'm not working at the dental office Nick and I run, I like to..." She put a finger to her lips. "Well, I used to love hiking; we have lovely woods behind our house. But I haven't done that in years. I run quite a bit, but typically when I'm stressed. Mostly to *have fun,* I just relax on the couch with Netflix and wine, when I get the chance." She smiled sadly, obviously unhappy with her own answer. "Oh, and I've always loved to write. I'd love to publish a novel someday."

"Well, we do not have Netflix here, but I am happy to say there are plenty of hiking trails in the woods—just please stay on the paths we have marked for your safety—and I should think you will find plenty of time to write during your stay, if you would wish to do so. It is peaceful here." His smile broadened. "And there is certainly no shortage of wine."

"I'll drink to that," Natasha said with a cackle, raising her empty glass.

At her words, the doors to the relaxation center opened and eight waiters appeared, each carrying white trays. They approached our table, and nearly in unison, placed our plates in front of us. They poured our drinks and took the menus from us, checking to make sure everything was in order before they left.

I looked up, realizing Manu didn't have any food in front of him. "I shall leave you now and let you talk, relax, and enjoy your meal," he said, standing from his chair. "And I certainly hope you do. You are in paradise now, my dears. Your only focus should be enjoying every moment of it."

I lifted the wine to my lips, letting the cool, rich texture sit on my tongue. Behind us, the water could be heard slapping against the sand, bringing with it a humidity that had the back of my shirt clinging to my neck.

He skirted away quickly, and when he was inside of the building, Andy broke the silence with as much class as could be expected.

"Holy shit, this is delicious!" Pineapple sat atop his pork, and I snorted watching him dig in. Emily picked at her salad, though I didn't see her take a bite.

"Had you eaten today, bud?" Brad joked, and Andy flipped him off.

"This is really great," Megan agreed, plucking a mandarin orange from the salad in front of her.

"I can't believe we're here," Natasha said, taking a sip of the yellow mixed drink in her glass. "Like, this is really happening, you guys."

"It's wild, right?" Laura agreed. "This place is breathtaking."

And so the conversation shifted, from our usual talk of the day-to-day to our newfound existence in paradise. I had the vague feeling that we were all just waiting for the other shoe to drop, like none of us—Emily aside—could believe it was really happening.

It was our first night on the island, and the first night we'd all get to spend together.

Little did I know, it was also the only night we'd all be alive.

# CHAPTER ELEVEN

## LAURA

After our dinner plates had been cleared, we were all stuffed and exhausted, and over the horizon, the sun had begun to set into the sea.

"Let's go watch the sunset, Nicky," Megan said, her excitement contagious as she leaned into him and he kissed her forehead. They were so in love it was nearly sickening.

I looked at Brad, who was staring out over the water stoically. "Want to go, too?" I asked.

He nodded less enthusiastically, standing up, and I watched as Nick pulled Megan's chair out, though Brad was already several paces away from the table by the time I caught up to him. "Wait up!" I called.

The others followed behind, each couple getting up and stretching at their own pace. We made our way to the shore, and Brad turned to me. "What do you think, babe? Sand or a chair?"

"A chair, please," I said with a laugh. "I'd never manage to get up from the sand." It was a joke, but the pain in my knees had begun getting worse and, try as I might to ignore it, my hips felt sore from day-to-day movements anymore—a definite sign I was no longer the eighteen-year-old he'd met so long ago. Emily was a constant reminder of everything I wasn't anymore. We started toward the white chairs on the sand, stopping abruptly as Nick darted into our path with Megan on his back.

*"Sorry,"* he called, Megan squealing with delight as he launched them both into the water. Brad took my hand, leading me toward the chairs as we watched Nick and Megan play in the water, laughing loudly and splashing each other like two teenagers. I couldn't help smiling. It was a perfect picture, really. The sunset behind them, both of them undeniably beautiful, even soaking wet and jet lagged.

I sat down in the white chair, nearly tipping it over as I managed to sink in and Brad slid his toward me, surprising me by putting an arm around my shoulders. Maybe this place would be good for us after all.

"I love you," he whispered, resting his chin on my shoulder. I leaned my head onto his.

"I love you, too."

"Alright, you love birds," Natasha said, laughing as she hurried around in front of me and took the seat to my right. "Dear God, how do you get in this thing without falling on your ass?"

I snorted, reaching over and holding the chair steady so she could sit without tipping the chair on its side. "I don't think you do."

Without a word to her, Jaren took off his shirt, laying it over a free chair and hurrying into the water as well. "Has Jaren been working out?" I asked Natasha, surprised at the abs I'd never noticed before. Then again, it wasn't all that frequently I saw him without a shirt on.

She raised a brow, following my gaze. "Who knows what he does… He bought one of those ab machines off some guy who brought his car into the shop a few months back. Ten bucks says by the end of the year, it'll be used to stack clothes on."

"He looks great," I told her, wiggling my brow and elbowing her playfully. "This week could be really great for you two."

"I have ears, you know," Brad said, shaking his head. "Sometimes it's like you girls don't care about our feelings at all." He crossed his arms, batting his eyelashes excessively.

I laughed out loud, sliding my feet further down in the sand, where the earth began to grow cool. "I'm just saying. Natasha and Jaren are bound to have a great time reconnecting. We all are."

She rolled her eyes. "Yeah, well don't get your hopes up. I don't plan on getting too cuddly with someone who can't change his drawers for a week." She snorted again, obviously feeling the three glasses of a cocktail called Yellow Bird she'd had at dinner.

I tsked, clicking my tongue at her. "You're awful."

She shook her head. "He's a grown man, baby. He can stick up for himself. Anyway, don't let me ruin your time with your man. You have clean clothes, don't you, Brad?"

He guffawed. "Plenty of 'em. And I'm giving some to Jaren too...*drawers* and all."

She cackled. "Don't do it for my sake."

"Where's Andy and Emily?" I asked, looking behind us when I realized they weren't around.

"I think Andy went to order them some extra drinks over at the kayak rental shack," Brad said, pointing to where Andy could be seen waiting at the small, round pergola a few yards back.

"Do you think Little Miss is going to swim in that full face of makeup?" Natasha asked.

"Twenty bucks says she's going to make Andy take her picture and not even drink it," Brad said, winking at Natasha.

She shook her head. "You should know by now I'm not taking any losing bets, Brad."

"Shh..." I quieted them as Andy was handed two tall, red and yellow frozen cocktails. He moved to hand one to Emily, but she turned around too quickly, missing the gesture, so he followed behind her instead, carrying the drinks carefully, as if they were eggs in an egg-and-spoon race. They made their way so far away from us I was sure they were going back to the huts, but eventually they stopped, and Emily reached for a drink, pulling her phone from inside her bra.

Natasha sighed apprehensively. "She sure is pretty, but poor Andy..."

"Poor Andy?" Brad asked with a sarcastic chuckle, so excitedly I elbowed him.

*"Watch it."*

"I'm just saying," he rubbed his chest where I'd hurt him, "she's half our age, *loaded,* and..." He sighed, folding his arms over his chest. "I'm just saying Andy is, like the girls would say, *living his best life,*" he teased, using a phrase Britta overused.

I grimaced. "Yeah, for now. But how long do you realistically think it'll last? I mean, it's Andy."

"Even young and perky gets boring after a while," Natasha agreed.

"I don't know. Have you seen the way he watches her? He's like a puppy dog," Brad said.

"He's obviously just infatuated because she's the first girl in the history of the world not falling all over him. He's having to put in the work on this one. Maybe it'll be good for him," I said.

"Like I said, he's a puppy dog chasing a bright, shiny new bone." Brad jutted his head in the direction of the two of them. We watched as Emily positioned herself in front of the sun, pressing her lips to the side of the glass, and Andy snapped a few photos on her phone.

"Yeah, well, someone needs to put that puppy down," Natasha said. "Lord, it's pathetic."

I stifled a grin of my own. "I just want him to be happy. Maybe she's the one."

"She's *a* one," Brad agreed, clearing his throat. "And this is the first time I've ever seen him date someone for longer than a week. He seems…I hate to say it, but he does seem happy."

When they were done taking the photo, Emily traded the drink for her phone, looking through the pictures. When she appeared to have found one she approved of, she stuck the phone back into her dress and surprised me by looking directly at us.

At once, the three of us looked away, and I felt heat rush to my face. "Real smooth, guys," Natasha joked.

When we looked back, she was still staring our way, a small smile on her painted red lips. She was perfect, in an intimidating way that I couldn't deny. Sure, she was half my age, but it was more than that. There was something so confident about her, a confidence that most women never knew. At any age.

Interrupting my thoughts, Natasha nudged me. "She's coming over here. She's coming over here. Stop staring."

I looked down, then back up, realizing she was right. They were headed back our way, nearly to us at that point. When they reached us, she bent down, sitting directly in front of me, her legs bent carefully behind her.

Andy took a seat next to her, his legs crossed, both drinks still in his hands and his palms bright red from the cold.

"Hey," she purred.

"Want me to help you out?" Brad asked, taking one of the drinks and burying its base in the sand so it stayed in place. Andy did the same with the other one.

"I saw you guys watching." She rolled her eyes with fake humility. "So embarrassing, I know. But the poses that look ridiculous in real life make for the best shots online."

"Sorry, no. It wasn't that at all. We weren't trying to stare. I just find what you do so fascinating," I told her.

"Oh, you probably think it's super shallow," she said, waving me off. There was no bitterness in her voice. "I know it's silly, but it pays the bills, ya know. There are worse things…" She trailed off, flicking her long, dark hair behind her shoulder. "So, are you guys having fun?"

"It's beautiful, Emily. We can't thank you enough for inviting us," Brad said, taking some of the pressure off me.

"My pleasure. Really. I never get to do these things with people I actually know, let alone *like,* so this is great for me." She paused. "I hate that you had to leave your daughters at home, though. I know you must miss them."

The thought of Britta and Elena sent a stab to my heart. "I do," I admitted. "Very much. But I know they're having fun with my parents."

"And what about you, Natasha? You have children, right?"

"A son. He's seventeen." Her eyes brightened. "About *your* age, right?"

Andy gave her an irritated look of warning, but Emily didn't seem to notice or care about the condescension in her tone. "Just about. Very cool." She nodded rhythmically, like she was dancing to music no one else could hear.

"I'm so curious about what you do, Brad. You said you bring water to foreign countries? Andy had only told me about your accounting, but I think that's so cool." She leaned forward, zeroing in on Brad, who didn't seem to mind giving her the extra attention. "Do you ever need donations? I love getting my followers involved in worthy causes." She smiled sweetly, and a sick feeling washed over me.

"Yeah, absolutely. It's a worthwhile cause, and the way these people live, it's just…it's amazing how resilient man is, you know?"

"Or woman," she said, her tongue resting on her too-white teeth.

"Yeah," he said, hanging on to the ending sound. "Woman, too." His eyes darted to mine nervously, and I hoped he could feel the tension. I was not a jealous person, but it would take a woman more confident than I am to watch their husband watching someone so beautiful, so interested in him, without feeling at least a pang of spite.

"How did you get into social media?" I asked, drawing her attention back to me as Nick, Megan, and Jaren emerged from the water, making their way up the shore toward us.

"Oh, gosh, it just kind of happened, you know? I posted about what I did, my life, and it just…" She snapped her fingers. "Took off. You know how it goes." *Oh, right, of course.*

"You must enjoy it," Brad said. "All that freedom…I'm not sure what I'd do with it."

My stomach tightened.

"It's great," she agreed. "It gets lonely sometimes…" She blinked slowly, then looked at Andy. "But it's still great. Beats a desk job, right?"

Andy smiled. "Beats getting your knuckles torn to shreds at a shop."

"You love your cars," she said, puckering her lips and grasping his chin, shaking it back and forth playfully.

"Hey, I could learn to live without 'em if it meant doing stuff like this all the time," he told her, the statement rolling over her expression slowly. Her smile faded.

"You know most of the time I have to travel alone."

He nodded. "Yeah, of course. I'm just kidding." Though he wasn't, and that was incredibly obvious to everyone.

"What did we miss?" Nick asked, as he and Megan finally reached us. Their wet clothes clung to their bodies, Megan's long blonde hair stringy and a shade darker than usual. Her smile was infectious. An island employee rushed toward us, holding out three towels, which they each took graciously.

"Thanks, Nani," Megan said, bowing slightly as she began to dry her hair.

When the woman walked away, Nick asked again, "Sorry, what did we miss?"

"Nothing," Emily said, "we were just chatting."

"Yep, just chatting," Natasha agreed, a too-perky, patronizing grin on her face.

"I think we're going to go dry off," Megan said. "Will you guys be out here long?"

"Ye—" Andy said, but Emily cut him off sharply.

"No. I plan to get up early and do yoga on the beach at sunrise, and I need a full eight hours or I won't be of any use to anyone tomorrow, so I think I'll go to bed. You're welcome to stay, though, babe." She nodded at him. He seemed unsure of what to say.

"We're probably going to stay awhile, aren't we, babe?" Brad asked, already seeming sure of that fact. "If you want to hang with us for a bit, Andy."

"Yeah," I agreed. "You're welcome to stay with us, Andy. At least until the sun sets. I'm not sure how late I'll stay out after that." A yawn escaped my throat. "Unless I fall asleep out here."

Nick looked reluctant to leave, though Megan was already pulling him away, waving happily at us as Emily stood to leave, too.

"You going to bed?" Jaren asked Natasha, who shook her head.

"I'm about to get one of those pretty little drinks Andy has and stay right here." She paused. "You?"

"I'll stay, too… If that's okay?"

She shrugged. "It's a big beach."

I could remember so well when things were good between them. They'd met in college, and for such a long time, they were the picture of happiness. I wasn't sure where it went wrong, but it made me incredibly sad to watch it play out in real time.

When he walked away, I looked at Natasha. "He tries…"

"That wasn't trying," she said firmly, her tone sharp. That was the end of the conversation, and no matter how badly I felt for her husband at times, I'd always side with my best friend. I knew her better than anyone, which meant I saw her pain when Jaren was at his most irritatingly obtuse.

"She's great, isn't she?" Andy asked, interrupting my thoughts as Emily walked away.

I smiled, trying to decide what to say, when Natasha spoke up. "She treats you like you don't exist, Andy."

Andy's jaw dropped, and the smile faded from his lips as he attempted to come up with a response.

"Now, that's not fair." Brad came to his rescue.

"And why the hell not?" Natasha pressed. "She's barely looked at him all day. I'm sorry, Andy. She seems like she's a sweet enough girl, but she's totally self-obsessed."

Andy paused. "Do you all feel that way?"

His question was met with silence. Finally, Brad cleared his throat. "I think she's great, Andy. Honestly. But as long as you're happy, that's all that matters."

Torn between my husband and best friend, the truth and a lie, I chose silence.

"I thought you'd all be excited that I've found someone I'm serious about."

I wrinkled my nose at his words. "Are you? Is it serious between you two?"

"Yeah," he said. "This trip was my way of showing her how serious I am. I think..." I held my breath as I waited for him to finish the sentence. "I think I'm ready to settle down. Stick it out. See what happens."

"Does she want to do that?" Natasha asked skeptically. "I think you should talk to her before you make any big decisions."

The life deflated from Andy at her words. "I really thought you guys would be more supportive. Aren't you always telling me I'm too old to keep dating around?"

"Yes," I said, giving him an assertive nod. "And if you're serious about her, and she's serious about you, then we're so happy for you, Andy. We just don't want you to get hurt."

Andy pressed his lips together. "I won't. You guys know me. But just wait, you'll see. This week, you guys will get to know her better and see how great she is."

I hoped he was right, because he truly did seem the happiest he'd ever been. When I glanced up to where she was, as she headed back to the huts, it surprised me to see that she had stopped just a few yards away and was staring back toward us again. Had she heard what we said?

Her gaze was locked on Brad, a small smile on her face. My blood ran cold.

When she noticed me staring, she lifted her hand in a small wave, then turned abruptly and walked away. I looked at Natasha and Brad, though neither of them had seen the exchange.

The only proof that it had happened were the goosebumps lining my arms.

*She doesn't like Brad.*

*And even if she did, Brad would never act on it. He loves me. He loves Andy.*

Still, I couldn't get the image of him staring at her completely out of my mind. I refused to look for her again, though I could swear I felt her stares burning into the back of my scalp.

# CHAPTER TWELVE

## NICK

The sound of crashing waves and distant laughter pulled me from sleep, and I wondered, briefly, where I was and why the hell I was soaked in sweat. When I opened my eyes and looked around, I saw wooden walls that were not my own, white curtains blowing in the wind from the open windows, and then, the ocean. Crystal blue, vast, and utterly terrifying, yet incredibly beautiful in the most inexplicable way.

I sat up in bed, realizing Megan's spot in our bed was empty. Where had she gone? The white sheet fell down my bare chest, and I slid one foot off the bed, the air only slightly cooler out from under the sheet. I wiped a hand across my brow as I walked across the room, pulling my sweat pants over my boxers as I tried to determine where the laughter was coming from.

As I neared the door, I could see them—Megan, Emily, and Laura—sitting in the sand, facing the ocean. They were dressed in capri yoga pants, Laura's sensible black to match the sports bra she wore, Megan's a floral pink and yellow that matched her T-shirt, and Emily's black with cheetah print patterned patches and random cut outs. Her crop top matched. Fashionable, I guessed, but they looked ridiculous, if you asked me.

"Get your head out of the gutter," Brad said, pulling me from my thoughts, which hadn't quite entered said gutter, but were definitely nearing it as the women stood, bending straight over, arms to either side. Emily appeared to be leading them.

I laughed, accepting the plastic cup of coffee Brad held out. "What the hell are they doing?"

"Yoga, apparently," he said, slurping his coffee.

"Don't they know they're supposed to be sleeping in?"

He scoffed. "I planned to sleep in until noon. Laura was up at the crack of dawn to go running."

"Running? Why, is she stressed?" Laura only ran when she was stressed. "Doesn't she know we're on vacation?"

"I guess she didn't get the memo." He snorted, brows darting up. "Anyway, when she came back, Emily invited her to do yoga, and they've been out there ever since."

"How the hell can anything that looks like that be relaxing? It looks painful."

"I don't know, and I don't care. They can keep it up, far as I'm concerned. I much prefer to see my wife like this than in her sweats at home."

I didn't laugh, because he had no idea how lucky he was to get to see her in her sweats, and I so badly wanted to tell him that. Instead, I took another sip of the scalding coffee. It was black when I'd have preferred creamer, but I wasn't a complainer.

"I think the guys are wanting to play some basketball later. You down?"

I nodded too quickly, then backtracked. "Well, I'll have to check with Megan before I agree. She may have something planned. We hadn't discussed it."

Brad waved my worry off. "Emily's already talked them into going to the spa for the day. My guess is we won't see them until dinner. Laura gets in the spa, and you can basically forget doing anything else."

I nodded, my lips pressed together. "What about Natasha?" She was the only one not participating in their yoga.

"According to Jaren, she's still snoring."

I laughed, because of course she was. That was Natasha for you. "Now that's my kind of vacation. We need to get her to teach our women a thing or two." I ran a tongue over my teeth in thought, then yawned loudly before taking another sip of my coffee.

At the mention of his name, Jaren and Andy walked out of Andy's hut together and headed our way.

"Morning," I said as they grew nearer.

"Morning," Jaren said.

"Did Brad tell you?" Andy asked. "About the game?"

"Yeah, sounds cool."

"You're in?" Andy asked.

"Yep, count me in."

"Awesome," Andy said, nodding to Jaren, who blinked his eyes sleepily, obviously not completely awake. I realized then he was wearing a shirt that was obviously a size too big—likely Andy's.

"Oh, shoot, Jaren, I meant to give you clothes last night. Did you get everything taken care of, or do you still need stuff?" I jutted my thumb in the direction of my open doorway.

"Nah, it's cool. I think I've got everything." He looked back out at the girls on the beach, apparently wrapping up their session as they noticed us gathered together.

"You wouldn't think they'd all get along, would you?" Brad said stoically.

"Do you think they do?" Jaren asked.

"Well, I know Natasha doesn't like Emily," Andy said, flat-toned.

"Natasha doesn't like anybody," Jaren said with a sniff.

"Natasha just doesn't know her, man. None of us do," I pointed out. "She seems nice enough."

"She's perfect," Andy agreed. "You'll see."

"Enough about that," Brad said finally, clearing his throat after he downed the last of his coffee and crushed the cup. "I'm going to get changed. Now that we're all up, it's time for breakfast and to hit the gym. I'm dying to see what a *state-of-the-art* gym looks like. Sound like a plan?"

"You said it," Jaren said. "It's gotta be better than my garage setup."

"Yep, I'm in. I'm starving," I said, my stomach grumbling with agreement.

"What are you boys up to?" Emily asked, approaching the group first. She pulled her hair out of the bun, letting her long, dark locks fall down around her face, the roots coated in sweat.

"Making plans for when you ladies disappear into the spa all day," Andy told her.

"You mean you don't want to join us for mani-pedis?" she asked with a grin and wrinkled nose.

"Not if I was held at gunpoint." He laughed.

"Well, don't let me *hold you up*," she jeered, poking his chest playfully. "I'm dying to get to hang out with the ladies." She leaned forward to kiss Andy, and when his hands went around her waist, he drew the kiss out, her tongue pushing forward into his mouth. I looked away, scratching the top of my head awkwardly. We were used to watching embarrassing displays of affection from Andy and the women he dated, but Emily had seemed the least receptive to it until that moment.

When the kiss ended, she turned around, her eyes locked with Brad's, her face flushed red. She touched Brad's arm gently, but only for a second. His gaze locked on hers, seeming lost in the moment. I don't think anyone breathed until she spoke again. Her words came out so low, I almost had to lean in to hear them. "See you boys later."

I watched his Adam's apple bob as he swallowed then looked

away, his neck flaming scarlet. What the hell just happened? Had I been the only one to feel the tension of the moment?

Laura was staring off toward the ocean, her jaw locked in place, and I knew I wasn't the only one. When I looked at Andy, his lips were still red from the kiss, his eyes locked on Brad. Though he appeared lost in thought, there was something in his expression that led me to believe he was thinking the same thing I was. *What the hell was that about?*

# CHAPTER THIRTEEN

## ANDY

We changed into shorts and tennis shoes and headed to breakfast, and then later to the gym within the hour. I purposefully lagged behind, trying to catch Nick's attention, when Brad and Jaren walked onto the basketball court.

"You doing okay, man?" I asked, keeping my voice low as he knelt over the bench in the locker room, tying the lace on his tennis shoes.

He glanced up, his dark hair hanging in his eyes. "Yeah…" He paused, obviously confused. "You?"

I inhaled, running a palm over my face. "Yeah, yeah… Megan seems great."

"She is," he said. "Emily seems great, too. I'm sorry everyone's bustin' your chops about her. You know they're just messin' with you."

I scratched the back of my neck. "Thanks. Listen, I wanted to check in about the whole…*Laura,*" I lowered my voice as I said her name, "thing. I haven't been able to talk to you alone since you told me, and then the next thing I knew, you were engaged."

His expression went stiff, and then one side of his mouth upturned. He exhaled through his nose and rested a hand on my shoulder. "I'm fine, man, honestly. The night I told you about Laura, we'd been drinking too much. It was stupid. I honestly don't even remember most of what I said. Whatever I felt for her is in the past. It's nothing to worry about." His eyes darted toward where Jaren and Brad waited for us in the distance. "You haven't said anything to him, have you?"

"*No*," I assured him, shaking my head, "no. Of course not. I wouldn't. I mean...if you were having an affair that would be one thing, but feelings? Especially ones that were in the past? Never." He lifted his hand from my shoulder. "I just wanted to be sure you weren't rushing things with Megan. I mean, I know I'm the king of *not* rushing things, but it's for a reason. I mean, you've seen Jaren and Natasha." I chuckled, stopping our footsteps and lowering my voice again. "I love them separately, but together, it's a nightmare. I'd never want that for myself, and I wouldn't for you, either."

He looked across the room, where I could hear the thud of the basketball being dribbled in the airy gym. "Thanks, man. Honestly, I appreciate it. But you don't have to worry about me, okay? Megan is *the one.* She's perfect." He raised a brow, laughing with an obvious intent to change the subject. "But can we talk about Emily?"

While she was my favorite subject, there was something in his expression that told me I needed to push harder. My friend was suffering... He was in love with a woman who'd never want him back, and I was torn between my loyalty to my best friend and the desire to comfort my equally good friend in his time of need. Still, there was nothing left to say. If he didn't want to open up, I couldn't force it.

"She's perfect," I said after a pause, my default response when anyone asked. "*So hot.* And funny. She's super smart, too."

"She seems great."

"She is." It was all I could say. Mostly because it was true, she *was* great, but also because, in truth, I didn't know that much about her.

She was still very much a stranger to me.

A gorgeous stranger who was making me rethink everything I believed about dating and relationships and…life.

The kind of stranger I never wanted to let go.

# CHAPTER FOURTEEN

## NATASHA

Emily was cool.

Honestly.

Spending the day with her, I was realizing that maybe I had it all wrong. Sure, she was self-obsessed and vain, but she was young and beautiful, and that came with the territory. She reminded me of Nolan, except that she actually seemed to have her eyes on the future, and she'd built quite a nice future for herself after all.

"Seriously, though," she said through her laughter, "what's the deal with you and Jaren, Natasha? You're not old enough to hate each other yet." We were sitting in the spa, all dressed in white robes, green mud caked on our faces and our feet soaking in something that felt strangely similar to those Pop Rocks candies Nolan had loved as a kid.

I shook my head, my lips thinning, though I couldn't resist the smile that played at the edges of my mouth. "We don't hate each other," I said, and Laura's brows drew down. "We *don't.* At least, I don't hate him. But… I don't know. It's just time, right? We've been together… God, nearly twenty-five years. We got married straight out of college, had Nolan shortly after." I blinked, realizing how long ago that was as I said it. "We've been together longer than we were ever apart. And, at this point, we've found every way possible to get on each other's nerves." I took a gulp of the mojito in my hand. "I love him. He gave me my child. He has worked all his life. He is a good man...but life has beaten us up, I guess. And it was our marriage that took the brunt of the force."

Emily looked as though she may cry, her dark eyes locked on mine. "I'm so sorry."

"No need to be sorry," I said. "We're adults. We've made our bed. Once our son turns eighteen in a few weeks, we're going to file for divorce and get on with our lives. Before we really do end up hating each other."

Laura gasped at my words, and Megan put a hand over her lips, but Emily remained unmoving. "Oh, don't go all dramatic on me, you two. It's not like we're the picture of wedded bliss."

Laura cocked her head to the side, watching me closely. "Yes, but...I didn't realize things were so bad. Bad enough to contemplate divorce."

"We aren't *contemplating* divorce, we're *getting* divorced," I said. "It's fine. Honestly, we're both better for it. I'm just glad it's happening before I'm too old to enjoy myself again."

"Well, I want you to be happy, but what will happen to our group? What will that mean? Do we have to see you separately?" Laura asked, reaching across the salon chair and putting her hand on mine. "I'm so sorry, Natasha. I wish you'd told me."

"You won't have to do anything different. Aside from adding an extra space at the table when I get my boy toy." I winked, though the idea of Jaren bringing someone else sent ice through my veins that I forced myself to ignore. "It'll be fine," I swore, and I hoped to God it was true. "We aren't divorcing you guys, just each other. I swear we won't make it weird."

She nodded, but I knew she wasn't convinced.

"Sometimes, splitting up while things are still amicable is for the best. I think it's really brave of you two to realize where you're broken and look for something better. Something to bring you happiness," Megan said.

"Thanks," I told her, draining the last of my glass. "Where is our lady? I need another."

"She should be back soon," Emily said, brandishing her empty glass. "I need one, too." She looked at Laura. "You two are the same age, right? You and Natasha?"

"Mhm," Laura said. "She's a few months older."

"Why do you have to do me like that?" I asked, a hand to my chest, a growing grin on my face. "'Yes would suffice."

Laura wrinkled her nose at me. "Hey, when it was us getting into bars, you were proud you were older. Now is my time to shine," she said with a dry laugh, taking a sip of her wine.

"So did you and Brad get married straight out of college, too?" Emily asked. "Or did you meet after?"

"We met in college," Laura confirmed. "Around the same time Natasha and Jaren did, actually. But we got married a few years after college. We had a," she smiled to herself, "long engagement. I got cold feet quite a few times, and we ended up with an impromptu wedding in his parents' backyard."

"She says that," I added, "but nothing Laura does seems impromptu. It was gorgeous and looked better than I could've done given six months to plan it, let alone, what? Like a week?"

Laura nodded a confirmation. "Something like that."

"And you two have been friends since college, too?"

"The four of us, yeah," Laura said. "Brad and I, and Jaren and Natasha."

"So where do the rest of the group members fit in? I know you and Nick work together, and obviously you're," she pointed to Megan, "Nick's fiancée and Andy's Brad's best friend..."

Laura drank the last of her wine and set the glass down on the table beside her chair. "Yeah, Nick and I have been friends all our lives. We went to school and then college together, so we've always been close. We opened our dental practice right after college. Nick's family had the space and sold it to us, so it all worked out perfectly. And he met Megan…" She looked at Megan. "A year ago?"

Megan nodded. "Yep. That's right."

"So, she's been part of our group since then, and Andy and Brad were best friends in college, too. But Andy didn't really hang out with us until after we graduated, just because it was always a couples thing."

"I love that," Emily said. "You guys are literally the cutest." She paused, spinning her empty glass around in her long, outstretched hand.

"We're very blessed to have such great friends, and Andy is among one of my best. He's really such a great guy, and he seems so smitten with you," Laura said.

Emily pressed her lips together, waving her off. "Oh, no. We're just having fun. He's a sweet guy, but it's not serious."

"Have you told him that?" I grimaced, shocked by her words as I thought back to what Andy had said the night before. Megan and Laura looked just as taken aback.

"Andy really seems to care about you," Megan said cautiously.

"It's true," Laura added. "I've never seen him so serious about a girl, and I promise I'm not just saying that. In college, Andy got really hurt by someone he was dating who cheated on him, and I've never seen him open up since that ended…" Her eyes drilled into Emily, and there was a warning in her tone. "Until now."

Emily smiled, but it was tight-lipped. "Well, like I said, he's sweet. I care about him, too." She inhaled. "I didn't realize he'd been cheated on in the past. He never told me. You all must know so much about each other. I can't imagine the kind of secrets you must have between all of you."

"Secrets?" Megan squeaked. I was shocked by the sudden

change of subject, though Emily looked relieved to be in control of the conversation again.

"Yeah, I mean...there has to be something, right? Something you're keeping from the others or...from yourselves." She rested her head back in the chair, staring at the ceiling. "Friendships like these are rife with all sorts of scandalous things."

"I don't know. I think we're pretty boring, honestly," I said, wishing that the lady would return to refill our drinks. I was losing my buzz.

"Yeah, totally," Laura said.

"Mhm," Megan agreed, though I noticed her hands were gripping the arms of her salon chair so tight her knuckles had turned white.

"I don't buy that," Emily said. "I mean, statistically, between you all...there has to have been at least one affair, one secret life, and one murder."

I swallowed, my throat tight. When she looked at me, she burst out laughing. "I'm kidding, obviously. Oh my God, you all look terrified."

We laughed, but it was unenthusiastic.

"Well, honestly, Emily. We can't thank you enough for bringing us here. It's been so fun, and I think we all really needed it," Megan said, her voice shaking slightly.

"Yeah, I agree. You're a godsend with this," Laura said. "Brad and I haven't been on a proper vacation in, well...maybe not ever. Not like this, anyway."

"Us either," I agreed. "I can't believe you get to do stuff like this for work."

Emily smiled, seemingly pleased with herself as the waiter finally appeared with fresh refills for us all. "Sorry, ladies. We're running a bit behind today." She took our empty glasses. "If you need more before I come back, just shout across the hall. I'll be around."

"Thank you, Mina," Megan said, because of course she already had the staff members' names memorized.

When she left the room, I lifted my glass to my lips, swallowing a gulp in hopes of bringing back my quickly fading buzz.

"Anyway, like we were saying, thank you. I really can't believe this is happening. It's like a fairytale," Megan said, and I had to hide the fact that I was rolling my eyes. God love her, she could be so cheesy sometimes.

"You're all *so* welcome," Emily said. "Seriously, don't mention it. I'd do anything for my new besties." She tilted the bright red cocktail to her lips and paused, "And besides, the more I get to know you, the closer I get to all those secrets…right?"

# CHAPTER FIFTEEN

## ANDY

By the time dinner came, we were all exhausted. Who knew vacation could be so much work? We took the same seats at the table we'd taken for every meal thus far, almost as if they were assigned, and immediately began looking over the various options on the menu. While most of the others chose similar food each time, I wanted to eat something different for every meal.

"How was your day?" I asked Emily, my voice low. I'd missed her—as insane as that was to say. We didn't live together, didn't know each other on a level where I should miss her after just a few hours apart, but I did. It was the strangest feeling.

"Fine," she said, tucking a stray piece of hair behind her ear. After her day at the spa, she'd changed into her bikini, tying a white wrap around her waist, and had sunglasses on top of her head. This night was much more casual than our first meal on the island. At this point, we were almost all sunburned, and we'd chosen light, loose clothing to ease that pain.

"You look beautiful," I told her, and it was true. Despite her casual clothes, she wore a full face of makeup; her long, dark hair had been straightened, and the top half was pulled back.

"Thanks, Andy," she said, looking up at me finally. "How was your day? Did you have fun with the boys?"

"We kicked his ass," Nick teased.

"Cheated is more like it," Brad argued, shaking his head.

"Don't be a sore loser, Walker," Nick spat back lightheartedly.

"We'll get 'em next time," I called over Emily.

"Tomorrow?" Jaren asked.

"I don't know about that," Laura responded, putting a hand on Brad's chest with a grin. "I would like to spend a bit of time with my husband on this trip." Her eyes danced between mine, and warmth spread in my stomach. She'd never know it, but I considered Laura my closest friend after Brad, the nearest thing I had to a sister. We'd been through so much together, and she'd been right there through most of my life. I couldn't help caring about her so deeply—but those weren't the kinds of things you said to your best friend's wife. My feelings weren't romantic, for the record, not like Nick's. I just genuinely liked her. She was a warm person, always had been. I admired that in people.

"I agree," Nick said quickly. "I plan on relaxing with my girl tomorrow." He wrapped an arm around Megan and kissed her head. "But tomorrow evening, it's on."

I laughed, holding out a fist for him to bump. "You've got a deal."

The waiter came and we placed our orders, and within twenty minutes, our food was in front of us. That night I'd ordered jerk chicken with coconut rice. Predictably, Emily had ordered a salad. It was all I'd ever seen her eat. She reminded me that it was because she had to keep herself in shape to keep up her page, but I believed a carb now and again wouldn't do that much harm.

"You okay?" I asked, watching her pick at her meal. She was the only one who'd ordered a salad that night. Even Megan, the vegetarian, had ordered black bean and green chile enchiladas.

She ran her fork through the salad, nodding, but not looking up at me. "Mhm."

I leaned down closer to her. "You sure? You're being really quiet."

"I'm fine, Andy," she said softly.

"You don't seem fine," I said, laying down my fork. Though we were trying to be quiet, it was obvious we were drawing attention to ourselves. "Did something happen today?" I shot a glance toward Natasha. After all Emily had done for us, if someone had done anything to upset her, I wasn't sure there was any coming back from—

"No," Emily said, laying her fork down without taking a bite and lifting her glass instead. She took a sip of her wine.

"Are you sure? If someone said something to—"

"Why are you pushing, Andy?" she asked, her voice raised. The table fell silent.

"Because..." I felt my face flame red with heat. "Because I care about you."

"Why?" she demanded. "Why do you care about me?"

I scoffed, turning in my chair to face her. "Are you kidding me? Because you're amazing, Emily. You're the most beautiful woman I've ever seen. And you're kind and fun, and...I care about you, okay? Why is that a bad thing?" I should've been embarrassed to say all that in front of my friends, but I didn't care. Emily meant more to me than my pride.

"People always say they care, but it's a lie. We all sit around lying to each other, keeping secrets... We put up this wall of what things are supposed to look like and pretend things are perfect, but at the end of the day, someone always cares less and someone always gets hurt."

"Should we give you two a little priv—" Laura started to say, pushing her chair back, but Emily interrupted.

"I just don't want either of us to get hurt here."

"I know that, but I would never hurt you," I vowed, reaching for her hands, but she pulled them back. She pushed her chair away from the table and stood abruptly. "Emily, please..."

"I need to go back to the hut and lie down. I'm not feeling well."

"Okay. I'll come with you. Should I ask for a to-go box in case you get hungry later?" I stood, too.

"No, Andy, please don't," Emily said, hurrying past me. She lowered her sunglasses over her eyes and stormed away. When she was out from underneath the pavilion, she called over her shoulder, "Please don't follow me. I just need a minute."

I watched her disappear, her shape overshadowed by the sun on the horizon as she got further away. Then, feeling awkward, I smiled feebly and sank back into my chair.

"What the hell was that about?" Nick asked, brows raised. Jaren shook his head slowly, looking back toward the huts.

"I'm sure she's just tired, Andy," Laura said, staring at me as if I were a hurt animal rather than a grown man who'd just had his shit handed to him in front of his friends.

"Did something happen while you were at the spa today?" I demanded, my voice a low growl. Nothing else made sense. They had to have done something. What was I missing?

"No," Megan answered quickly, and the girls shook their heads in unison. "She seemed fine. Honestly. We all had a great time."

"So it's something I did, then? It has to be." I felt tears prick my eyes and looked away, frustrated at myself for getting so upset. I barely knew her. I shouldn't care. It had been so long since I had. Why had I let myself care about her so much?

"No. I don't think you did anything, Andy," Natasha said, her tone less harsh than usual. "She was being kind of weird at the spa, too. Not upset or anything, just...well, she kept talking about secrets there, too. I thought she was joking, but maybe I was wrong."

I felt a sinking feeling in my stomach. "What did you tell

her?" *What do they know?* I looked at Brad, the keeper of all my secrets and the one who knew every stupid or embarrassing thing I'd ever done.

"Nothing, Andy. We swear she seemed fine. I don't know what happened to upset her. Just..." Laura paused. "Just give her a bit to collect herself, okay? I'm sure she'll be fine with a bit of time to clear her head. It's been a long day for us all." Her eyes turned weary as she said it, the crow's feet on either side deepening as she watched me closely.

"A long *few* days. We're all still exhausted from the flight and the boat ride. Plus spending all this time in the sun and heat. We're not used to it. Any of us," Brad added, clearing his throat and rubbing his palm over his lips. "I'm sure that's part of it."

I picked at my food, scooting further into the table. Emily vacationed for a living. She should've been used to it, but I wasn't going to argue. "Thanks, guys. I'm sorry about...*that*." My skin burned hot with embarrassment, anger, and confusion. I wanted to follow her, if not to confront her then to hide away from the scrutiny of my friends' gazes after what had just happened, but I couldn't.

"Don't mention it," Nick said.

"Just don't try to one-up us for public fights," Natasha joked, trying to get me to smile. It was no use.

"Yeah, we hold the title for that," Jaren said, smiling at her. "Reigning champs."

"Seriously, Andy, it's fine," Laura said when I couldn't bring myself to smile.

The waiter appeared with refills for those of us who'd already emptied our glasses, and Brad sighed. "Right on time."

Everyone laughed.

Everyone but me.

# CHAPTER SIXTEEN

## LAURA

I slid under the covers next to Brad, curling up in the bend of his arm, and felt his warm breath on my scalp. Staring through the glass of our windows, I could vaguely make out hints of light on the ocean's surface, though it was almost entirely a black abyss out there. The moon was covered in thick clouds, giving an eerie glow to the places the light touched.

"You've been quiet tonight," Brad said, interrupting my racing thoughts.

I swallowed, unable to say anything. If I did, I feared everything would come roaring out of me, and I couldn't have that. I had to figure out what to do—what to say.

"Have I? Sorry, I guess I'm just tired."

He nodded, his stubble rubbing the top of my head. It had been years since I'd seen him with a beard, but during our time on the island, he'd decided to give up his morning shaving routine. By the end of the week, I was sure he'd have a full face of hair.

*Think about that. Think about something else. Think about anything else.*

"Oh, yeah? Did you have a big day relaxing?" He was teasing, but he had no idea what my day consisted of, not really. "How long's it been since you've been to the spa? Years, right?"

I sighed, forcing a smile, though he couldn't see it. "Yeah, I guess so. I'm not used to that much pampering anymore. Ever, maybe. They really dug into my back during the massage, too, so I'm sore."

His fingers traced a line across my upper arm. "I'm sorry, babe." He paused. "You're being too quiet. Are you worried about the girls?"

Tears pricked my eyes, and I blinked rapidly, hoping to keep them from falling down my cheeks. "Of course I am. I hope they're having fun. I wish my parents had mentioned that they'd spoken with Manu, though. It would make me feel better about them being able to reach us if they need us."

"Maybe they just assumed we knew," Brad offered. "Besides, it was the first time they've seen the girls since Christmas. It's not like they stood much of a chance of getting a word in edgewise." I smiled, thinking of the chaotic drop off, each of the girls relaying their entire previous six months to my parents in rapid succession. He squeezed my arm gently. "This is good for us. I know you're not loving not having our phones, but this is what we wanted, right? A chance to reconnect. A chance to put down the phones and talk again. How long's it been since we just lay in bed and talked like this?"

I buried my head deeper in the bend of his arm as he pressed a kiss to my forehead. He was right. It had been so long since we'd had a quiet moment to ourselves, so long since we'd had a day without interruptions from the girls, from work, from friends. Life had us swept up in the whirlwind, and it was easy to forget why I'd married Brad. Why we'd fallen in love in the first place. This island was bringing those reasons front and center—reminding me how good of a man I had. Reminding me of who we used to be. Before technology. Before kids. Before jobs. "It is nice," I whispered, twisting a piece of his arm hair gently as I felt a tear glide down my cheek without warning.

Brad's voice interrupted my thoughts. "We just have to enjoy ourselves while we're here. It'll be over before we know it… You're, I mean, you *are* glad we came though, right? It's been fun, hasn't it?"

I swallowed, my throat tight because I could never tell him the truth. I had to lie—had to keep lying. It was the only way.

"It's been the most fun. We deserved this." I leaned up to him, pressing my lips to his and praying he wouldn't see the tear on my cheek. He wrapped his other arm around me, groaning slightly as he adjusted, keeping his lips on mine.

I had to end the questions.

I wasn't sure how much longer I could hide the truth.

# CHAPTER SEVENTEEN

## NICK

The steady *tick, tick, tick* on the glass of the door startled me, but mostly because I was staring at the door and no one was there. I blinked with eyelids heavy from sleep and looked around. Had it been a dream? Had I imagined it? Outside was a vast ocean of darkness, hints of moonlight glinting off the sand just outside the hut.

Megan was asleep, curled up with her back to me, blissfully unaware of whatever noise I'd heard.

I waited for a moment longer.

Two.

Silence.

If I'd heard something, it may have been a bird, or some other beach critter. Whatever it was, it was gone. I closed my eyes, beginning to drift back to sleep almost immediately, when I heard it again.

*Tick, tick, tick.*

My eyes darted back open, staring around the dark room. I hadn't imagined it, whatever that meant. Something was outside my hut making noise. But what?

My heartbeat picked up speed in my chest as I sat up from the bed, trying to force my eyes to pierce the darkness. I could see the white outline of the sliding glass door, but nothing beyond it. If someone was knocking on the door, I was sure I'd be able to see them, even just slightly, but there was nothing.

Only darkness.

I pulled on my sweatpants and T-shirt, walking across the hardwood floor as quietly as possible. I had nothing to protect myself with if someone was a danger to Megan or me. But who could it be? Who would want to hurt us? Who would be knocking on our door in the middle of the night? And why? Were we in danger?

I tried to force the ludicrous thought away. Of course we weren't. We were on an island with fewer than fifty other people total, and seven of them were my best friends. There was no place safer.

I reached for the door, pulling it open, and looked out. The wind had picked up, blowing sand across the moonlit beach, but there was no one on our porch. I took another step, looking to my left, down the row at the other huts.

Each was silent.

Dark.

Everyone was asleep but me.

I stared out at the ocean, feeling my chest tighten. It was almost scary at night, how dark and empty it was. It could swallow you whole, and no one would ever know.

"Hey," a whispered voice called to my right, and I jumped, letting out a jolted scream that set my face ablaze. It echoed through the silent night, and I was sure others would wake because of it. I turned to face the person approaching me, trying to make out their shape in the darkness.

"Jesus Christ, you scared me," I said, a hand on my chest as relief flooded me. "What the hell are you doing?" I looked back to where Megan was sleeping in the bed, relieved to see she hadn't moved. Carefully, I slid the door back into place, moving toward my surprise guest.

"Sorry, I didn't mean to scare you," Laura said, keeping her voice a low whisper. "I was at the window, and I thought you saw me."

"No, I didn't..." I could finally make out her face in the moonlight, just flashes of shadows and hints of light. I knew it was her—by her scent on the wind, the lilt of her voice, and the way my heart was speeding up as she drew nearer. "What are you doing? Are you okay?"

"Yeah," she said, but there was hesitation there. "Can we talk?"

Now it was my turn to hesitate. "Sure..."

She waved a hand beside her, drawing me toward the side of the hut where she'd been standing at the window, but continued until we were several yards away from the huts, barely able to see them in the distance. I wondered exactly what she could see while she tried to pull me from sleep...what I looked like in a fit of sleep. Could she even see in clearly? Did she want to? Why was she here? What did she think of me? I didn't know anymore. I cringed at the thought, keeping pace with her. "You're scaring me," I said. "Is something wrong?"

She stopped when we were far enough away I assumed no one could hear us, no longer shaded by the awning, but hidden from the huts by a group of palm trees. In our hideaway, nothing else existed. No one else. We couldn't see the huts. Couldn't see the ocean. The cluster of palm trees and shadows provided the perfect cover from the rest of the world, but not each other. In the dim moonlight, I could make out her face finally, the slight bump of her nose, the long eyelashes, the perfect bottom lip.

*The worry.*

I couldn't focus on anything else, because all I could see was the worry in her expression. Something was definitely wrong.

"It's about Emily."

The statement shocked me, and I let out a slight sigh of relief. "What about her?" Had she noticed the connection between Emily and Brad, too?

"Something's...*off* about her. Have you noticed?" She wrapped her arms around herself as the wind picked up. "I'm worried she's up to something."

"What do you mean?" I resisted the urge to reach out and hold her, keep her warm. A droplet of rain hit my cheek, but I ignored it. Above us, I could hear the gentle lull of rain beginning to hit the tree leaves that were providing us shelter. I should've been concerned about getting caught in the storm, but my only worry was Laura.

"I just...I don't think she invited us here for the reasons she said she did." She tucked a piece of hair behind her ear, wiping away a raindrop from her forehead.

"What reason could there be?" She was talking about Emily and Brad...she had to be. Emily wanted Brad, that much was obvious, but would he ever act on it? I swallowed, my throat dry at the thought. *He'd be an idiot.*

"I don't... I don't know," she said, raising her voice slightly above a whisper as the wind picked up again. "I just have a strange feeling about her. I don't think we can trust her."

I nodded, still not quite sure what she was saying. "Is this about her and Brad?"

She was still, watching me closely. "What about her and Brad?"

"What did Brad say when you told him?" I asked, trying to change the subject. Maybe I was way off.

"I haven't told him... I wanted to talk to you first." She looked down, her bare feet kicking the sand. My stomach lurched at her words. She'd chosen to come to me first. I was the one she'd thought of. The one she trusted.

"Why me?"

She cocked her head to the side, giving me a knowing look. "You're my best friend, Nick..." She paused, her hand unfolding from where it had been wrapped around herself and reaching for my arm. "And you never act like I'm crazy for telling you things that might be crazy."

"It's not crazy," I said, though I still wasn't sure what we were talking about. Her palm spread warmth through my arm instantly. "I just—I'm not quite sure what you're talking about. Do you think she's dangerous? Or do you think she's not serious about Andy?" *Do you think she's in love with your husband?*

"I don't—" The wind picked up and cut off her sentence, and she buried her face in my chest to block the sand that blew through the air. I wrapped my arms around her, afraid I'd never be able to let go, and prayed the wind would keep up. Let it blow forever if that was what it would take to keep us there. Together.

Eventually—all too soon—it died down, and she stepped back. "It's probably nothing," she said finally, shaking her head. "I shouldn't have woken you up."

"Hey," I reached for her, lifting her chin so she had no choice but to look at me. She seemed fragile, so shaken up, and I wanted terribly to understand what had happened to bring her to such a state. "You can always come to me. You know that."

She nodded, moving a piece of hair from her mouth as the wind whipped it around. "I do know." Her smile brightened, but there was a sadness still hidden in the depths of her eyes. "You'll always love me, won't you?"

"Always," I promised, because it was true, but not just in the way she meant.

"Are you okay, Nick?" she asked. "I mean, not just now, but... in general. Are things with Megan okay?"

My jaw tightened, and I pulled my hand away from hers, probably too quickly. "Things are great. Why do you ask?"

"I'm glad to hear it," she said, her hand brushing my arm again. We were a mesh of skin bumping against each other in a confined space, hot breath, and frozen time. So close I could smell her skin, yet unable to breathe her in. The darkness surrounded us, giving way to thoughts I normally wouldn't let surface. "I want you to be happy. You know that, don't you?" She touched my arm again, my body and mind at war as our skin met.

I didn't dare pull away, but I stared at her, ice filling my veins. "What are you doing, Laura?"

"What do you mean?" she asked, her hand not leaving the underside of my forearm.

"Why are you asking about Megan? Why are you looking at me like that?" It was a look I recognized, but one that wasn't welcome. Not here. Not like this. Not when she'd deny it in the daylight. Not when she'd break my heart doing so.

"I care about you, Nick. I'd never want to do anything to hurt you…" She pulled her hand back, her face going into her palm. "Everything is so messed up." Her voice cracked as she whispered the words.

I touched her shoulder, and she looked back up at me, a hint of tears in her eyes. "What's messed—"

Without warning, she pushed up on her toes, her hands cupping my face, and lips meeting mine. My body filled with warmth, then fire, raging through me like she'd lit a match. The sound of the crashing waves and the whipping wind created a vortex—only room for the two of us inside. Nothing else mattered. No one else existed. Time disappeared.

She wrapped her arms around me further, and I pulled her into me, expelling a moan laden with emotion. How long had I waited for this moment to come again? How long had I hoped it would?

She stepped back, and I pushed her against the palm tree, my hands sliding under her shirt. The warmth of her skin under my palms sent lightning throughout my body.

Was any of it real? Was it truly happening? Her fingers laced through my hair, tugging at it playfully as she nipped at my lips. There was so much unexplored passion between us, so much unsaid. Her hands went to the waistband of my sweatpants, and my heart galloped in my chest. There was no going back.

This *was* happening. I lifted her up against the tree as her legs wrapped around me. I wanted it to last forever. I wanted this moment to be how I spent the rest of my life. I couldn't move fast or slow enough. Couldn't breathe, couldn't think.

It was bad, but so good.

It shouldn't happen, but I'd die before I stopped it.

I loved her.

I'd always loved her.

Her hands gripped my back, and I wondered if she felt the same. In that moment, nothing mattered.

Nothing but her.

Me.

The two of us. Moving together. Our bodies melding as one; years of love, desire, and passion between us taking shape.

And then, minutes later and all too soon, it ended. We fell apart, gasping for breath, our skin slick with sweat.

Like a douse of cold water, she stepped away from me, pulling on the shorts I'd stripped away. I adjusted my own pants, trying to slow my racing heart as I figured out what to say. What to do. The reality of what we'd done sat evident on her face. There was so much being said in the silence between us.

She put a hand to her lips, taking a step back. "Oh my God. What did we do? I'm so sorry, Nick..."

I reached for her hand, but she jerked it away. "*Sorry?* No. Don't be. We should talk—"

Before I could finish a sentence, more tears filled her eyes, and she shook her head. "I can't. I'm sorry. I have to go. I'm sorry." She pushed away from me, sand flying up behind her as she ran away, disappearing in the darkness, just a glint of moonlight across the sand and then she was gone. The rain began to fall faster, harder. As if it had held off just for us.

I sighed, lifting my hands to my own lips. Was I even sure I was awake? Had it really happened? I was tempted to throw myself in the ocean to make sure I wasn't dreaming. Let the cool water confirm what I knew—that I'd gotten what I'd wanted for so long. And that it may have ruined everything.

Instead, I sighed, confused as hell, and began to walk back toward my hut. I should've gone after her, forced her to talk to me. But what was there to say? And what if whatever she had to say would only hurt worse?

I shook my head, forcing myself to keep moving. When I reached the stairs of the hut and looked up, I froze.

*No.*

I squinted, but the flash of white I'd seen in the doorway—the blonde hair—was gone. I hurried up the sand-covered stairs, not sure what to say or do or believe or think. It wasn't possible. It couldn't be. How would I ever explain this?

When I reached the door, I took a deep breath, counting one, two, three, and slid it open. The sliding glass door felt heavier than I remembered, and I let out a sigh as I realized Megan was still in bed. The sheet rose and fell with her steady breaths. I'd imagined it. Imagined her. She hadn't been at the door. Watching me. Watching Laura run away. She'd been asleep. I was safe. No longer innocent, no longer faithful, but safe.

I swallowed, the weight of what had happened crashing down on me. The weight of what I'd almost lost. I moved toward the bed slowly, taking steady steps. My breaths were too loud, coming out distraught and ragged. I lifted the sheet gently, one inch at a time, then eased myself in next to her, every move calculated and thought out. Would this be the one to wake her? Finally, I let the sheet cover me, another breath escaping my throat as I listened for her to make a noise.

If she moved, I'd apologize.

If she'd seen, I'd grovel.

If she was, by some miracle, still asleep, I'd gotten way too lucky.

# CHAPTER EIGHTEEN

## ANDY

How mad at me could she have been? What had I done that was so wrong? I walked along the beach, my legs soaked with the cool water from the tide. Wherever she was, she was avoiding me. That much was obvious. So, it had to be my fault. Something I'd said. Something I'd done. Something the women had said about me.

Was it possible they'd do that to hurt me? I didn't want to believe it. Try as they might to annoy me, I had to believe they cared about me. Laura and Natasha especially, though I'd always done my best to make Megan feel welcome in our group, too.

Why weren't they doing the same for me?

Why didn't they like Emily?

I wiped a hand across my face as a raindrop hit it. The wind had picked up, whipping my clothes wildly. Wherever she was, she needed to come home. I was starting to worry. I'd been walking back and forth between the relaxation center, checking the spa, the library, the theater, the gym, the kitchen, and then back to our hut.

Manu told me the forest was too dangerous to walk at night when we couldn't see the path, but if she didn't turn up soon, I was going in there. I wouldn't leave her. I couldn't. Whatever I'd done, I'd make it up to her.

I heard something in the distance, and I looked left. The shape of someone moving near a clump of palm trees caught my attention. I froze, watching carefully and trying to make out where the noise was coming from. *Who is that?* "Em—" I stopped when I realized it wasn't Emily. But there was a woman...

I could see the flash of white in the clump of palm trees, different than the first glimpse I'd seen. Two people. *What the...?* I heard her voice on the wind, when it wasn't blowing fast enough to drown out all other sounds. *What is she—*

I stopped in my tracks, refusing to walk a step further. It wasn't possible.

*No.*

Nick's hands were wrapped around Laura's legs, holding her up, her back against a tree. I squinted my eyes, sure I was seeing wrong, but even in the moonlight, I could see the embrace. The kiss. Her head to the left, his to the right. Upon further inspection, I noticed the clothing strewn about in a heap on the sand.

*No.*

My heart sank, my breathing catching in my throat. How would I ever tell Brad? How could Nick have lied to me? How could this be happening?

I sucked in a sharp breath and walked away, torn between wanting to stop them, wanting to get the image out of my mind immediately, and wanting to get away as quickly as I could before they could see me. The stress of the situation had my heart pounding. I was angry, confused. Everything I thought I knew was called into question. Nick had just told me a few hours earlier that he was over Laura, so why would he lie? And how could he look Brad in the face knowing the lie would destroy his world?

I took a step further, toward the water. I should've said something, confronted them, but what was there to say?

I needed to do something, but who should I go to first?

Nick, to be lied to again?

Laura, to demand the truth?

Brad, because he was my best friend?

I couldn't catch my breath, my head pounding with impossible options as I pushed forward, walking along the shore and kicking sand as I went. It was a mistake to come. To bring these people. Emily and I were falling apart, and now this? Now I'd have to break my best friend's heart? Should I wait for the vacation to end? To say anything now would ruin the trip for everyone. But to wait would ruin it for me. I'd never lied to Brad—about anything—and I didn't want to start now.

As the wind picked up again, new rain droplets hitting my face, I caught a glimpse of someone moving up by the huts. Several yards away and in the dark, I couldn't make them out, but I knew it had to be Laura as she ran past where Nick's hut was. I needed to talk to her. I had to know the truth. She had to know I knew she'd been lying.

I picked up my pace, moving toward her quickly. "Hey!" I yelled, keeping my voice low. I didn't want to wake everyone up, but with the noise of the wind and the crashing water, she couldn't hear me. I moved faster, but I'd lost her; she'd ducked into the shadows of the huts. Maybe to the safety inside.

Had she seen me? Did she know? Was that why they broke apart? I spun around, looking for Nick. If they knew what I'd seen, what would they do? As I spun, something in the water caught my eye.

Something moving in the water.

No, not moving.

*Floating.*

I swallowed, stepping closer. Was it a fish? It was too large.

The dark mass floated toward me, just an unreflective bump in a sea of white ripples, rising and falling with the tide.

My throat went tight as I moved forward, letting the water meet my ankles and then my knees.

*No.*

As it grew closer, it was unmistakable. I reached for her, touching the hair I'd once loved to see piled atop her head. The hair I'd played with when she lay in my lap. I gripped her arm, staring at the hand I'd held in the car. The air around me felt like it had turned to Jell-O, as if everything was happening in slow motion. My vision blurred, my thoughts jumbled. The cries escaping my throat were animal-like as I pulled her to me. I flipped her over, staring at her face in the moonlight.

*No.*

"Emily, *please,* no. No. *Emily?*" I patted her face, shaking her. Trying to press my lips to hers in the ever-moving water. Another scream escaped my throat as I dragged her to shore, my body shaking, fighting against the current and the waves and the growing storm around and within me. Nothing felt real. It was a nightmare come to fruition. It wasn't possible. We weren't moving. I couldn't save her. I couldn't save myself.

It wasn't possible. I wanted to let go. To drift out to sea with her.

*No.* I couldn't give up. There was still a chance.

"Emily!" I screamed, the sound of the ocean soaking up my voice like a sponge.

No one could hear me.

No one could see me.

No one knew what had happened.

No one knew the world ended.

*"Emily!"*

Please, God, no. I wasn't particularly religious, but in that moment, I prayed. I prayed harder than I'd ever dreamed possible. Screams ripped from my chest, guttural sobs tearing through me, the water slapping me in the face. My mouth was full of sea water as I begged for her to be spared. For this to all be a nightmare.

*Bring her back.*

*Save her life.*

*Don't take her from me.*

*I'll do anything.*

I prayed and I cried and I fought the current and I pushed and I breathed into her cold mouth. I did everything I knew to do. I fought for her harder than I would've fought for myself.

The ocean slapped me in the face again, nearly ripping her from my arms, but I clung to her for dear life.

In the end, it didn't matter.

By the time I made it to the shore, she was already dead.

# CHAPTER NINETEEN

## NATASHA

I'd been tossing and turning all night, but at that moment, I was lying awake thinking of all that had happened. Between the group, but also between Jaren and me. What had gotten us to the place we were in? I remembered so many fights over the years, arguments over things that didn't matter in the long run. Screaming fights over things I couldn't even remember anymore.

What Emily said in the spa really got to me. More than I wanted to admit. Sure, I knew my friends knew Jaren and I had problems, but they were around us all the time; they knew our truths. Emily was a stranger. She knew nothing, and yet she knew something I would've never volunteered without being asked. Why had I told her anyway?

What if she brought it up to Jaren?

A sickly feeling washed over me as I pictured the way she'd been looking at Brad lately—Brad, a happily married man.

What if, knowing the issues Jaren and I were having, she tried to go after him? I couldn't have it.

I shouldn't have cared. But I did.

Outside the hut, the wind was howling. Rain pattered on the

roof and the windows. The sliding glass door was closed, but even with the overhead ceiling fan, the open windows were doing nothing for the heat outside except allowing rain to pour inside. I stood up to close them, though I dreaded doing it. I was drenched in sweat, my mind wandering between stress about my marriage, stress about Emily, and the possibility of running headfirst into the ocean to cool off. My husband, insistent on sleeping under a sheet and blanket even in the hottest of environments, was still in bed, sleeping peacefully. I was sure by morning, our bed would be a puddle of sweat.

The wind picked up, howling again, but this time it sounded practically human.

No.

It *was* human. Someone was screaming.

I flipped on the bedside lamp on my table and hurried across the room. Jaren rolled over, one hand over his eyes. "What are you—"

"Something's wrong."

The sound died off, but I knew what I had heard. I walked to the sliding glass door and slid it open, suddenly aware that there were no locks on the doors, and wondering what we would do if something went wrong.

Jaren was sitting up in bed then, one eye still closed. "What are you talking about?"

"Someone—"

There it was again. A cry of pain—of agony. Someone was hurt. I looked at Jaren, who jumped from the bed at the sound.

"What the hell was that?"

"I don't know," I said honestly, the wind whipping around me, cooling me as the sweat dried on my skin. Through the darkness and the storm, I couldn't make out a thing. "Put your shoes on." He reached for his shoes as I did, tossing on a T-shirt as we rushed out the door and across the sand. The beach was dark—it didn't seem like anyone else had been disturbed by the noise.

Jaren moved in front of me, a hand out to keep me behind him as we made our way toward the roaring ocean. The rain pelted us, blurring our vision and stinging our skin, soaking us even more than we already were. "Did it come from this way—*what's that?*" He pointed straight ahead, and I moved around him, trying to catch a glimpse of what he was staring at. I put a hand up over my eyes to shield them from the rain.

*No.*

*"Andy,"* we said at the same time, dread filling my veins. Without another word, we took off, rushing toward him as quickly as our legs could move in the dense sand. He was face down, the tide slapping his sprawled out body, though he wasn't moving. I could hear his quiet sobs the closer we grew, his voice hoarse. How long had he been out there?

"No, no, no, no, no," he sobbed, not looking up even as we grew near, our shadows cast across him.

"Andy?" Jaren yelled. "What's going on?"

My blood ran cold as we reached him and I realized what I was seeing. The places where I'd thought the sand had washed away, creating dark, shadowy rifts, were actually strands of hair. Dark hair. Andy wasn't face down in the sand, he was lying on top of someone.

He was lying on top of someone who looked incredibly dead.

When Andy lifted up, Emily's body was contorted. Even in the moonlight, I could tell. Her head was twisted to the left, her hips and legs pointing to the right. Even for someone flexible, the position didn't look comfortable. The rain slapped her in the face, though she didn't move or seem bothered by it. She was incredibly pale—even more so than usual, and I'd wager a guess that her lips would be blue if there were enough light for us to see them. I knew what had happened, and yet I couldn't make my brain form the words.

Jaren went into action immediately, bending down and grabbing the body. "Andy, move." He dragged her back across the shore, his feet digging in as he struggled to move backward through the shifting sand and raging storm. "Come on." He sighed, breathing out of his mouth heavily. "Help me."

Andy stared in horror, watching it all unfold but not moving. I ran around in front of them, grabbing under one of her arms and helping Jaren move her to dry sand. Once she was away from the tide, we laid her down gently, straightening her body out. Jaren leaned over her, pressing his ear to her lips as I hurried to bring Andy to us.

I threw his arm over my shoulder, helping him to stand. As we moved to safety, away from the ocean's lapping tongue, I checked him for injuries as best I could in the small amount of light I'd been given. He was completely drenched, his hands pruney. Was that from the ocean or the rain? I put a hand to his head, brushing his hair back when we reached the dry sand, standing just a few steps from Jaren, who was working tirelessly performing CPR he hadn't taken lessons on in twenty years. To my surprise, he seemed to remember it, his years of lifeguard training in college paying off well.

We watched in silence as he pounded rhythmically on her chest, pausing to blow breaths into her mouth every few pumps. I needed to do something—to ask Andy what happened, to call for help, but I was frozen in fear.

Did I want to know what happened?

Had Andy done something awful?

How could I even think that?

After a few minutes, Jaren stopped, his head hung low, arms dropped to his sides. Rain dripped from his hair onto the sand. "Is she..." I trailed off. It was too hard to say. Besides, I already knew the answer.

He nodded, not looking at me. "She's gone. I'm sorry, Andy."

A scream erupted from Andy, causing me to jump back with shock. He pushed away from me, falling to his knees beside her body. "She can't be…no. She can't be." He pounded on her chest and blew into her mouth over and over, copying what Jaren had done, but he was doing it all wrong.

"Andy…" I leaned down, trying to stop him. Jaren leaned across her body, forcing him to stop. He was protecting her.

"You're going to damage her body even more," Jaren screamed. "You aren't helping her, Andy. You can't help her." His tone was strong, in command. "You have to stop. We need to get help—call Manu, get the police. There's nothing we can do for her anymore. I'm sorry. She's gone."

Andy stopped fighting against Jaren's arms, his shoulders dropping as he sobbed silently.

"Andy, what happened?" I asked, dropping to my knees and pulling him toward me. He leaned his head into my shoulder stiffly, remaining silent. "Andy, talk to us. What happened?" I demanded, stroking his hair. I needed answers. I needed to know what to say when people asked. "We have to go get help." I lifted his head to look at me. "Is there anything we need to know before we do?"

His face contorted with disbelief. "What are you talking about?"

"Andy, you know we'll protect you," Jaren said, and I was so thankful he was backing me up finally. "If we need to know something before we get the police involved, you can tell us."

He backed up. "What are you—*I didn't do this.* You know I didn't do this."

"Of course not," I said, trying to pull him back to me. "Of course not." It was a stupid thought, but it was there. *It's always the husband.* Boyfriend in this case.

"Go get help," I whispered to Jaren as Andy fell back over Emily, giving in to his sobs. "I'll stay with him."

Jaren started to move, but stopped, his jaw tight. "Let me stay. You go."

"I—" Was he worried about me? Lightning struck, lighting up the sky momentarily, and I heard thunder rumble in the distance.

"Don't argue," he said. "Go." When I stood, he added, "And wake up Nick or Brad. I don't want you walking across the beach at night alone. Especially not in this storm."

I nodded, fear taking root in my bones at his words.

Was I in danger? Were we all?

What happened to Emily?

What was going to happen to the rest of us?

# CHAPTER TWENTY

## LAURA

"*Wake up,*" a voice called. Someone was shaking me in my sleep. "Laura, get up."

I opened my eyes. *Something's happened to the girls.*

Brad was staring at me, standing on my side of the bed, worry plaguing his expression. "Get up." *He knows.* I'd changed clothes when I got home, hidden away all the evidence. How could he know? Maybe it was the girls after all.

"What's wrong? What happened?" I sat up, throwing the cover away from me and searching for my phone before realizing it wasn't there.

"Something's going on outside. Put on your shoes." He walked away from the bed and toward the door, already dressed. The floors beside the windows were soaked, and I noticed, for the first time, the sounds of the rain hitting our roof. It was still storming. Harder now than when I'd made it home. How long had I been asleep? I glanced at the time. It couldn't have been more than an hour, and yet it felt like I'd been sleeping for days. I moved to the windows, shutting them quickly, drying my hands on my clothes.

"What are you talking about?" I grabbed my flip flops from

under the edge of the bed and slid them on, hopeful he wouldn't question why my hair was already wet. I cursed myself for trusting that we'd sleep through the night, that my hair would be dry by morning. Even with so much on my mind, I should've pulled it up in a bun or something. My thick hair retained water for hours once wet. If he asked, what excuse did I have? I'd gone for a walk? I'd taken a middle of the night shower?

He was staring out the open sliding glass door, the worry on his face bringing me back to reality. There were more important things than my own panic. "What is it? Do you see anything?"

"Natasha's outside talking to Nick. They seem upset." He slid the door the rest of the way open as my blood ran cold and I rushed forward.

*No.*

"Brad, wait!" I moved quickly, trying to stop my husband from discovering whatever it was he was about to discover—there were too many possibilities. Had Natasha found out? Had Nick told her? "Brad, stop! Please! Wait!"

He didn't stop, though. Didn't wait. Not when I reached the door, not when I hurried down the porch, my flip flops slowing me down as I reached the sand. The rain slapped my face, blurring my vision as I tried to keep up. I bent over and pulled my shoes off, tossing them back onto the porch and hurrying behind him. "Brad!" I screamed, no regard for the fact that Andy and Emily should've been sleeping next door.

Natasha and Nick were deep in conversation, oblivious to the storm, and I spied Megan standing beside Nick, her arms crossed and a sour expression on her face. What was happening? What did they know?

Brad reached them before I did, and I struggled with whether to speed up or slow down. As I grew nearer, I noticed the distraught expression on Natasha's face.

"What happened?" I asked, pulling her into a hug as soon as I reached the group, not bothering to wait for an answer. She never cried, never worried, so if she was upset, something was very, very wrong.

Nick's expression was washed clean of emotion, raindrops dripping from his hair and clothes. Megan looked as though she were going to be sick. Natasha wrapped her arms around me, and I realized she was shaking, trembling with sorrow.

"What is it?" I asked again, looking at Nick.

He swallowed, shaking his head.

Why was no one answering me?

Brad cleared his throat finally and spoke the words that would've sent me crashing to my knees if Natasha hadn't had her arms around me.

"It's Emily. She's dead."

My arms dropped from her shoulders, my body suddenly shaking as well, as if I had no control over it. My knees were so weak, I was sure I'd collapse at any moment. "What do you mean *she's dead?*"

Natasha pulled away from me, wiping a hand across her face to clear the water, though it had little effect. "She drowned, Laura." She pointed toward the sea, raging and lapping with fury. "Jaren's down there with Andy. He really needs us right now, but I have to go get Manu. We need to call the police. It's bad. Andy's...it's not good."

"Oh my God," I whispered, unable to form coherent thoughts. Nothing made sense. "How did this happen?"

"We don't know," Natasha said. "Andy isn't talking. He's just crying, screaming... I've never seen him so upset. We heard him screaming. It was what woke us up. Jaren sent me to get Manu, but he wanted me to wake someone up to walk there with me. I was on my way here when Nick walked outside."

"I heard the screams, too," Nick explained. "I was coming to see what was happening when I ran into Natasha."

"We were coming to wake you next," Natasha said.

"This is terrible," Megan cried, tears mixing with rain on her cheeks. "Poor Andy."

"I can go get Manu," Nick said, not looking at me. "You ladies shouldn't be on the beach alone. Go down and take care of Andy, okay?" He looked at Megan, who nodded.

"Of course, Nicky. Be careful." She leaned forward and kissed his cheek, and I inhaled a sharp breath, hoping no one would notice the knee-jerk reaction.

"Want me to go with you?" Brad asked, and my chest tightened. *No. Say no.*

"No," Nick said, way too quickly. At least we were on the same page about that. "I'll be okay. Take care of the girls." He looked at me briefly, giving a quick nod before spinning around and hurrying across the sand.

Together, we made our way back down toward the ocean's edge, where I could see Andy and Jaren sitting facing each other over Emily's lifeless body. Heavy rain came down all around them, but they made no move to shield themselves from it.

How had this happened? It felt like a dream. A nightmare. An impossible tragedy.

How was this possible? I couldn't catch my breath as tears welled in my eyes.

How had we come to this?

How had so much changed so quickly?

Would Andy ever survive this?

I wrapped my arms through Natasha's and Megan's, to comfort them, but also to support myself. I wasn't sure I could get any closer. It was too much. It was all too much. Jaren sat silently, letting Andy grieve. It was enough to destroy me.

Megan unlatched her arm when we grew closer, crying loudly as she walked over to where Andy sat. She touched his shoulder, and he looked up at her, searching for something only someone as peaceful as she was could give. She took his hand. "Oh, Andy." He fell into her arms, her face twisted in just as much agony as his was. Together, they cried, and she rubbed his head and whispered softly in his ear. I was thankful for Megan in that moment. More thankful than ever before. She was a warm energy we desperately needed that night. The only warm thing left, it seemed.

I just had to put what had happened with Nick—the fact that I'd betrayed her friendship and my marriage in the worst way—out of my mind for the night.

We sat in silence. Natasha and I gripped on to each other to keep us steady, to keep us *standing*, while Brad made his way down to sit beside Jaren. No one moved after that. No one seemed to know what to say. I felt like I was going to be sick. Maybe pass out. Maybe both.

"What happened?" Megan asked Andy at one point, through her tears.

He seemed to have no answer.

None of us did.

Minutes passed—maybe hours, maybe lifetimes—before Nick reappeared with Manu. Manu was dressed in white sleep pants and an oversized, short sleeved linen shirt in a different shade of white than his pants. His short hair stood up on one end, near his ear, and he wore glasses, water clinging to their lenses.

There was no greeting, no warm wishes for us that evening. Instead, his face was solemn. He approached us carefully with bare feet and watchful eyes, as if we were the threat.

We stared at him. The only sounds were the roaring of the ocean, the thuds of rain hitting the sand, and the whistling of the wind. He took in the scene, his eyes bouncing between each of us, landing on Emily's body several times. Finally, he spoke, his voice carrying a heavy weight in the night.

"What happened?"

I looked at Andy, holding my breath.

"I found her," he said. Simple. Straight forward. He found

her. But found her where? And why? And how? Those were the answers Manu needed to know...answers we all needed to know.

"Where?" he asked first, his voice completely calm.

Andy looked to the ocean. "She was floating. I—I wasn't sure it was a person, at first. But I was looking for her... I swam out. She was...she was already gone." I forced the vision of her floating body out of my mind.

"You brought her back to shore?" Manu asked.

Andy nodded.

"Did you know she had gone swimming?"

Andy shook his head. "She left dinner early, said she was going back to the hut, but when I got there, she wasn't there. I've been walking around looking for her ever since. I thought she was just out for a walk, clearing her head."

My blood ran cold. Why didn't he tell us that? Why hadn't he asked us to help him look for her? Then another, more devastating thought hit me. If he was out looking for her, what had he seen?

"Were you all looking for her?" Manu looked at Nick, who shook his head, wiping rain from his eyes.

"We just found out she was missing."

"Andy, why didn't you tell us?" Brad asked. "We would've helped you look for her." He didn't say it, but the truth hung there in the air. If we'd been able to help look, maybe we could've found her in time. Maybe she'd still be alive.

"I wanted to talk to her alone. I knew she was upset, and I thought having you guys find her would just make it worse." He inhaled a sharp, haggard sob. "I didn't think she would— I didn't think—" He gave up trying to speak, putting his head in his palms instead.

"We will have to call the police and tell them what has happened," Manu said, his voice grim. "But I am afraid the high winds during the incoming storm have taken out the phone lines. I cannot send my men out in a storm like this to get help. There is no choice. We shall have to wait until the storm passes."

"How long will that be?" Natasha asked.

"We are nearly in the heart of it now," he said, raising his voice as the wind picked up as if to agree with him. "I hope by morning it will have cleared, but even still, we will have no phones. I will have to send a crew back to the mainland to get help."

"We have to leave her so the police can collect evidence," Jaren said.

"We can't leave her here," Andy said, gripping her hand. "Not like this." No. He was right. The thought of leaving her outside in the storm, alone, dead…it was enough to make me start crying again, harder this time. What were we going to do?

"No," Manu agreed. "We cannot. Any evidence will be washed away by the rain and the ocean. I will have some of the staff take her to the infirmary until the police arrive." He paused.

"Are we in danger here, Manu?" Megan asked. "Are there… other people on the island? People who could've hurt Emily?"

He pressed his lips together, gripping his hands at waist level. "The currents get strong at night. Perhaps Emily did not realize and decided to take a swim. It is a tragedy, but I do not want you to be afraid on my island. You are safe here, as it is only inhabited by my staff, myself, and…well, you all." The wind howled again, and I stepped forward from its strength. "This was a terrible accident, but I do not believe you are in any danger. Please do not fear."

His words did little to comfort any of us, I knew, and Andy's continued sobs supported that theory. Whenever I'd hear him crying, or look over at him, I'd cry harder. What were we going to do? How would he ever survive this? "Andy," Manu said, practically screaming over the storm and Andy's cries. "Would you like to come with us to take her to the infirmary? Perhaps you would like to say goodbye to her somewhere a bit more"—lightning struck, interrupting his words—"a bit more peaceful."

Andy nodded, not moving from her side, and Manu looked at us. "I should think the rest of you would like to get inside, get dry, and warm up. Please return to your huts, if you will."

I looked at Andy. I didn't want to leave him, not like that. He shouldn't be alone.

"Andy, do you want us to stay?" Brad asked, reading my mind.

"Come with us, Andy," Nick said. "Let's get inside and dry. There's nothing you can do by getting sick yourself."

Andy shook his head. "Please just go," he cried. "I want to be alone with her."

Manu took two respectful steps back. "I am going to wake the staff to help."

Andy nodded, then looked up at Brad, then Megan, then Nick. It was me his eyes landed on when he spoke. There was a darkness there. A fury I didn't understand. "Just go. I don't need you right now."

The words stung, the tone underneath them even worse. "Andy, please, we want to help—"

*"Go,"* he said harshly. Then, again, he bellowed through the storm. *"Go!"* At his command, I took a step back, and then another. The group followed my lead, and we walked back to our huts in silence. Sorrow ripped through my chest as I tried to figure out why Andy had seemed so angry with me specifically. Was it just my imagination? It felt so real. I didn't know what to do. I wanted to comfort him and had no idea how. We split up into our huts without a word, and Brad and I stood in front of the sliding glass door, staring out into the dark night, the sky turning white with lightning more frequently as the storm raged. From there, we couldn't see Andy. Emily's body may as well have been a figment of our imagination, but we knew they still existed out there. Beyond where our vision reached, our

friend was experiencing the worst heartbreak of his life, and we were completely powerless to help him.

"What happened?" Brad whispered, his breath on my ear.

I shook my head in horror, staring out into the dark night through the glass as I swiped away another tear. I couldn't stop myself from crying every time I thought of Andy. "Do you think it was an accident?"

Brad didn't answer, but I hadn't expected him to. How could any of us answer something so horrible. It had to be an accident, didn't it? If it weren't, it meant someone had killed Emily on purpose. And, if that was the case, that meant someone on the island was a murderer.

Which meant any of us could be in danger.

Any of us could be next.

# CHAPTER TWENTY-ONE

## NICK

The next day started off as a strange mix of awkward and solemn. Andy hadn't shown up to breakfast, and still, no one knew quite what to say. Megan cried all night, I couldn't sleep, and from the looks of it, we weren't the only ones. The sky was cloudy, and though the storm had died down, the evidence that it had happened was all around us—limbs and debris spread across the once-pristine beach. Workers were out there, cleaning it up, acting as if nothing had changed. Perhaps hoping we would, too, but we couldn't.

Like it or not—understand it or not—everything had changed.

We sat at the breakfast table in silence, and as I thought about it, I realized I didn't think anyone had talked the entire morning. Was this what the rest of our trip would be like? If so, I would've preferred to go home.

"Should we check on Andy? Or ask Manu how last night went?" I asked, finally breaking the silence as I picked at my food.

"Let him sleep," Natasha said. "Lord knows he deserves that much."

"When do you think the police will get here?" Laura asked.

"Soon," Natasha said. "By dinner, I'd think. They've probably already sent a boat out for help, right?"

I shrugged, though she wasn't looking at me. Brad, who she was looking at, nodded. "I'd say so."

"Maybe we should just all go home," Jaren said, huffing out a breath as he read my mind. "I mean, I don't think any of us feel like vacationing right now. We should get Andy back, help him figure out what's next."

"What *is* next?" Megan asked. "Does he need to contact her family? Or will the police do that?"

"I don't know," I said, when no one answered right away. "I don't think any of us knows how this is going to work. All we can do is be there for Andy. And, honestly, I'm with Jaren. I'm okay to leave if everyone else is."

Slowly, I watched all the heads around the table nodding.

"I'm going to check on him," Brad said finally, pushing back from the table. His breakfast was completely untouched. "I won't wake him if he's asleep, don't worry. But I'm not going to let him lie around alone all day. If I were him, I can tell you I wouldn't be sleeping."

"I'll come with you," Laura said, starting to stand up, but Brad put a hand out.

"No, just...let me have a minute alone with him, okay?" He leaned his head toward his shoulder, and she nodded.

"I can't eat anymore anyway," Natasha said as he walked away. "I'm going back to the hut to change clothes." She put a hand on Jaren's shoulder as she stood. "You coming?"

He nodded, standing to join her. Together, they tossed napkins onto their plates and left the table. Megan pursed her lips, staring around before clearing her throat. "I think I'm going to go back to our hut, too. Come with me, Nicky?"

I looked at Laura, the only one left at the table, and I couldn't help feeling conflicted. She stared down at her plate, chewing slowly as if lost in thought. "Yeah, I'll meet you back there, okay? I need to go check in with Manu about a few things."

"O-okay," Megan said, caught off guard because I hadn't mentioned it until that moment. Namely because I hadn't made it up until right then. "Do you want me to go with you?"

"No, it's okay. It won't take me long." I waved her off, my heart swelling with hope as I waited for her to continue leaving. Thankfully, after a moment's pause, she pushed her chair back.

"Okay, then. See you soon." She looked down at Laura, leaning her head down to meet her line of vision. "You okay? Want me to walk you back to your hut?"

My chest tightened. *No.*

"It's okay," Laura said, giving her a small smile. "I'm going to wait awhile. I need to eat something, even if I don't want to."

Megan nodded, looking between the two of us. "Okay..." She was obviously uncomfortable leaving us together, and I should've just left with her, but I couldn't. There was something I had to know. A few things, honestly.

Finally, she sighed, walking away practically in slow motion. She wanted me to follow her. I should've. Instead, I stayed still, watching her as she grew further away. When there was enough distance between us, I turned to Laura, two seats down from me. "We need to talk."

She seemed a million miles away, and when she looked up at me, it was like she was just realizing I was still there.

"Hm?" Her brows furrowed. "No, I can't talk about last night right now, Nick. Not with everything going on."

"It's *about* everything going on."

Her eyes widened. "What are you talking about?"

"That," I said, pointing to her hands, where she'd gathered them in her lap, nervously picking at the skin around her nails. "You only do that when you're stressed about something."

"Of course I'm stressed," she scoffed. "For so many reasons. I feel terrible about what we did. Wracked with guilt. And on top of that, one of our friends just died, Nick. Where have you been?"

"I know that. Don't you think I feel terrible, too?"

"I have no idea how you feel." She chewed her bottom lip, and I was sure it was going to start bleeding soon if she didn't stop.

"Laura, look at me," I begged, reaching forward and touching her chin. She jerked back as if my skin was scalding hot. "Please don't shut me out. I'm here for you."

"I don't need you to be here for me. We made a huge mistake—monumental. Everything is ruined, and it's all my fault. I can't even blame you. I did this." She put her face in her hands.

"It's not your fault." I lowered my voice. "I could've stopped it just as well as you could've. We didn't. So now we have to deal with it."

"Jesus Christ, Nick. Do you not think there are more important things right now? Emily is dead!" she shrieked. Patches of pink were beginning to emerge on her pale skin. "I can't do this right now."

"I'm not trying to make you do anything. I just wanted to check on you. We're all dealing with a lot. I wanted to be sure you're okay. I'm worried about you."

"How could I possibly be fine?" She closed her eyes, shaking her head. "There's so much going on... Everything's just piling up, and— How could I be fine? Are *you* fine?"

I let out a huff of breath in frustration. "You know that's not what I meant. I just...you can talk to me, you know? I'm here for you."

"I need to go check on Andy," she said, pushing her chair back from the table. I reached for her hand on instinct, and she stared down to where I'd touched her. I wondered if she felt the same pulse of electricity I had.

"You can't touch me like that, Nick. Not now." She put one

protective hand over the place my palm had been just a moment before.

"I'm sorry," I apologized. "If you want me to forget last night ever happened…" I couldn't make myself finish the sentence. It wasn't possible. It meant too much to me. Why didn't it seem to mean as much to her?

*"Emily just died,"* she cried, tears welling in her eyes. "I can only deal with one tragedy at a time. The disaster I've made of my life—of our lives—will just have to wait." At that, more tears began to fall down her cheeks, and she broke out in sobs, her shoulders shaking. She fell into my arms without warning, and I held her steady.

"Shhh," I whispered, rocking her back and forth. "I'm sorry. I didn't realize you were taking it so hard. I thought… I mean, because of what you said last night… Well, I didn't think you really liked her." I shouldn't have said it. As soon as the words left my mouth, I groaned internally. It was the worst possible thing to say. She tensed in my arms.

"What are you saying?"

"Nothing, I just…I know you care about Andy, and of course it's tragic, but Emily herself, well, she wasn't really our friend, was she? You told me just last night you thought she was dangerous." Why was I still talking? I couldn't end the rambling.

Her eyes were wide with unexpected rage when she pulled away from me. "Do you think I don't know that? Do you think I don't remember all the horrible things I said about her last night? Andy cared about her, whether I liked her or not, and whether I trusted her or not. And she's dead now, so what's your point?" She shook her head, still half out of it. The purple bags under her eyes said she hadn't slept either. "That I'm a horrible person? That I'm a monster? That I can never take it back?"

I shook my head. I didn't dare touch her, despite the fact that my fingers were moving her way instinctually. "No, God no. Laura, of course not. You aren't a monster. I could never think that about you. My point is..." Suddenly, a strange thought hit me. Took the breath straight from my lungs. It was impossible. Ridiculous. I shook my head, arguing with myself internally.

But why was she so upset?

More upset than what seemed warranted.

We hadn't really known Emily. And it wasn't as if they were close. "What, Nick?" she asked, studying me. I couldn't make myself say the words. They were awful. Terrible. I felt sick at the weight of them on my tongue.

"*What,* Nick?" she asked again when I'd been silent too long.

"You walked home alone after...after what we did."

Her face grew stony. "So?"

"Did something happen?" I asked hesitantly. "I mean, did you see something? Did you maybe run into Emily? Did she try to hurt you?"

Her jaw dropped, and she glanced behind us. "Are you serious?" she demanded. "Are you really suggesting that I..." She trailed off, a hand on her chest. "Nick, you know I'd never do anything to hurt her."

"I know that," I said, my heart thudding in my chest. "But I know how upset you were yesterday, and then after everything that happened. I mean...you weren't thinking clearly. That's understandable. Did she do something to you? Maybe you were acting in self-defense..."

"What are you talking about?" she demanded, yelling in a whisper. *"I didn't do this, Nick!* I went straight back to the hut. I never saw Emily, and even if I had, do you honestly think I'm capable of murdering someone? Where is this coming from?" Her eyes narrowed at me, so much pain in them, but I had to know the truth.

"I...I'd never suggest you could do anything like this, it's just..." I took a deep breath and forced myself to continue. "Last night when you came out of the hut, when you asked what happened and we told you…"

"Yeah?"

The truth was there, pounding against the walls of my brain, begging me to say what I knew. Four words. Just four little words that would make her hate me even more than she likely already did. But I had to say them. I had to. "You…didn't look surprised."

Her hands were back in her lap again, and when she caught me staring, she pulled them apart. "What are you talking about?"

"You didn't look surprised when we told you Emily was dead. If…if anything, you looked…well," I closed my eyes, "you looked relieved."

Her back straightened. "*Screw you,* Nick. I can't believe you're asking me this, and I can't believe you'd think I'm some monster capable of it. I thought you were my friend—"

*"I am—"*

"Apparently not. I thought you knew me better. I'd never have asked you this. *Never.* I know you, trust you." She stood up abruptly, dusting her hands on her shirt.

"I'm not saying you did anything, I was just asking a question. I'd never tell anyone, even if you did, you know that. I'm trying to protect you, Laura."

*"There's nothing to protect,"* she squealed, her voice too loud. She lowered it. "Please just…just leave me alone." With that, she stormed away, and I watched her go, so conflicted on what to do.

Last night, two unthinkable things happened—one very good, and the other devastating.

I needed to deal with them both. But how, without knowing the truth? Why had Laura kissed me? Why had she let what happened, happen? Why had she been so upset about Emily today?

*What happened to Emily?*

As those questions swirled through my mind, a new one began to form. Two. Three. They took root. Begging to be answered.

Why hadn't Laura answered my question directly? Why hadn't she come out and told me she was innocent?

The last question was the loudest—screaming and clawing at things inside the ripples of my brain: What was I going to do if I discovered she wasn't?

# CHAPTER TWENTY-TWO

## NATASHA

"Hey." The voice behind me caused me to jump, and I looked up from my book, lifting my sunglasses as Nick took a seat next to me in the empty beach chair.

"Hey…" I stared at him. "Where's Megan?"

"She went with Laura to get some food for Andy. Brad says he's not doing well."

I clicked my tongue and closed my book. "Poor Andy. The first girl he actually seemed to care about in years…"

"I know," he said softly, shaking his head and staring off at the horizon.

"You planning to go for a swim?" I asked, gesturing to his swimming trunks and bare chest.

"Nah, just getting some sun." He looked down, his arms resting on his bent knees. "Nothing feels right to be doing right now, you know?"

I did know. Oh, how I knew. No matter what, I felt like I was behaving wrong. We couldn't enjoy ourselves. We couldn't relax. We barely knew her, so we couldn't grieve. Andy didn't want anyone around, so we couldn't comfort him. Every move, every single decision felt wrong.

"I think we're all just doing the best we can to be there for our friend." I paused, because what I was about to say might sound crazy. "Do you think Manu was right? That she just went for a swim and got stuck in a current?"

The answer came after some hesitation. "I don't know. It's possible, I guess." He looked at me then. "But not the most probable answer."

"I hadn't seen her swim in the ocean at all. Truth be told, I hadn't seen her go near the water. So, what would make her decide to go for a swim last night? Why would she do it alone?"

Nick's brows drew down, and he shook his head. "I just don't know, but I don't want to think about the alternative."

"What? That someone did it? Hurt her?"

He nodded. "It's one or the other."

A cold chill ran over me, and I wrapped my arms around myself to warm up. "But who?"

He rubbed his hands over his knees, not responding at first. When he did, he wouldn't meet my eyes. "I don't know. I need you to tell me what happened at the spa yesterday."

"What do you mean?" I asked, taking in his serious expression.

"When you guys left, everything seemed fine, but when you came back, Emily was obviously upset about something. Did anything strange happen? You said she kept talking about secrets. Was that it? Nothing else weird? Nothing to give you a hint what she might've been talking about?"

"No, nothing. Not that I know of, anyway." I paused, because it was only a partial truth—something *had* happened. Something strange. But I wasn't sure what I could tell him. Honestly, I wasn't even sure what I knew.

"Everything was fine the whole time? You all got along? No drama?"

I pursed my lips at him. "Why are you asking so many questions, Nick?"

"Because I want to know the truth. When you left, Emily seemed fine. Something happened between going to the spa and meeting for dinner, when she was obviously upset about something. And the next time we all saw her, she was dead. Did someone tell her something? About Andy? Or...or was there some sort of a disagreement?"

"No, Nick, there was no disagreement. I'm telling you everything was fine. We had a nice time, a few drinks, and a bunch of laughs. She seemed totally okay at the spa. Something must have happened after she left."

He put his fingers over his lips, squeezing them mindlessly, lost in thought. "Where did she go after the spa?" he asked.

"I have no idea. We all split up, went back to our huts. I didn't see her again until dinner."

"So she must've gone back to see Andy. I wonder if she seemed upset when she got back. He didn't mention if they'd been fighting..."

"Are you going to ask him?" I asked, unable to hide my grimace. "I mean, it doesn't seem like the best timing."

"The police are going to be asking when they get here anyway," he said. "I don't want to push him, but if we *are* in danger, I think we all want to know."

"Well, we know it wasn't any of us, so who could it be? One of the workers? Manu? I mean, he seems like more of a lover than a fighter, you know? What are the other options—you think there's a serial killer in the jungle?"

He shook his head, not grinning at what was supposed to be a joke. "I have no idea, but I'll be glad when the police get here."

I lowered my glasses over my eyes as the sun peeked out from behind a cloud. "I know one thing. I'll be glad when we can get off this island."

"Some vacation, right?" He patted his knee with a scoff, staring back out across the water.

"Some vacation..." I paused. I wanted to help, but I didn't

want any fingers pointed at the wrong people. "Hey, Nick, look…I don't want to start anything, or…or point fingers at anyone. I like Megan. I know I don't always show it, but I do." I paused, chewing on the inside of my lip.

"What about her?" he asked defensively.

"It's probably nothing, but you could ask *her* what happened at the spa."

"Why can't you just tell me?"

"I've told you all I know, but there was one point when Emily and Megan went outside for a while. We'd been waiting on our drinks to be refilled for a while, and Emily offered to go get them. Megan went with her."

He studied my face, not saying anything. "I'm not saying anything happened," I went on. "It was probably nothing. But maybe Emily said something to her." I shrugged one shoulder. "It's worth a shot, anyway."

His lips were tight as he nodded then patted my knee. "Thanks. I'll ask her. You're right. At this point, we all may know more than we realize. We just need to piece it together. Thanks, Natasha."

"Anytime," I told him, opening my book again as he pushed up on his knees, standing up with a groan. "I'm just your average armchair detective. Happy to be of service."

He paused, knowing me better than most people and recognizing the sarcasm I used as a shield. "You're going to be okay, right?"

I nodded, thankful my sunglasses would hide the imminent tears. "Always. Let's just all get home alive, okay?"

His nod was a salute, a promise. When he spoke, it was a vow. "I'll do everything I can to make sure that happens."

# CHAPTER TWENTY-THREE

## ANDY

"Knock, knock," Laura said, saying the words rather than actually doing the knocking. The sliding glass door was already cracked, but she pushed it the rest of the way open, and she and Megan stepped through.

"We brought you chicken noodle soup and iced tea," Megan said. "Comfort food and something to keep you cool."

"The *world-renowned* chef made chicken noodle soup?" Brad asked from where he sat by the window. He'd been with me all day, sitting quietly, waiting for me to talk, but I had nothing to say. I felt empty, hollow. This was my worst nightmare come true, and I had no one to understand it. None of them liked Emily, anyway. They didn't care that she was gone. They didn't understand how I was feeling or how much I was hurting.

"Special request," Laura quipped, easing down on the bed. She rubbed my ankle carefully. "Andy, do you want to eat something?"

I grunted a response, not bothering to move.

"Come on, sweetie, you need to eat something," Megan said, sitting beside Laura. They looked up at me as if I were a child. Someone to coddle.

"I'm not hungry..." I croaked, my voice hoarse from hours of screaming and crying. Exactly like a child. I squeezed my eyes shut. I just wanted it to all be over. I wanted to talk to Manu and tell him I wanted to go home early. To be alone. It was too hard being here.

"Well, how about a drink, then?" Laura asked. She leaned closer to me when I opened my eyes, setting the Styrofoam cup and bowl on my nightstand and moving to open a window—all the windows. "It's so hot in here, and you haven't had anything to drink. You're going to dehydrate if you don't get something in your system."

"Newsflash, Laura, I already have a mother. I don't need you to tell me what to do—"

*"Easy,"* Brad warned, giving me a cold glare. "She's just trying to help."

Laura didn't miss a beat as she moved back toward the bed, a breeze now carrying across the room. I didn't want to admit how good it felt. I wanted to be hot. Miserable. It was still a better end of the deal than what Emily got. At least I was alive. "We're really sorry about Emily, Andy."

"Yeah, I'll bet you are," I muttered, hardly moving my lips.

"What's that supposed to mean?" Brad asked, standing up then. If he wanted to fight, I could take him down. I was taller than him, stockier. But I didn't care. I didn't care what he did or what I did. I couldn't feel anything except pain. A vast, empty pain that dulled everything else.

"You know damn well what it means—Laura and Natasha already admitted they didn't like her. She just wanted to be accepted. She brought you here, to this island, to get to know you all, and instead you shut her out and made comments about her age and how badly she treated me. You didn't even try to get to know her." I looked at Laura, whose shocked expression brought me a strangely heightened sense of pain. Why was I doing this to someone I cared so much about? It was like I couldn't control myself. Maybe I wanted them to hate me. Maybe that was easier than caring. "They're probably glad she's —she's—" I couldn't bring myself to say the word. It was too awful.

"Oh, Andy, what a terrible thing to say," Megan said, shaking her head.

Laura stood still, staring at me. "I never said I didn't like Emily. Some of the things she did—the way she treated you—bothered me, but only because I care about *you* so much, Andy. You're like a brother to me, always have been. I'm protective of you. I know you're hurting right now, but that doesn't mean you should forget who cares about you, who's always been there."

"You're all always nagging me about not settling down. I'm too old to keep dating around apparently, but when I finally find a girl I care about, a girl nice enough to bring us all here, she's not good enough for any of you. You treated her like crap… Don't think I didn't notice. And now, because she's gone, you want to pretend you were just a saint to her—"

"Name one time I treated Emily badly," Laura challenged.

"Laura—" Brad interrupted.

"No, I want to hear him do it. I want him to tell me a single thing I ever did to her." She looked at me again, scarlet patches on her skin. "Because, yes, I may have thought *privately* that she may not care about you enough, but I never said anything of that nature when she was around. I was nice to her, Andy. I treated her well, tried to make her feel welcome. I cared about her because I care about you." Tears were in her eyes then, really cementing the shitty feeling in my stomach.

"You should've protected her. She went to the spa with you, and she came back upset. You should've taken care of her. If someone made her mad, you should've fixed it." Tears blurred my own vision then, and I wiped them away furiously. "I trusted you with her, Laura, trusted my friends to make her feel welcome, and when she came back to me, something was all wrong. And now she's dead, and I don't even know why. She wouldn't have gone in the water, not at night and not alone. So what happened? Hm? What happened when you were at the spa? What happened to Emily?"

"I wish that I knew, Andy." She took another step toward me, her tone changing. "Honestly, I do. When I saw her last, I thought she was fine. I mean, she kept talking about secrets and…she acted strange, but not like at dinner. And we did everything we could to make her feel welcome." She looked at Megan, who agreed quickly.

"It's true. I thought we were all getting along well," Megan said. "I really did like Emily. She was a sweet girl."

"Why *was* she talking about secrets so much?" Brad asked, watching Laura. "Did anyone ever figure that out?"

"I think maybe she was just being coy…" she said, staring at Megan. They both seemed apprehensive.

Megan took a breath before saying, "She kept talking about how there must be a ton of secrets in the group. I think she was joking, but…she did mention it quite a few times."

"She had to have mentioned *something*." I furrowed my brow. What could she have been talking about? I'd spent the whole previous evening thinking about it, questioning everything I'd said or done since we'd arrived on the island, but finding her body had cast all my other thoughts aside.

"I don't know. She didn't elaborate, and we told her there weren't any secrets," Laura said. "It wasn't like she talked about it the *whole* time. She just brought it up once or twice. We were trying to enjoy ourselves, too. Like Megan said, I just assumed she was teasing, I guess. No one pushed her for an explanation."

"Was she asking about me? About…my past? All the women I've dated?"

"Oh, Andy." Laura took a seat on the bed next to me again, swiping away the tears on her cheeks. "You didn't do anything wrong. Is that what you think? That we told her something awful about you and that's what caused this to happen?"

I swallowed, unable to look at her, because until that moment, it was exactly what I thought. But hearing it out loud, I knew her better than that.

"I just want her to come back," I cried, covering my eyes with my fists. I'd been mad at them for treating me like a child, but that was one hundred percent how I was feeling. I was filled with such rage, such embarrassment, such sorrow.

"I know," Laura whispered, and I felt her hand on my back, rubbing cautious circles. I was drenched in sweat, but she didn't seem to care. I both loved and hated her for how much she cared about me in that moment. Why couldn't she just get mad at me like a normal person? "I know, Andy. I want that, too."

I turned away from her, unable to say anything else. The room was quiet after that; the only noise was the steady whistle of the breeze through our windows. I listened to it, letting it lull me nearly to sleep.

"Maybe you can give us a minute?" I heard Brad say, and though I didn't hear the women leave, I knew that was what had happened. I felt the emptying of the room, and I knew we were alone.

After a minute, I wiped my eyes and looked up at him. "I'm such a mess."

"Yeah," Brad said, matter-of-factly. "You are. We all are."

"She was the one, man," I said. "I really think she was."

Brad shook his head.

"What?" I asked.

"Andy, I know you cared about her, but was she really *the one*? I mean, did you love her or did you just...I don't know, did you just think she was interesting and hot?"

"What?" I curled my upper lip at the insensitive question. Brad had never been one to beat around the bush. "What kind of a question is that?"

"I believe you cared about her, man. I do. But I think a huge part of that was just that maybe you just enjoyed the chase more than you realized. It was exciting, right? And, now, that doesn't mean you don't get to grieve, because you do and we'll all be there for you, but you barely knew her. You have to keep perspective, right? You need to remember your friends and the people who are here for you. Who've been here for you through everything. I know Laura's a lot, but she's trying to help. We all are. Be upset if you want, but just don't forget who's been there for you."

I sniffed, rubbing a hand down my face. Was he right? I *thought* I cared about Emily, but did I? I didn't know as much about her as he knew about Laura, sure. But did that make my feelings any less real?

He jutted his chin toward the door with a dry laugh. "Anyway, thanks for coming to my TedTalk. Now, for the real therapy, let's go get a drink."

# CHAPTER TWENTY-FOUR

## LAURA

It was after midnight and Brad still hadn't returned. He and Andy had been absent from lunch and dinner both, but I knew they needed space, and my presence only seemed to make things worse.

Natasha could see the worry on my face. We were gathered on her bed, Jaren dozing off in the chair by the window as we waited up. Every bit of movement in the moonlight caused me to look that way hopefully, but no lights came on in Andy's hut.

"Maybe we should just go check," Natasha said finally, nodding. "Maybe they slipped in and went to bed, and we just missed them."

"Wouldn't Brad have come looking for me? He would've known I'd be here if I'm not there."

"I would think, but it won't hurt to get up and check. We aren't doing anyone any good by sitting here wondering." She stood from the bed and held out her hand. "You coming?"

I nodded apprehensively. The idea of walking on the beach at night terrified me, but I couldn't deny how nervous I felt at seeing Brad not return. What if something had happened? The very idea was enough to send me running out after him.

"We'll just check the huts, and then if they aren't there, we'll go up to the relaxation center and make sure they're *somewhere.* They should know better than to worry us so much."

"I don't think Brad's thinking about that too much. You didn't see Andy today, Natasha. He's in bad shape… I've never seen him so upset."

Her expression was grim. "That's how he was last night. It's bad." She nudged Jaren's arm gently. "Hey…"

He jolted awake, looking around. "What's wrong?"

"Nothing's wrong. We're going to check and see if Andy and Brad made it home yet." She paused. "Do you want to come with us?"

"Yeah, yeah," he said, standing up and adjusting his clothes. "What time is it?"

"After midnight," I told him.

His jaw dropped slightly as he rubbed his eyes. "And no one's heard from them?"

"No," I squeaked, not wanting to show him how worried I was, but I could see the same fear reflected in the tight line of his lips.

"I'm sure they're fine," he said. "But yeah, let's go check."

We ambled out of the hut, the cool wind much calmer than the night before. The beach had been cleaned like nothing ever happened. Every scrap of stray rubble had disappeared between breakfast and dinner, and the night was eerily reminiscent of our first night. As if nothing had happened at all.

I tried to push the thought from my mind as we checked Andy's hut, which was empty, then moved to mine and Brad's, which was also empty. We walked past Nick and Megan's, noticing the two lumps under their covers. They were sleeping peacefully, unaware of all that was happening. I couldn't help feeling the bitter sting of jealousy, not at their happiness, but at their peace. I hated fighting with Nick. Hated what he'd accused me of more.

Tears lined my eyes as we continued over the beach, and I refused to look out at the water. If Brad and Andy weren't at the bar or restaurant, and they weren't in the gym…where were they? Would I be spending my night searching for them as Andy had for Emily last night? Would my search meet the same grim end?

I couldn't bear to think of it.

We walked in silence, and I wondered if everyone was thinking the same thing. When we could see the lights from the relaxation center ahead, fear flooded me. They weren't outside at any of the tables. One less place to check. One less possibility.

"We'll look inside," Natasha whispered, as soon as the building came into view.

I nodded, fighting back tears as I moved. If I tried to speak, I was sure I'd let out the sob that was tight in my chest.

We moved past the table that had been cleared since dinner and up toward the door. Jaren reached for it, holding it open so we could pass through it first. To the right was the doorway that led to the spa. Straight ahead was the hallway that led to the gym. To the left, the kitchen. We chose left, turning and walking into the small, restaurant-style dining room, and my heart leapt, relief washing over me.

"Oh, thank God," Natasha said, taking the words straight out of my mouth. Her voice carried across the quiet room, over the sound of beachy music, reminiscent of what had played on our boat ride over, playing softly from a loudspeaker in the corner of the room. Brad and Andy turned their heads from where they sat at the bar.

"Hey," Brad said, his cheeks pink the way they looked only after he'd had a few too many drinks. "What's up?"

"Are you two planning to come home soon?" I asked, glancing out the dark window.

"It's getting late," Natasha added. "We were worried."

Brad glanced at his wrist, though he wore no watch. "What time is it?"

"After midnight," I said.

He put a hand to his forehead. "Holy shit. No way…" He patted Andy's back. "We've gotta call it a night, man."

"One more for the road," Andy said, from where his head rested on the bar.

Brad looked at me, a question in his expression.

"You both look like you've had enough," I said softly. "Let us help you get home."

"There she goes, Mom-ing again," Andy sang, lifting his head up sleepily and laying it back down.

"Andy, please—" I started to say.

"I'll wait with them if you want," Jaren said. "Make sure they get home safe. I can walk you two home and then come back for them."

"No," Natasha said. "I don't want you walking back alone either. Laura and I will be fine. We should stay in pairs at night."

Jaren didn't appear to agree, but he gave in. "Are you sure?"

I chewed my lip, worried as much about Natasha and me walking home alone in the dark as I was about Brad and Andy walking home alone and drunk in the dark or Jaren walking alone, period.

"Yeah, it's fine," Natasha said, gripping my arm. "But I want all three of you home soon, okay? I'll wait with Laura at her hut. I'm talking twenty minutes, tops."

Jaren nodded and leaned in, kissing her lips. She looked as shocked as I did.

"Be careful," he whispered. "Go straight there."

Her fingers went to her lips, and she nodded, her eyes growing misty. "We will. I'll see you in a minute?"

"See you in a minute," he promised, and I felt Natasha pulling me away. I waited for Brad to worry, to call after me, to say we should wait, but he didn't. Instead, I watched him hold up two fingers to the bartender, ordering another round.

I ducked my head, spinning around to leave with Natasha, trying to hide the sheer terror I felt as we opened the doors and looked out into the black night.

Deep down, I couldn't deny the voice in my head saying that this wasn't a coincidence or bad timing. Something bad had happened to Emily, something worse than an accident, and the longer we stayed on the island, the closer I felt we'd be to meeting the same dreadful fate.

---

THE NEXT MORNING, I stared at my phone, wishing it would do more than tell me the time, which was 6:07 a.m. My alarm was scheduled to go off in just thirty minutes—I couldn't bring myself to remove the notification about yoga on the beach every morning this week with Emily.

With a heavy heart and pounding head, I stood from the bed and unplugged my phone, switching off the alarm. I walked up the stairs to use the restroom and brush my teeth, swiped on deodorant, and tiptoed back down the stairs to the first floor. Outside, the sun was beginning to peek over the horizon, providing the light I so desperately craved. I wanted to get outside, my legs were itching to move, but I wouldn't dare when it was still dark.

My footsteps were quiet on the wood flooring, but not quiet enough to keep from waking my husband. He rolled over in bed as I was pulling my workout pants on, one hand on his forehead as he groaned.

"Oh, God." He released a long, drawn-out sigh and laid his head back down. "I feel like death."

"Well, I'd imagine so," I teased, trying to bite down the sting of his word choice. "After a hard night of partying like you were a college kid, not a forty-year-old man, I wouldn't expect you to feel well."

He winced, his eyes still shut. "I'm sorry, *Lor*. I didn't plan to drink so much." I watched him prop himself up on his elbows. "Are you mad?"

I slid the shirt over my head, covering myself with one arm as I maneuvered the sports bra over my shoulders. No one should've been up, but that didn't stop my uneasiness at our open windows, despite being too lazy to shut them for just a second's change or walk back up the stairs to undress there. "No, I'm not mad. I wish you would've given me some sort of heads-up as to what was happening or where you'd be, but I'm not mad." I tugged a pair of socks from my suitcase and sat down on the edge of the bed to pull them on. "How's Andy doing?"

He rubbed his palm over his face. "Not any better than he was, honestly."

"When are the police supposed to be here?" I asked, sliding my feet into my shoes next. "I thought they'd be here yesterday, but Manu said something about having to send a boat out. I haven't seen them."

"We asked, too. Manu said the phone lines are still down, and without a way to contact the catamaran company, they have no way to get to the mainland."

"You mean there aren't any other boats here at all? I thought he said something about sending employees back to the mainland when the storm calmed down. I thought they'd already be there and back by now."

"There is one, but as luck would have it, it's being repaired right now. When I asked him what they normally do in an emergency if they don't always have a working boat, he said they have a board-certified surgeon and two nurses on staff here to treat patients in case of an emergency. I guess they didn't plan to have to leave the island with phones being down, so it wasn't a priority to get it fixed. According to him, it's an unfortunate coincidence."

I scoffed, unable to believe what I was hearing. "It's a bit more than that, don't you think? That's not safe! What about when someone needs to get home? What if there was an emergency with the girls?"

"Well, normally, they'd have the phones, I guess, so getting the catamaran back would only take a day or so. It's not like this is a normal circumstance, and the resort is new. They're learning. I'll bet they never make this mistake again. For now? His words exactly were, *the island provides.* So, I guess we just wait."

Once my laces had been tied, I stood up, hands on my hips. "I don't like that. How long will it be until the phones are back up? This is such a safety hazard."

He nodded, laying his head back on the pillow once more. "I'm sure they're working on it as quickly as they can."

"You don't seem concerned."

"The only thing I can be concerned about at this exact moment is making sure I don't projectile vomit across the room." He squeezed his eyes closed, pinching the bridge of his nose.

I blew air from my lips, watching as my hair flew up and out of my face. "Okay, well, I'm going for a run before it warms up too much more."

"Don't stress, babe. Everything's going to be okay."

I nodded, though he couldn't see me, and even if he could, he had no way of knowing that was true. Everything was far from okay as it was, and I didn't truly believe that was going to change any time soon.

As I walked out of the hut, I heard him call, "Stay close," which was further proof that he was just as worried as I was.

I hadn't run in months, but it was the only thing that worked to relieve my most debilitating stress. I had to move, to free my mind and think only of keeping moving.

I jogged down toward the water until I hit the wet sand, packed enough to run on, popped my AirPods in—incredibly thankful Bluetooth still worked on the island—and began to run.

Within minutes, I felt my stress begin to melt away. It was the most beautiful, miraculous thing, the way my burning thighs made everything else disappear.

The beach was breathtaking in the morning with no one around. As the sun came further above the horizon, I watched its reflection dancing on the waves and saw the silhouettes of birds that crossed in front of it.

It was peaceful and reminiscent of the first morning when we'd boarded the boat, sailing away from the life we'd known and preparing for our long ride to the island—and the first glimpse when it came into view.

I remembered the way I felt, hopeful, but also a bit fearful of what was to come. Why hadn't I trusted that gut instinct? Why hadn't I said no to this trip altogether?

But no matter what, whether we'd come or not, Emily would've been here, wouldn't she? She was the one chosen out of what must've been hundreds or maybe thousands of applicants. If we weren't there, would she still be alive?

Maybe, if it was truly an accident. Maybe if something hadn't upset her, she wouldn't have tried to swim.

But if it was murder...if someone actually meant to hurt her...I had to believe that us being there or not hadn't affected her death. Right? Because, if not, that would mean it was one of us who'd killed her, and that wasn't even an option.

I glanced behind me as a chill ran over my arms, feeling sick to my stomach. I could still see the huts in the distance, though they were getting smaller the farther I got from them.

In the far distance, I could see the tiniest hint of the relaxation center, its lights still off for another hour. The small dots of white lounge chairs speckled the beach. It was completely desolate, except for one dark shadow sitting in the front row of chairs.

I slowed my jogging for a second as I pulled an AirPod away from my ear, the music stopping in an instant. What was he doing? I took in the familiar shape, the face I knew so well as I grew near.

He wasn't looking up, he either couldn't hear me or didn't care that I was coming.

Was he asleep?

Or...*dead*?

"Andy?" I called, moving faster in a hurry to get to him as the worst possible scenario swam through my head. *Please, no.*

To my great relief, he looked up finally, staring at me as I made my way to him. I stopped, my hands on my knees as I tried to catch my breath. His eyes were red and bloodshot. He'd either been crying, still drinking, or both.

"What are you doing out here?" I asked, when he hadn't said anything.

He jutted his chin toward the ocean. "Emily wanted to watch every sunset while we were here." His lips quivered, and I was assured the redness in his eyes was from tears. "I couldn't even make it to the first one. I was tired, jet lagged. I told her there'd be...plenty more." He sniffed, rubbing the back of his hand underneath his nose.

"Andy, you didn't know. You can't keep blaming yourself for what happened. It was an accident—"

"No," he cut me off sharply. "No, it wasn't an accident."

"What are you talking about?"

"Emily didn't go swimming that night. It wasn't an accident. Someone murdered her." He stared straight ahead, conviction in the deep timbre of his voice.

"Y-you don't know that, though, Andy. You shouldn't think like that."

"I do know." He nodded, swiping a hand under his nose

again. “I didn’t want to believe it, but I know what happened to her.”

My blood ran cold. “What do you mean? You know what happened to Emily?” Was he delirious? He didn’t seem to be. In fact, he seemed to be in much better condition than my husband was.

“Yeah, I do.” The answer came out as a dry laugh.

“What is it, Andy? What happened to her?” I asked, sinking down into a crouched position, my hands resting on my knees. “Why didn’t you say something sooner?”

“It’s complicated,” he said, twisting his lips in thought. “If I tell you, you have to swear you won’t say anything. Not until… not until I’m ready.”

“I swear, Andy.” My heart thudded in my chest, and I wasn’t entirely sure I wasn’t dreaming. What was he talking about? What did he know?

He pushed himself up, pointing toward the woods behind the relaxation center. “Come with me.”

He was walking away before I had a chance to comprehend what he’d said, but I let the words wash over me. “Where are you going?”

No answer came as he continued to walk, headed around the far side of the building. And then, despite every muscle in my body screaming that I should turn the opposite way, despite a nagging voice telling me it wasn’t safe, I followed him.

And then, I disappeared, too.

# CHAPTER TWENTY-FIVE

## NICK

I was up by seven without prompting from Megan, my nerves on edge. I wasn't sure how much longer I could stay on the island. I waited on the porch for her, struggling to form thoughts around how worried I felt. I was used to being cool, collected, and in control, so this was entirely new and unwelcome for me.

I kept staring at the place where we'd found the body, just a few yards from where I was sitting. Emily was the first person I'd ever known to die. Both my parents, both sets of my grandparents even, were still alive. Her death shook me to my core, and having to sit around with nothing to do but think of it made it worse.

I wanted answers. I wanted to know the truth.

The sliding glass door opened and Megan walked out, her long hair tied back in a braid. She draped an arm over my shoulder, her lavender perfume surrounding me.

"You couldn't sleep, either?"

I shook my head. I felt weak for caring so much. Emily meant nothing to me, and I was acting like I'd lost someone I'd known my whole life. I tried to reason that it was the shock of it all that had affected me, but I knew it was more than that. Everything just felt wrong about what had happened. Everything felt wrong moving forward, too.

"I can sleep fine, I'm just having trouble staying asleep for long," I said.

"Same here." She shivered, wrapping her arms around herself as she walked around me and took a seat in the empty chair to my left. "Is anyone else awake?"

"I haven't seen anyone." As soon as I said it, I heard a voice coming from one of the other huts. We turned our heads, staring out as Brad's door opened and he peeked his head out. "*Spoke too soon*... Morning," I called, waving a hand over my head. He looked terrible—his hair disheveled, eyes red and bloodshot.

"Mornin', have you seen Laura?" he asked, wincing from the sound of his own voice.

"Long night?" I chuckled. "You look like hell."

"I feel like it," he agreed, reaching the side of the hut but not climbing up the stairs. "I was up most of the night drinking with Andy, and *apparently* I'm not twenty-one anymore. Who knew?"

"Did you ask if we'd seen Laura?" Megan asked, her voice filled with concern, reminding me of the question, too.

Brad nodded, rubbing the back of his head as he stared off down the coastline. "Yeah, she went for a jog an hour ago. I thought she'd be back by now."

I stood up, placing my hand over my eyes and staring out into the blinding, rising sun. "Did she say where she was going?"

"You know Laura. She likes to run when she's stressed... which is an understatement for all of us right now. She may have just run farther than I expected."

"Maybe she is just planning to meet us for breakfast instead," Megan offered. "If she finished her jog around the time we usually meet for breakfast."

Brad didn't look too sure. "Yeah, maybe."

"Let me grab my shoes, and we'll go check. Did you check on Jaren and Natasha? Maybe they've gone up to breakfast already and she met them?" I said, standing up.

"I didn't think of that. I'll check and see if they're still home," Brad said. "Meet you right back here." With that, he jogged toward the last hut, while Megan and I made our way inside and slipped on our shoes and brushed our teeth.

A few minutes later, we walked back outside. Brad was waiting for us in front of the hut. "You could be half right. Natasha and Jaren are just waking up, but Andy wasn't in his hut. Maybe he met Laura, and the two of them are already waiting for us at the pavilion. I told Jaren we'd meet them up there."

"Sounds good," I said, feeling relieved of my fear as I realized Laura and Andy were likely together. I pulled the door closed behind us, and together we headed toward the relaxation center.

After a few moments of walking in silence, Megan let out a weighted breath. "Well, at least Andy's up and out of bed, right? On his own. That has to be progress."

Brad nodded. "I hope so. He was in bad shape last night."

"Poor guy. First girl he actually seems to care about, and this happens…" I clicked my tongue thoughtfully. "What do you even say to someone dealing with something so…*big?*"

"You say that you're there for them," Megan said. "That you love them and you'll be there for them no matter what." She slid her hand in mine, intertwining our fingers. "I hope the police come today. I think it'll give him some finality. It just feels weird, knowing they're just keeping her body here." She shivered, and I saw the hairs on her arms stand up with a chill.

I grimaced but didn't say anything. It was true. I hated the thought that we were in such limbo here. The promise of isolation, privacy, and a chance to disconnect in order to reconnect, had quickly turned into our own personal purgatory, yet it was hard to process that while we were surrounded by such paradise.

"The way Manu talked, we may be stuck here until the end of the week, when the boat returns, unless they realize the phone lines are out and send someone sooner to fix them," Brad said. I didn't like the sound of that. The thought of staying on the island for much longer made me sick. I didn't think I'd ever be able to look at the ocean the same way again, not when it had taken so much from us. And once we were back home and at work, I'd have a chance to talk to Laura in a neutral, private environment. I needed that more than I was willing to admit. We had to discuss what had happened, or I was going to burst.

"Surely they know the storm caused outages," Megan said, bringing me out of my thoughts.

"I hope so," I agreed. "I can't believe they don't keep a boat here for emergencies. That seems reckless."

"I guess that's something we'll have to add to our review," Megan said softly, though the joke was tepid.

When we could finally make out the outline of the pavilion, I saw Andy sitting at our usual table, but much to my dismay, as we got closer, I was sure he was alone. Brad stiffened beside me, noticing it at the same time.

"She's not there."

"She may have just gone to the restroom," Megan offered. "Let's check with Andy."

I refused to look out at the water. I wasn't going to be searching for Laura—she was fine. Definitely alive. Definitely fine. This wouldn't be like Emily. It couldn't.

She was *fine.*

We reached the table finally, the rest of the walk completed in total silence, and when Andy saw us, he looked up. He didn't seem to be in much better shape than Brad; his eyes were bloodshot, and he was still wearing the clothes I'd seen him in last. He had two pieces of toast in front of him, though it looked like he'd only been picking at them. There were no other plates at the table to indicate he wasn't dining alone.

"Hey, Andy," Brad said. "Have you seen Laura this morning?"

Andy's brows drew down, and when he spoke, he kept his voice low. "No. Why would I? She isn't with you?"

"She went for a run earlier, and she hasn't come back."

Andy shook his head. "I've been here for half an hour, and I haven't seen her coming or going. Maybe she ran the opposite direction?"

"Maybe," Brad said, his lips tight. I wondered if he could feel the same panic setting in that I was feeling. I wanted to be respectful of Andy, not bring up any memories that he was trying to suppress, but this felt eerily similar to Emily's disappearance. My heart bounced around in my chest like a wild horse, and I had to stand completely still, pretend to be less freaked out than Brad, less worried than Andy.

"We should go look for her," I said, trying not to jump to it right then. Why weren't we already going? What were we doing just standing around?

"Agreed," Brad said, locking eyes with me, the panic evident. *Thank God I'm not the only one.*

"You guys want some help?" Andy asked, standing up. "I can't make myself eat right now anyway."

"Thanks," Brad said, nodding. "I say we split up. Nick, Megan, you two go that way," he pointed past the relaxation center, "and Andy and I will go this way. We'll stop by and ask Jaren and Natasha to help, too." He glanced at the watch on his wrist. "What do you say, we'll meet back here in an hour?"

"Sounds good," I said, tugging Megan to follow me. I couldn't stay still any longer. I was going to scream if I didn't get going. I took off running, the sand making it difficult to move very fast, but I pushed through anyway. I had to find her. "Laura!" *Where are you?*

# CHAPTER TWENTY-SIX

## NATASHA

"Laura!" I yelled, staring into the woods, slick sweat on my skin. A mosquito buzzed near my ear, and I swatted it away, licking my dry, chapped lips. I needed water, but I couldn't stop the search until we'd looked everywhere. Jaren was walking back toward me, his head hung down. "Nothing?"

"No sign of her." He swiped the back of his hand across his brow. "I'm hoping the others had better luck."

"She wouldn't have just run off," I said, shaking my head. "We can't give up. This doesn't feel right." I narrowed my eyes at the woods, praying for a glimpse of her. Praying she'd run out laughing, like it had all been a prank—albeit the most insensitive prank in history.

"We aren't giving up. Let's go check back with the others. They said meet up in an hour. For all we know, they've found her." He put an arm around my waist, shocking me with his touch. "If not, we'll come back and keep looking."

My eyes softened as I looked at him, my heart swelling with appreciation. "Thanks, Jaren."

He gave a short nod. "You know I've got you."

Fear knotted inside me as we continued our journey back to

the others. Where was she? She wouldn't have wandered off, not knowing what we were all dealing with already. I knew her better than that. But then, where was she? Why hadn't she returned? I felt bile rising in my throat as I tried to force the thought away. This wouldn't be like Emily. It couldn't. Laura was still alive. I couldn't lose her.

We were the last of the group to make it back. They were all red-faced, sweaty, and exhausted, but Laura was nowhere to be seen.

"You didn't find her?" I asked, the last bit of hope evaporating from my chest.

Nick shook his head, one hand on his scalp. "No. What do we do? What should we do?"

Brad was sitting beside Andy, his elbows resting on his knees, head hung down. "Where could she be? This doesn't make any sense. She wouldn't have just disappeared. She must know how worried we are."

"Where else might she have gone?" Megan asked, rubbing a hand over Nick's back. "You guys know her best."

As anger gripped my organs with scalding fingers, I stepped away from Jaren. "Give me just a minute."

"Where are you going?" he called, but made no move to follow me as I waved him off, shaking my head.

The answer didn't matter as I shoved through the doors and into the building. Moving past the bathrooms just inside the doorway; past the dining room, its chairs still turned over the tops of the tables; the spa, its music playing gently in an effort to soothe me despite the anxiety coursing through my veins; the library, whose fiction couldn't be stranger than our truth; and the gym, its floors and equipment pristine, begging me to come in. Everything's fine, it seemed to say.

But everything wasn't fine. Nothing was fine. My friend was missing, my other friend was dead, and someone here had to know why. Had we walked into a trap? Was this all a setup?

Maybe I sounded like a conspiracy theorist, but that's how it was starting to feel.

Making my way down the hall, further than I'd gone before, I read the sign that hung on the wall, searching for just one thing.

**Gym ↓**
**Library ↓**
**Spa ↓**
**Dining Room ↓**
**Pool ↑**
**Office →**
**Theater ←**
**Infirmary ←**

*Office.* The arrow pointed to my right, and I turned abruptly, moving my feet as fast as I could along the wood floor.

"Miss?" I heard an employee call from behind me, but I didn't dare stop. I wanted answers, and I wanted them now. If Manu wasn't involved in whatever was going on, he surely knew something. And, if he didn't, he needed to help us get to the bottom of it.

The door ahead was tan, with a white linen wreath hanging on it, and a sign beside the door that let me know I'd come to the right place. I reached for the handle, turning it swiftly.

*Click.*

It was locked. I groaned, lifting my hand to the door and rapping against it. "Manu? Manu, it's Natasha. Can I come in?" I pounded on the door again, growing impatient. *"Manu!"*

"Ma'am, can I help you?" An employee was behind me, his hand on my shoulder. "Mr. Manu is very busy…if I can help, I'd love to be of service to—"

"I need to talk to him," I said, cutting the man off.

There was a faint clicking noise, and the door swung open.

Manu stood in front of us, a frazzled look on his usually calm face. When he saw me, he smiled, clasping his hands together in front of his chest. "Thank you, Fraser," he said, waving the man off. "I can take it from here." When I felt his hand leave my shoulder, heard the footsteps retreating, I released a breath. Manu smiled again, waving me inside. "Now then, what can I do for you, Mrs. Natasha?"

I stepped forward, still not far from the doorway as I attempted to catch my breath. Manu walked across the open and airy office, taking a seat at an executive desk in the middle of the room. It felt so out of place there. The room was filled with plants, an open skylight above us, all wicker furniture. The clock on the wall was made from a slab of a tree root, thick and shiny with sealant. The office was crisp, airy, and earthy, much like its occupant, all except for the desk, which would've fit in perfectly at any corporate building.

"Have you seen Laura?"

"Have I seen… I am afraid I do not understand."

"*Laura.* She's missing."

He leaned back against the desk, a blank expression overtaking his face. "I am so sorry… I am afraid I have not seen her. I had no idea. Who else knows?"

"Everyone," I waved my hand toward the open door. "We've all been looking all morning."

"Where was she last seen?"

"Brad said she went for a run this morning, but that was over two hours ago. No one's heard from her since."

Manu stood back up, his face solemn. His hands shoved into the pockets of his white kaftan. "Oh, my. That is serious, then. I will have my staff assist you in your search."

"Manu, do you know something about what's going on?" I demanded, taking another step toward him.

His expression didn't change. "What do you mean?"

"First Emily, now Laura... I can't believe it's just a coincidence."

His eyes searched my face. "What other option is there?"

"If someone here is hurting us...picking us off one by one, and you aren't involved, you need to protect us. You need to get the police here."

"My island is a peaceful place, Natasha. I can assure you that no one under my staff intends to harm any of you."

"You've got a dead body down the hall, and my best..." A sob stopped the word from leaving my throat. I sucked in a breath, composing myself. "My best friend is missing. Newsflash, Manu, this isn't a peaceful place. Someone is doing this. They have to be. Laura wouldn't have just run off. Emily wouldn't have just gone for a swim." I waved my hands wildly as I talked, unable to control the anger swelling in my chest.

He reached for my shoulders, but I stepped back. No way was he going to touch me. There was no way I could bring myself to trust him—trust anyone, for that matter. When I pulled away, he stepped back, allowing space between us. He clasped his hands together once more, his eyes softening. "My island *is* a peaceful place, Natasha. At least, it was before this week. Before *your* group arrived."

"What are you saying?" I suddenly felt unable to catch my breath.

"I wish I knew what was happening. Trust me when I say, my staff and I are just as concerned about it as you are. This is my livelihood. I have worked my entire life to create this island, to make it what it is, and I am terrified that this week will undo all that I have built. My staff are worried for their safety, worried for their jobs. I know that you have lost a friend, and I am terribly sorry for that, but I need you to understand that we are doing all we can to make sure you have the best time you can in the most...unthinkable circumstances." A noise to his left caused him to look away, across the room, where the wall was blocking most of my view. "If there is a killer on this island," he said, looking back at me finally, "we have to protect ourselves, too."

"What are you talking about? If it's not you…and it's not us. Who could it be?"

He stared at me, not speaking for a long and uncomfortable amount of time. My breathing grew loud, the only sound I could focus on. What was he doing? What was he waiting on? I stared back, feeling my chest rising and falling. My hands balled into fists. "Manu, *who?*" I demanded.

"Come with me," he said, holding his hand out and wagging his fingers at me, as if pulling me to him. "Let me show you something."

The words sent chills down my spine, and I turned away from him, my brain screaming with danger. I needed to go. I needed to get out of there. I wasn't safe, and no one knew where I was. With no further thought, I pushed away, turning from the room, thankful I'd left the door open, and darting from its confines.

I dashed down the hall, past the worried-looking Fraser and another employee I didn't recognize. I didn't stop running until I'd made it out of the building and to the safety of my friends.

As safe as we could be while trapped on a deserted island with a murderer.

# CHAPTER TWENTY-SEVEN

## NICK

"What's wrong? What happened?" Brad demanded, his eyes wild as he grabbed Natasha's shoulders. She'd come barreling out of the building like the place was on fire, so even those who weren't too worried before, definitely were now. Megan gripped my hand, her other hand over her mouth before Natasha even began to speak.

"Manu...wanted to show me something," she said, clutching her chest. I waited for her to go on, but she didn't.

"Show you something? Show you what?" Jaren asked.

"You're hurting me, Brad," Natasha said, pulling away from his grip. Brad let go of her immediately.

"I'm sorry—I didn't—" He looked horrified.

"What did Manu do?" I asked, stepping forward, no time for any further conversation. "Did he know something about Laura?"

As she struggled to catch her breath, she looked behind her, where the door remained closed. "Let's...go...over here." Waving a hand over her head, she walked away from the pavilion and down toward the shore, leading the way. We followed her cluelessly, and I wondered if everyone felt as confused as I did.

When she stopped walking, I heard her voice over the rushing waves before she turned around to face us. "He swears he doesn't know anything about Laura, or about Emily. He says his staff are just as worried as we are, and he's going to send them to help us look for her."

"Okay…but that's a good thing, right?" Megan asked, her voice patronizing.

"We're trapped here, you guys. Literally trapped. I just don't feel safe. I feel like…what if they want to pick us off? One by one? We're stuck here. No boat. No phones. No way home." She bent down, placing her weight over her knees. "We're trapped and…and we flew here, so we obviously have no weapons. No way to protect ourselves. We can't do anything about any of it. We just have to wait here for…for what? I mean, it was Emily who set this all up. What if she found out what was going on? What if they took her out first because she discovered the truth—"

"You aren't making any sense," Andy said, shaking his head as he moved toward her. He put a hand on her shoulder. "Just breathe, okay? Just breathe."

As I listened to her talk, watched the panic set in, the weight of our situation hit me like bricks. We *were* trapped. No way to contact our families, no way to call for help. We only had Manu's word that he'd even spoken to our emergency contacts. For all we knew, no one in the world knew where we were. No one would be looking for us, and even when they started to, they'd have no idea where to look. "Why isn't she making sense?" I asked, chills lining my skin. "She's right, isn't she? We don't know what's going on? We don't know what happened to Emily or what's happened to Laura. We don't know when or if the police will be here. We don't know who or what we're up against. It's us against the staff, the people who know this island. We have no idea what's in the woods. We certainly can't swim. We've got this stretch of beach, but that's it. If someone wanted to hurt us...we've walked right into their trap."

As I said the words, Megan began to cry. Her blue eyes blurred with glistening tears, and as much as I wanted to comfort her, I couldn't. Because none of it mattered. We *were* trapped. Probably going to die. And there was nothing any of us could do.

Natasha rested her face in her hands, sinking all the way down until she was sitting on the sand. "Laura didn't even want to come. We convinced her. If I had just stuck to the no I said originally, she wouldn't have been here. She only agreed because we all did. If I'd just said no, she wouldn't be here. *We* wouldn't be here."

Throughout the group, I could see a new level of panic setting in. All around me, glassy eyes were filled with tears and hopelessness. "Okay, we can't just sit here. We have to do something," Brad said. "We aren't just giving up."

"What can we do?" Jaren demanded. "What is there to do? Nick's right. We have nowhere to go."

Natasha let out another sob, her arms wrapped around her knees, head tucked between them.

"Okay, why don't I take Natasha back to the hut?" Andy offered. "You guys can keep looking for Laura, and once she's calmed down, we'll join you."

"No," Natasha said adamantly. "No. I want to help look for her."

"I know, but you're soaking wet," he said, pointing to where the tide had begun hitting her jeans. "And you're upset. You should calm down, and if anyone can relate to what you're feeling...it's me."

Natasha ran a hand over her legs, feeling the damp denim. "Yeah, okay. But we can't give up on her. And we should stick together. I don't think it's safe for anyone to be alone right now."

"Okay, so where should we go?" Andy asked. "We can meet them after you change, and we'll all search together."

"Maybe we should try the forest next?" Megan asked. "It's the one place we haven't gone, and I agree, we shouldn't be alone. Groups of twos at a minimum, but I'd feel safer if we stick together as a full group as much as we can."

Realizing her hand was still in mine, I stroked her skin with my thumb. I wouldn't let anything happen to her—not if it took my life to do it. If something had happened to Laura, I wasn't sure I'd survive it, but the idea of losing Megan, too, was enough to bring me to my knees then and there. I had to hold it together for her. It was my fault she was in this mess.

"Okay, let's go," Andy said, holding out a hand for Natasha to take. "You guys go ahead to the edge of the forest. Natasha and I will meet you there."

"Hold up," Jaren said, wagging a finger in the air. "I need to change shoes anyway." He gestured toward his sandals. "I'll just go with Natasha, and we can meet you there."

Andy paused, his face stoic. "Oh…well, okay."

"Thanks, Andy," Natasha said, slipping her hand in Jaren's. "We'll meet y'all in just a minute, okay?"

We nodded in unison, and I looked at Brad. "I think I'm going to change shoes and put on some sunscreen, too. You and Andy want to meet us up there or come with us?"

Brad looked down at his own shoes, though I could tell his mind was entirely elsewhere. "I'll be okay. I just want to get going." He nodded toward Andy. "You ready?"

Andy's jaw locked as he nodded, not saying a word, and the two walked up the sandy hill. Tugging at Megan's hand, I led her back to our hut.

"It's going to be okay," she said, releasing my hand to rub hers over my back. "We'll find her."

"Do you really think so?" *Do you really want us to?* If she knew the truth about what Laura and I had done, I was sure she'd feel differently. Unable to meet her eyes, I locked my gaze straight ahead. Our destination. If I looked at her, I was sure I'd break, and I couldn't afford to do that. We had a mission. Shoes. Sunscreen. Search. Laura's life may depend on it. The thought of her somewhere in the forest was devastating. The thought of her dead was unfathomable. I just had to keep moving. Until we found a body, there was still hope.

"I know so," she said. "I understand your panic, but until we find Laura, I think it's premature." I couldn't tell if she was just trying to put on a brave face, as tears continued to fall. "We'll find her," she repeated.

"I can't—" We reached our hut, and I climbed the stairs, interrupting my sentence as I tried to compose myself. When Megan passed through the door, I followed her and shut it behind us. As I turned around, she was staring at me, her eyes as inquisitive as ever.

"You can't lose her," she finished for me.

I nodded, no sense in arguing or trying to lie. She'd see right through it. "She's my best friend. My business partner. She's been there my whole life..."

Megan was solemn as she reached for the sunscreen. "Do you love her, Nicky?"

I opened my mouth, but no sound came out.

"I know you've said that you don't, not like you love me, but I don't think that's true. I see the fear in your eyes right now, and I think it goes deeper than friendship. You look like Brad. Like Andy. I've told you I will love you through anything, as long as you don't lie to me, but I need to know the truth now." Tube in hand, she squeezed a glob of white into her palm and soaked her shoulder in it, rubbing circles before switching sides. "What am I dealing with here? Am I going to lose you?"

I shook my head. "You're not going to lose me. Of course

not." My mind went back to the night on the beach—to the flash of white in the window. So much had happened since the night Laura kissed me. It felt like ages ago, so how had it only been days? "I loved Laura for a very long time, it's true. But she chose Brad. She chose him years ago, and I respect her decision. I've moved on, too. I love you. I'm *in love* with you." I stepped forward, taking the sunscreen from her.

"Did she love you back?" she asked. It was the one question no one had ever asked. I'd never spoken the truth aloud. Not to my parents, not to my brothers, and certainly not to my friends.

"I don't know…" I said finally, applying sunscreen to my forearms to stay busy.

"You'd know," she pressed, putting a hand on my arm to stop me. "If she loved you back, you'd know."

I looked up at her, our eyes locked. A moment in time, a moment of truth. "Yes," I choked out, the word almost silent on my breath. "At one time, she did. It was brief. Fleeting. Before they were married. Brad had gone to Haiti for two years with his company. They were building a well, or a water treatment site, something… It never should've happened. Laura and I were still in school, and she was lonely. It was a mistake." I swallowed. It felt so good to finally speak about the secret I'd kept to myself for so long. "When he came home, we broke it off. We haven't spoken about it since. It doesn't matter anymore. It was a lifetime ago."

She watched me, her eyes darting between mine as I spoke, soaking up every word I said. When she didn't react right away, I added. "You can never tell anyone. Please. Laura would never forgive me if she knew I'd told you. If it got back to Brad, it would destroy her."

Megan nodded seriously, taking the vow. "I'd never tell a soul, Nicky. You know you can trust me." She leaned forward, pressing her lips to my cheek. "Thank you for telling me the truth."

"Are you mad?" My throat was incredibly dry as I waited for the answer.

"Of course not. I wish you'd told me, of course, but it was before our time. I don't have any right to be mad. I just want to know everything about you. And Laura is part of your story. I know that, and I appreciate it. I appreciate her *not* choosing you, so I could have a shot." When she smiled, I saw the hint of sadness, and I felt my chest tighten. I hated this. "I love you with every part of my being, and I know you love me back. I will always be here for you, unless you ask me not to be or give me a reason not to be." She squeezed my hand, then moved to rub my sunscreen in, putting it on my shoulders and the back of my neck. "As long as you are honest and you still want to be with me, I'm here."

I swallowed, closing my eyes. What did I want anymore? Truth was, I had no idea.

*Laura.*

I wanted Laura found. I wanted Laura safe.

Anything other than that could wait.

The rubbing stopped, and my eyes shot open. "You do still want me here, don't you?" She leaned around to look at me.

I took her hand in mine, kissing her fingertips, the taste of the sunscreen on my lips. "You're the best thing in my life." It wasn't an answer, but I didn't think she wanted to hear the one I would've given her if pressed. In that moment, with Laura missing and the truth of what had happened between us all those years ago hanging in the air, all I wanted was the one woman I could never have.

I wanted to tell her the truth—that I'd never stopped loving her, never stopped wanting her. I wanted to scoop her in my arms and never let her go. I wanted to burn our lives to the ground, who cared about the casualties, and start fresh. I wanted to love her the way I always had without having to hide it anymore.

"It's okay," she said, a new tear in her once-dry eye as she twisted her mouth to avoid crying. "Laura was your best friend. I know how scared you must be and how confusing it must be for you."

I froze, my body stiff with fear as I dropped her hand. "Was?"

"Huh?"

"You said *was*. Past tense." The blood in my veins was suddenly icy. "Megan, do you know something about Laura?"

A smile played on the edge of her lips. "What are you talking about, crazy? Of course I don't."

"Why would you say it like that?" I took a step backward, toward the door, and she followed.

"Like what?"

"Was? You said she *was* my best friend. Not is."

"Nicky, you're acting crazy," she said, a dry laugh in her words. "Laura *is* your best friend, of course. I just misspoke. Wasn't it you that said earlier how *I'm* your best friend now? I didn't mean anything by it." There was a pregnant pause while she waited for me to respond, but I couldn't. My body seized with panic as my hand made contact with the door behind me. In one quick motion, I spun around, pulled it open, and darted out.

I knew what I saw in her eyes. What I'd heard in her voice. I knew she'd had something to do with it. I knew she knew what happened to Laura.

Who had I brought into my life? Into Laura's life?

*What had I done?*

# CHAPTER TWENTY-EIGHT

## NATASHA

Nick rushed into the hut without knocking. When I turned around, thankful I'd just pulled the jeans up over my hips, I was prepared to chastise him, but judging by the look on his face, now wasn't the time.

"What's wrong?" *Laura. They found Laura.*

"I think Megan knows what happened to Laura," he said, breathing heavily, a hand flat on his stomach just below his ribs.

"What do you mean?" Jaren asked, stepping forward, his expression serious.

"I have to tell you something," Nick said, his eyes deadlocked with mine. His words sent chills across my arms. "You're not going to like it, but I have to tell you." He crossed the room and pulled the windows closed. "You should sit."

I crossed my arms. "I think I'll stand."

Jaren didn't move either. "Tell us, Nick. What's going on?"

"I don't have time to lessen the blow." His lips formed an 'O,' and he blew out a breath. "So, here goes. Laura and I used to be...involved."

The words ran over me, filling me with dread. Not because it was a shock, but because I needed to decide how to react. Jaren had no idea I knew. Nick had no idea I knew. Should I pretend I didn't?

"Involved how? You were having an affair?" Jaren asked, freeing me up to continue deciding how to proceed.

"No, not an affair," Nick said. "Well, it was an affair, sort of. Maybe. I don't know. It was years ago. Before we graduated. Before they were married. Nothing has happened in years... until the night before last."

"The night before last?" I perked up. Now this was new news.

"Laura..." He hesitated, a grimace on his lips as he prepared himself. "She kissed me."

*"What?"* I demanded. My heart thundered in my chest. Why hadn't she told me?

"I don't know why. It was the night Emily died. She came by my hut, and she was talking about Emily...something about what happened at the spa. She said she didn't trust her...and then she just, she..." He shrugged. "She just kissed me."

"And then what happened?" I asked.

He hesitated. "The sort of thing that usually follows kissing." His face was beet red as he ran a hand over the back of his neck. They'd had sex? He couldn't mean that, could he? Was he really admitting it to me? In front of Jaren. I'd have to make sure Jaren kept her secret, like I'd sworn to do all those years ago. "And then, it was over," Nick went on when no one responded. "I don't know what happened. It was a moment of weakness. She called it a mistake."

"Was it?" I asked.

"I don't—I-I don't know. She ran off before we could talk about anything, and I went back home. I'm telling you this because on the night that it happened, I could've sworn I saw Megan watching us from the hut."

"Why didn't you say anything sooner?" The cold chills were

back, and I was staring out the window, searching for Megan then.

"Because I thought I was wrong. When I got inside, Megan was asleep. I convinced myself I was seeing things, and then we found out Emily had died. I practically forgot what happened, and I didn't think about it again until Laura went missing."

"So you think Megan did something to her?" Jaren asked.

"I don't know what to think. She was talking about Laura just now, and she said something in past tense… Isn't that how cops always know someone's guilty on those cop shows?"

I raised a brow. "I don't know. That's a stretch. I mean, did you ask her? Couldn't it have just been a slip-up? You came running over here like you'd found her with a bloody knife." Was that all he was talking about? For all we knew, he was jumping to conclusions.

"I asked her why she said it like she did—why she said it in past tense—and she gave me an answer, but it was something in her eyes, Natasha." He was pleading with me again.

"I don't know, Nick. I can't really see Megan hurting anyone…" I wanted to believe him because I wanted answers, but they also needed to make sense. Why would Megan have done anything to hurt Laura? Even if she caught them together, why not confront Nick? Why not tell Brad? It didn't make any sense. Besides, I couldn't believe Megan the *vegan-vegetarian-whatever she was* would hurt a fly, let alone a living, breathing human.

I could see it in his eyes. Disappointment. He'd trusted me to believe him, but I wasn't sure I did. "I know you want to find her. To find answers for her and Emily, but we can't jump to conclusions. We can't turn on each other right now. We need to stick together." Jaren looked at me, and I could see he agreed.

"So, what are you suggesting? Laura's gone. We all just pretend like she's fine, like everything's fine until we know for sure something horrible has happened?" Nick demanded, running a hand through his hair.

I could see the fear in his eyes, feel it in the room. He'd likely never felt such panic—he didn't have kids. Wasn't all that close to his family. Laura was the most important person in the world to him, and she was missing.

I stepped forward and put a hand on his arm. "Nick, look at me." I couldn't let him see the panic I felt. It would only make his more real. Strangely, seeing him freak out only calmed me. I needed to find my best friend, but right now, Nick needed me more. Wherever Laura was, I would do this for her. I would be there for him like she would've been. "Look at me," I said again, watching as his cognac brown eyes flicked up to meet mine. "We're going to find her, okay? I don't know what Megan saw or didn't see, did or didn't do, but I know Laura. I know you. I know us." The smile on my lips was small, and I hoped he believed it. I needed him to believe it as much as I needed to believe what I was saying myself. "We won't give up until we find her. She isn't Emily. This isn't the end of her story."

He swallowed, and I watched his Adam's apple bob in his throat. His nod was slight, barely noticeable, but it was there. "We need to find Brad and Andy. We have to get back to looking."

"There we go." I patted his shoulder before bending down near the edge of the bed to pull my shoes back on. Jaren was strangely quiet behind me, but I paid no attention. Instead, once my shoes were on, I put an arm around Nick, casting a quick glance behind me to make sure Jaren was following, and led them both out the door. "Now, we need to get Megan first. Like Andy said, none of us should be left alone right now. We're going to keep an eye on her, but we have to play it smart, right?"

He nodded grimly. "She knows how upset I am. I shouldn't have overreacted."

"Right," I said. "Come on, I'll help you explain." We jogged up the stairs to Nick and Megan's hut as I played out the explanations in my head. What was I going to say? How would I make it make sense? And then, a much worse line of questioning... What if Nick was right? What if Megan *had* done something to Laura?

I swallowed back bile as it rose in my throat, forcing the question down with it. It wasn't possible. Laura was fine. She was safe. She had to be.

We walked into the hut, looking around.

*No Megan.*

"Megan?" Nick called, then looked at me. "Maybe she's in the bathroom."

"Maybe," I nodded, glancing back at Jaren, who was waiting awkwardly in the doorway. "Want to go check?"

"Yeah." Nick nodded without further coaxing. "She's probably upset. Give me just a sec." He jogged up the stairs, leaving my husband and me waiting in front of the bed.

"You okay?" I asked when we were alone.

Jaren nodded too quickly, then again slowly. "Yeah, I...I just don't know what to think."

"You know Megan couldn't hurt a fl—"

"No," he interrupted. "I mean, yes, I'm worried about Laura, too, and I don't want to believe any of us could be involved in what happened, but...how can you be okay with Nick telling you he and Laura were having an affair?"

I stared at him, my eyes taking in every inch of his face, the dark freckles across the bridge of his nose and near his eyes, the oversized bottom lip, his thick brows, matching the tight ringlets of hair he kept buzzed short. My husband was a handsome man; there had never been any question. Why was it only now, when we were all potentially in danger, that I was learning to appreciate him?

He cocked his head to the side. "I mean, she's your best friend. Aren't you freaked out that you didn't know?"

I should've lied. I considered it, briefly, but I was trying to do better. Be better. I wanted him to know the truth—every truth I could give him. I closed my eyes, bracing myself as I sucked in a breath. "I did know."

*"What?"*

"Laura told me…years ago. It was nothing. I didn't know about them hooking up here or whatever feelings she must've been having about that. She hadn't talked about Nick in that way in years." I kept my voice low, aware of Nick's footsteps on the top floor. "Not since the girls were born at all, but really not since college. I thought she was over him."

"How could you not have told me?" There was hurt on his face that I hadn't expected, as if he'd been the one cheated on.

"Laura made me swear not to when it happened…" I trailed off. "I didn't think you'd be so upset."

He ran a hand over his lips. "It's just…if you were keeping those kinds of secrets for her, what kind was she keeping for you?"

"Jaren, no. I didn't—you know I would never—"

"She's not here." Nick's voice behind us cut the conversation short, and I spun around.

"What?"

"Megan's not here," he said again. *"She's gone."*

# CHAPTER TWENTY-NINE

## ANDY

When I made it back to where I'd left Brad, the rest of the group had joined him. What was left of the group, anyway. Natasha, Nick, and Jaren stood next to him, watching me.

"Did you see Megan while you were gone?" Brad asked.

*Lie.* I forced my brows down, feigning confusion. *Lie better.* "Megan? Wasn't she with you, Nick?"

He shook his head, his face pale. Ashen. Terrified. "We had a, er, well, a disagreement. I went to talk to Natasha and Jaren, and when I came back, she was gone."

I gasped. *Too dramatic.* "Oh no. Maybe she was in the bathroom?"

"I already checked. She's not in the hut at all."

I looked away, thankful to not have the scrutiny on my face for a millisecond. How good of a liar was I? That was being tested in the moment. *I'll take a crash course in deceiving your friends, please.*

"Guys, I don't like this," Natasha said, running her hands over her legs. "This is starting to feel really, really bad. First

Emily," she said her name softly, as if to lessen the blow, but it didn't help, "then Laura. Now Megan."

"We haven't found Laura," Brad said firmly. "For all we know, she's fine."

"She wouldn't have just left us here to worry," Nick argued. "And where did Megan go? How did she manage to disappear? I only left her alone for ten minutes."

"Well, she couldn't have gone far. Andy went back to the huts just now. If she'd been walking outside, he would've seen her," Brad pointed out.

"Yeah," I said. *A lie, but not entirely.* "I would have. I didn't."

"Maybe we should check in with Manu again?" Jaren asked.

*"No,"* Natasha said, almost as quickly as I did. "If there's one thing we know, it's that we're on our own in this. Manu said he'd sent out staff to look for Laura, but he hasn't. Since Emily's death, we haven't seen him outside. He hasn't joined us for meals. I don't know what's going on here, but we can't trust anyone but ourselves. We have to search for her, for *them,* alone. And we can't split up anymore. Not for any reason. We have to believe we're safest together." She looked around at each of us, assuming her role as the unofficial leader. "Deal?"

"Deal," came the echoed responses.

She was trying to protect us, but she didn't know how wrong she was.

I couldn't tell her. Not yet.

We weren't safe together.

Not even close.

# CHAPTER THIRTY

## NICK

We walked through the jungle all afternoon, but there was no sign of Laura or Megan anywhere. When we emerged, my feet were blistered, and I'd run through every possible scenario—ranging from bad, she'd run off with an island man to live out her days, to horrific, she'd dehydrated on her run, died, and was being eaten by a swarm of wild hogs, to worst, she'd been kidnapped and was being tortured to death. I couldn't deny the fact that I was more worried about Laura than Megan, that it was Laura my mind wandered to when it was left to its own devices. Meandering through the quiet jungle, that described practically every minute.

It's not that I didn't care about Megan. Of course, I did. If I was wrong, which I was starting to realize I must've been with each passing moment, I was going to feel horrible. I should've stayed with her. I was supposed to protect her, but instead, I left her alone and accused her of something awful. If something had happened to her, I'd never forgive myself.

I think Natasha knew I was beating myself up. Despite the permanent worry etched on her face, occasionally, she'd place her hand on my back, mumbling something about how we'd keep searching, how it was okay. She thought she was helping me, but I think it was to help herself just as much.

We all needed to hear it. We all needed to believe it.

But I don't think any of us did.

Deep down, we knew something had happened.

I think we all knew we'd never see her again.

I was hot. My skin burned despite the sunscreen I'd applied, and my body was sore. I didn't want to admit defeat, but as the sun started setting, the forest around us going from dark to darker, I knew it was time to call it.

The thought of them—either of them—spending the night in the jungle alone was enough to destroy me. I forced it from my head. Who was to say we were any safer closer to the coast? For all we knew, they were the ones protected in the forest, while we were exposed.

My stomach grumbled loudly, making its emptiness known. Try as I might to ignore it, I was starving. My throat was dry. As much as I wanted to deny myself any sort of nourishment until we found the girls, in the extreme heat, none of us would last long if we weren't able to get something in our systems.

"Does anyone have anything to eat or drink in their huts?" I asked. Brad cleared his throat.

"You read my mind," he said softly, no power left in his voice. I guess that's how we all felt. Powerless. Empty. No idea who or what we were running from…no idea who would be next.

"There may be some wine left in our hut," Andy said. "Emily had Fraser bring us three bottles of wine our first night, and she only managed to drink one. She brought the mixed drinks back the first night, so I think they're all still there."

"There were two," Brad said. "When I was in your hut, there were two. We could make those last between us for a while if we had to. What are you thinking? We should avoid the pavilion?"

"That's not a good idea. We can't live on wine right now. We don't need alcohol at all," Natasha said. "We need water. And food. We aren't going to make it much longer in this heat if we don't hydrate. I'm starving. My legs are weak, and my feet hurt. We need to keep our strength up."

"So, what do we do? It's not like we have many options," Jaren said, staring at her. "We go back?"

"We have to. Natasha's right. We can get a good meal at the pavilion. As long as we stay together, we'll be okay, right?" Brad said.

"Can we trust them? What if they poison us?"

Brad shook his head. "Why wouldn't they have already done that? They've had plenty of chances." He waited, each of our breathing growing heavy as we labored across the sand. "I mean, seriously guys, if they wanted us dead, don't you think we'd be dead? Why wait? Are they just dragging it out? Torturing us? One by one?"

"Picking us off, you mean? Why would they do that? What do they want?" Andy groaned.

"They wouldn't," Natasha said. "Brad's right. Whoever's doing this isn't just going to come out and do it… They're playing a game. They won't make it obvious. We have to find out who, and why, but we have to be alive and nourished to do that. We'll go to dinner together. Act like nothing's wrong. Like we suspect nothing."

"Fine," Andy said. "I don't care as long as I can get something to drink." He huffed out a breath as we trudged across the sand, my throat growing drier as we saw the glowing yellow string lights from the pavilion.

We took seats at the usual table, the obvious differences from our first dinner weighing on me. There were just the five of us now—three missing or dead. The pain of what had happened, what we'd lost, was evident in our heavy, vacant gazes. On our expressions. No one seemed to know what to say. It hit me then…would we ever recover from this? If we made it off the island, would what was left of our group still exist?

Would we ever be able to look at each other without being reminded of the pain? It seemed doubtful.

Before the waiters could appear, Manu walked through the door, looking relieved to see us. "Thank goodness," he mumbled, loud enough for us to hear. He made his way to our table, the hem of his dress-type outfit swaying with his quick steps. "We had not seen you all afternoon… We were starting to worry."

"We just went for a hike," Natasha said quickly.

"I hope you were able to enjoy yourselves," Manu said. He truly did look relieved. "Did you make it to the falls?"

"The falls?"

"If you follow any of the paths in the woods, they lead to the waterfall at the center of the island. It is a beautiful place." His eyes moved from me, to Natasha, then to Andy, Brad, and Jaren.

"We didn't make it that far," I said, though we'd spent the afternoon hiking, we'd strayed off the paths more often than not, checking in ditches and streams. We assumed if someone wanted to hide them from us, they wouldn't be on the main paths. Maybe the falls would need to be checked tomorrow.

"Perhaps another time, then," Manu said.

"Manu," Natasha said, her hands clasped together in front of her. She smiled, but there was something devious in her eyes. I wondered if he noticed. "When we talked this morning, you said you wanted to show me something. I apologize for running off, but I wondered if you could show us now."

Manu's warm expression filled with confusion, his brows drawn down, the crinkles around his eyes deepened. "I am sorry, Natasha. What do you mean?"

Natasha hesitated. Her jaw dropped, but she quickly recovered. "This morning. In your office. You said you wanted to show me something and I, er, *left* before you could. I was just thinking you could show me, *us*, now. Together."

"Forgive me," Manu said, his expression steady. "I must be

confused, but I do not recall what you mean. We spoke this morning in my office, yes, but I did not need to show you anything. Perhaps you misheard me?"

I stared at Natasha, who was doing her best to rein in either fear or anger—maybe both. "Oh. Yeah, maybe you're right."

He smiled and patted the table. "Anyway, I wanted to let you know that we were able to get the boat here on the island running, so we have sent for the local police. Two of our staffers headed out early this afternoon. I expect they will return tomorrow, and they should be able to bring the police and someone to repair the phone lines as well."

Relief fell through me—I mean that literally. Real and effable, I felt the cool, slick relief spread from my head, to my chest, sinking into my stomach, intestines, and toes. This could all be over. The police would be here soon. We'd be going home. It couldn't come soon enough.

"Well, I shall leave you to your dinner. I just wanted to check and make sure you had all returned safely," he said finally. "Have a nice evening."

With that, he offered a hand in the air as a salute and turned away from us. It was only when he made it back to the door and inside that I realized he hadn't asked if we'd found Laura, and he hadn't mentioned Megan's absence.

Was it because he hadn't noticed, or because he already knew what happened to them?

# CHAPTER THIRTY-ONE

## ANDY

The police were coming.

I'd have to tell them the truth.

About everything.

How could I? How could I make them understand?

They'd hate me. Brad would hate me. Nick would hate me. And even if they didn't hate me, they'd never understand. They wouldn't understand how I could betray my friends, hurt my friends...but I'd been hurt, too.

Still, we swore to stick together. No matter what.

We should've defined *what.*

Did *what* include murder? Did it include lies? Did it include secrets that hurt the ones we loved most?

Would they stand by me no matter what, like they'd promised? Or would this be the end for us?

I shook the thought from my mind, rolling over in the bed. The others had decided to stay in the same hut together for the night. They'd be safe together—in numbers. But I couldn't do it. They didn't want us to split up, but I had to. I couldn't breathe for all the lies I was holding in.

I'd never been one to keep secrets well, especially not ones like this. Secrets of such magnitude.

I needed to be alone, to come to peace with my decisions. To figure out what had brought us to this point. How it had all gone so wrong.

I thought of Emily, of the smile I'd grown to love. The laugh I'd never hear again. The only thing keeping me from experiencing the all-out grief I'd managed to bury, was the anger that burned so hot it stung. The anger over what had been done and how all of our lives would change because of it. I wasn't sure who to be the most angry with, and so the anger settled on myself. For being stupid. For believing that people were good and honest and loyal. Emily had lied to me. She'd broken my trust. Used me. Did that make it so she deserved what she got? Of course not. I'm no monster. But I was the one still suffering. The one weighed down with secrets, lies, and truths that burned. When the police came, I'd tell them everything.

And then, my world as I knew it would come crashing to a halt.

*I'm sorry... I didn't want this.*

# CHAPTER THIRTY-TWO

## NICK

*Where are you, Laura?*

*Where are you, Megan?*

The questions swam through my mind, driving me mad with worry. We'd chosen to hole up together in Jaren and Natasha's hut. No one said it, but I think it was because it was the only place without bad memories thus far. I couldn't step foot in our hut without seeing Megan's things and becoming overwhelmed with worry and regret. I didn't even want to think about seeing Laura's things…

It was enough to destroy me, and I was sure Brad and Natasha felt the same. Only Andy had chosen to separate from the group. We'd offered to go to his hut, but he said he needed space.

Giving him that, I felt, was the least we could do.

He was suffering the most…a definite loss, while the rest of us still clung to our shreds of hope. If the police were coming, they'd be bringing cadaver dogs. There was so much land to cover, but I had to hope that would mean we would get our answers soon. They'd either find them alive, or…

What would happen if their search turned up nothing? What would that mean?

My chest constricted as I considered the possibility that maybe they weren't on the island at all anymore. Perhaps someone had taken them...driven them back to shore. We couldn't be certain who had them and, if that was the case, I knew the statistics... It was unlikely we'd ever see them again. I adjusted in the wicker chair by the door.

Brad was curled up in the window seat, while Natasha and Jaren slept in the bed. We were taking turns keeping the post, and I'd been supposed to wake one of them up an hour ago, but I had no intention of doing so. They were sleeping, and they deserved to. There wasn't a tired bone in my body.

I only wanted answers. If it were up to me, after getting dinner, I would've been back out on the search, but it would be foolish, I knew. I couldn't see anything at night.

I stared out at the moonlit beach, reminded of the night with Laura, a night such a short time ago that felt lightyears away now. I should've told her how I felt then. Should've told her I would choose her again if she'd give me the option. Should've kissed her again. Should've begged her not to walk away. Refused to let her.

If I'd known it may have been the last time I'd ever get to kiss her, touch her, breathe in her scent—

I forced the thought away. It was too painful.

I should've been grieving for Megan, but I felt heartless. I wanted her to be okay, but I *needed* Laura to be okay. I think that told me all I needed to know about where my heart truly lay.

If we found them—either of them—I'd have to be honest about everything. I couldn't keep lying.

Not when the lie might've caused either one of the women I cared about most to die.

# CHAPTER THIRTY-THREE

## NATASHA

I was trying not to move, aware of the erratic breathing sounds coming from my chest. Nick had been moving in the chair beside the door—he hadn't been to sleep at all. Jaren's sleep had been restless, waking every few hours from fitful nightmares. The squeak from the window seat where Brad was reclined roared through the hut every few minutes as he tried to get comfortable.

None of us knew how to sleep because sleep required peace. Who could feel peace at such a time?

I wanted to find Laura. Knowing the police were coming soon brought me a strange sense of calm. Because I both wanted them to come—to save us, to get answers, to protect those of us who were left—and because I didn't want them to come—because their arrival would most assuredly equal finding answers to what happened, and those answers would likely bring more pain than I was prepared for.

Jaren's breathing quickened in my ear, and I knew he was awake again. It was going to be a long night.

I squeezed my eyes shut, forcing out the question, the truth I'd been struggling with since Emily died. It had been so hard to find Laura alone, though I desperately wanted to ask her about what happened. I didn't want to seem like I was accusing her of anything, which made the conversation harder to have. Now, it was likely I'd never be able to have the conversation. Revealing the truth now, the truth I'd kept to myself all this time, would only make me look guilty.

If Laura was alive, it would make it look like we'd been hiding something together.

If Laura was dead, the blame for the lie would fall directly on me.

If I never told anyone, there was a chance it would never come out. Especially with all the witnesses now gone. There was also a huge chance it meant nothing anyway.

But with the police coming, I had to make a decision in just a few hours. What was I going to tell them?

Would I tell them that Laura left the spa with Emily that day, too? That I'd hidden that initially, to protect my friend? Would I tell them how they'd been gone for several minutes, and when they came back Laura was alone and strangely quiet? Emily eventually made her way back, of course, and I didn't want to believe anything could've gone on between them, but with them both gone now, could I deny how worried it made me that I'd kept it to myself? Laura was my best friend. She didn't hide things from me, but she'd hidden whatever had been said between them. She'd been avoiding me purposely, I was sure of it. But the only witnesses to the conversation were gone, one dead. At least one.

What good would it do to bring it up now? If I told the truth, it would only further incriminate me. If I didn't, it meant I was giving up on my friends. Counting on them to never return.

# CHAPTER THIRTY-FOUR

## NICK

Like Manu promised, the next morning at breakfast, I heard the steady hum of a boat engine that warned us visitors were coming. Our meal was abandoned as we made our way toward the shore to watch the boat arrive. *Boats,* more accurately. Three identical, mid-sized boats pulled up to the shore. Their bottoms were bright blue, a solid red vertical stripe running down the center. There was an enclosed cockpit, each with two uniformed men inside, and two more standing near each bow. They were dressed all in thick, black uniforms, with heavy-duty bulletproof vests, black hats, and dark sunglasses.

They disembarked from their boats quickly as Manu and several of the island employees made their way down to the shore to greet them. The officers stood back, letting one—I was assuming their captain or chief, some sort of leader—make his way through first. He went straight toward Manu, as if he knew him. Had they been called out before?

"Why so many?" Natasha asked softly from beside me.

I shook my head, not daring to speak. The group of twelve armed men were doing little to calm my already frayed nerves as I watched them staring around the island, and then at us.

Manu spoke to the officer in charge, nodding in our direction, and I watched as the man turned to his team, said something, and nodded. Immediately, four of the men headed inside, following two island employees toward the relaxation center.

Another four began walking across the sand—I wondered how hot they must be in such thick layers—guns at the ready as they moved past us, too, fanning out as they appeared to be searching.

Manu and the officer in charge made their way over to where we were standing. My heart plummeted. I should've felt safe, but I only felt scared.

Manu spoke first. "My friends, this is Officer Knowles. He will be leading the investigation into Ms. Emily's death."

The officer nodded at us but didn't speak. The hard lines around his lips made me wonder how much time he spent grimacing. He had a faded tan line from his sunglasses as he lifted them up, glaring at us with eyes that left no room for comfort.

"He has asked to speak to each of you separately." He nodded at Jaren and Natasha. "Including those of you who are married. Andy, we will ask you to stay in your hut. Brad, in yours. Jaren, in yours. Nick, in yours. Natasha, I will have you wait in the spa. And Ms. Megan can wait in the library."

"Megan's gone," Andy said before I'd had the chance. "Like Laura."

"She has gone missing, too?" Manu asked, his expression practically wilting. If he truly had nothing to do with what was happening, I couldn't help but feel bad for him. The island had to have cost him millions, and our visit was ruining everything he'd built. With each person's disappearance, I saw him deflate a bit more.

I nodded. "Since yesterday."

The officer's expression didn't change. "Very well," Manu said. "Just spread out like I said, then. I can have your breakfasts brought to you if you would like to finish what you were eating. Please just stay where you were assigned to be until Officer Knowles says otherwise."

They were splitting us up. It hit me then, and outright fear began to settle in my bones once more. How could we let them split us up when we'd all agreed we were safer together? Then again, what choice did we have? My eyes flicked down to where the gun rested on the officer's hip. We had no choice. We had to do what we were told.

We'd be fine. Andy had stayed alone all night, and he was fine, I reminded myself. This was just routine. Whether or not I believed it, I had to accept it.

I closed my eyes, moving away from the group with apprehension as sweat began to bead at my temples. My palms were slick with perspiration, and I wiped them on my shirt, shoving them into my pockets.

Whatever was coming, we had to face it alone.

Like it or not, we were all alone in whatever was to come. As we separated, spreading out like corners in a square, that was more obvious than ever before.

*Please don't let this be the last time I see them.*

---

After an excruciating amount of waiting, I watched Officer Knowles and one of his men approach my hut. My palms were drenched with sweat, matching my back and the bends of my knees. I stood, then worried that it was confrontational and sat again, bouncing my foot against the floor in a jarring fashion.

I was increasingly aware of my scent in the room. Of Megan's scent. Of the fact that I hadn't cleaned up. Of the fact that I was about to be questioned by police. Weren't they supposed to ask if I wanted to talk to a lawyer? Maybe only guilty people did that. *Why didn't I clean up?* Did I have food on my face from breakfast? *Don't touch your face.* That was a sign of a lie. I'd watched too many police shows.

"Officers." I stood again, unbelievably aware of the sweat pooling above my upper lip as they pulled open the door and stepped inside.

"Sit," Knowles said, waving his hand at me. The officer behind him held a notepad. He was muscled and tan, bigger than his commander, but kept a few feet back, as if he knew his place.

"What can you tell us about the night Emily Bennett died?"

I took a breath. This was it. This was the moment I revealed the very truth that would ruin my life.

"At dinner, Emily kept talking about secrets. She was acting strange, and she left dinner early."

"What do you mean strange?" he asked, cutting me off before I'd even gotten started.

Was I first or last in his questioning lineup? I'd waited so long, I couldn't have been first, could I? Had he heard this story before? What did I remember? I wanted to be sure I was getting it right, but so much had happened since then.

"It just seemed like she was upset over something. Like she wanted to fight with Andy. She was quieter than usual...and, like I said, she left before she'd eaten anything."

"To your knowledge, had anything happened to upset her?"

"No. She was fine when she left that morning. Chipper, even. But I didn't see her again until dinner. Something had changed."

He glanced at the man behind him, who was scribbling notes on his pad of paper, then back at me. "How long had you known Miss Bennett?"

I scratched my head. *Touching my face.* Pulling it away too quickly, I felt my skin burn with embarrassment. "Um, Andy brought her to our group dinner...like, two months ago? And then again around a month ago? So, I'd met her twice before we came here. But I wouldn't say I really knew her at all. She kept to herself, even when she was with us. I mean, not to say that she wasn't friendly. She seemed nice, I just...you know how it is, we've all been friends for most of our lives. It's hard to get in a word edgewise between us all."

The officer's lips hardened. "Was there anyone in particular that didn't seem excited to have Emily joining your group?"

*Natasha.* The name was there on the tip of my tongue. Always the last to warm up to anyone or anything new. She kept her walls ten feet high, and it was only because I'd known her so long that I knew it was a defense mechanism. I shook my head. "No. Not really. We were all glad Andy had met someone to make him happy."

"And did he seem happy?"

"The happiest I'd ever seen him," I answered. "Andy wasn't really the type to date the same woman for very long, so the fact that he kept seeing Emily said a lot. I really think he was falling for her." My words surprised me, but they were the truth. His reaction to Emily's death had been that of a man in love.

Officer Knowles obviously had no use for love. He grimaced, releasing an almost-growl as he continued his line of questioning. "Okay, so back to the night she died… Miss Bennett left dinner early. Did you see her after that?"

"No. Megan, my fiancée, had a headache after dinner, so we came back to the hut for her to meditate. We went to bed shortly after."

"Megan, your fiancée, is one of the others who's missing?"

I nodded. "Yes. Now. As of yesterday."

"Okay, so that night, neither you or Megan were up again until the next morning?"

"Well, Megan fell asleep after her meditation, but it took me awhile to fall asleep. The storm kept me awake." I looked up at the ceiling of the hut. "These things aren't the most sturdy or soundproof. And then, Laura came to visit me."

"Laura?" The writing officer was really scribbling then, the sound of the scratching of ink on paper reaching me across the room.

"Laura Walker. Brad's wife. She's my best friend. Has been all my life. We own a dental practice together."

"And she's also missing now, correct?"

Again, I nodded. "She went for a jog the morning Megan disappeared and never came back."

"And why did Mrs. Walker come to see you that night?"

My forehead wrinkled. "I don't know…" I thought back to that night, the whipping wind, the rocks tapping on my window. Why had she come? It didn't make sense. "She wanted to talk about, er, about Emily, actually." But why? I was asking myself the questions I should've been asking already, but so much had happened I didn't have the chance. Why had she been asking about Emily? Initially, I'd worried she had something to do with her death, but now she was gone, too. So either she was innocent or someone found out what she'd done. *She wasn't a murderer.* I knew Laura. Had known her my entire life. She wouldn't have hurt Emily. She wouldn't hurt anyone.

*Except me.*

But not intentionally.

The officer watched as I argued internally, before shaking the thoughts from my head and meeting his eyes. "She said that she thought Emily might be dangerous."

That seemed to surprise him. "And why did she say that?" He folded his beefy arms across his chest.

"She said that Emily was talking about secrets at the spa, same as she was at dinner. Laura thought she may know something about one of us. Something she was going to use to exploit us. She thought we may be in danger."

"What could she have known? Did Mrs. Walker say?"

I pressed my lips together, trying to think. So much of that night was a blur. *Except the kiss. And the sex. The rough scraping of our skin against the bark of the palm trees. The sand around my ankles. The wind. The screams.*

"I don't know. Laura didn't say."

The man stared at me, neither nodding nor speaking. He waited for me to say more. Now was my chance. I should've spoken up, but I didn't. I hesitated, and the moment was gone.

"Did Mrs. Walker return to her hut? Or were the two of you together when Miss Bennett's body was discovered?"

"She'd gone back to her hut. I was inside, too. Trying to get back to sleep."

"Did anyone join you two when you were talking?"

"No," I said quickly. "Apparently Andy was walking around looking for Emily, but we never saw anyone that night. We went down there," I pointed out the window, in the direction that we'd been, "to talk so we didn't wake anyone up."

"And how long after that was it before Miss Bennett's body was found?"

"About an hour, I guess. I was dozing in and out when I heard screams. Megan and I hurried out to see what was wrong, and that was when we learned what had happened."

"Did anyone know about you meeting Mrs. Walker that night? Her husband? Megan?"

"No," I said. "Not them. No one at the time, but Jaren and Natasha do now. I told them because…" And we'd arrived back at my chance again. "Laura and I used to have a thing back when we were in college. It ended years ago, but Megan was always a little worried I still had feelings for her." I ran a palm over my face. "When Laura first went missing, I was worried Megan had seen us together and done something."

The officer walked to the window. "Where did you and Mrs. Walker meet, exactly?"

"Way down," I said. "We couldn't see the huts, and she couldn't have seen us unless she'd followed me. It was a stupid thought, I was just worried about Laura."

"And when you came back, was Megan awake?"

I shook my head. "She hadn't moved in all the time I'd been gone. The headache she'd had knocked her out."

"Okay." The officer turned away from the window. "Is there anything else you can tell us about the night Miss Bennett died?"

"I don't think so. By the time I got down there, Andy already had her out of the water. I'd gone to get Manu for help, and they took her body to the infirmary. No one really knew what to do. Andy was a mess...we all were."

"You were a mess? You stated a moment ago that you hardly knew her."

"She was still our friend, and Andy is our best friend. It just felt wrong." I shivered despite the heat.

"What happened the next day?"

"Nothing. We were all supposed to be trying to enjoy ourselves, but we basically just tried to keep Andy calm. Keep ourselves calm." I gave a nervous laugh. Why had I done that?

"And the next day was when Mrs. Walker and Megan disappeared, correct? Yesterday?" He paced across the floor.

"Yes."

"What's Megan's last name?"

"Graham."

The officer wrote it down. "We'll need a piece of her clothing for the dogs to do their search."

"Of course." I grabbed a shirt from her suitcase on the floor and handed it to him. He passed it to the officer behind him, who placed it in a bag right away and tucked the bag under his arm.

"Now, how did you know they were missing? Who discovered they were gone first?"

"Laura went for a jog in the morning, around sunrise, I think. By breakfast, she hadn't returned. Brad pointed it out to me, and we planned to go look for her. While we were getting ready to go into the woods, I left Megan in the hut to go talk to Jaren and Natasha…it was when I had the theories about Megan being involved in Laura's disappearance, and when we came back to talk to her, she was gone. We haven't heard from either of them since."

"Does everyone in your group get along with Mrs. Walker?"

"Everyone loves Laura. She is practically the glue holding us all together. She brought me into the group, Natasha, Brad. Brad brought Andy. Without Laura, I'm not sure if we have a group left."

"So there weren't any disagreements?"

"Well, of course, there were disagreements here and there. Which restaurant we should eat at. How much we should spend on the Christmas gift exchange. Who was hosting game night. But it was never anything serious."

"Did Mr. Walker know about your involvement with Mrs. Walker?"

"I'm not sure," I said, swallowing the excess spit that had filled my mouth without warning. Why did I seem unable to function normally? "Like I said, it was years ago. She is just my best friend now."

"Was that her choice or yours?"

"She is…happily married. I'm happy for her."

"That's not what I asked."

"It was her choice, I guess. She chose to break off our relationship because she'd started feeling really serious about Brad. It was…God, it was more than twenty years ago. I'm over it. We're both over it."

"So why was it that Miss Graham had suspicions about the two of you, then? Why did she see what none of your other friends did?"

"Megan saw what wasn't there. She worried about my friendship with Laura. How close we are. But she isn't jealous. It isn't like that at all. She trusts me. She knows I love her. We are engaged, for crying out loud."

The officer stared at me, still and quiet for a moment too long. "What about Miss Graham? She is a newer member of your group as well, correct?"

"Yes."

"How do the people in the group feel about her?"

"They like her, I think. She's been part of the group for just over a year. She is the first serious girlfriend I've had in years."

"Since Mrs. Walker?"

"Laura and I weren't even that serious. And, no, there've been others since her anyway. But not in about seven or eight years, I guess."

Knowles turned back to the officer, whose name I still didn't know, and nodded. The man stopped writing. "Is there anything else you can tell us about either the death of Emily Bennett or the disappearances of Laura Walker or Megan Graham? Anything at all that you think might be able to help our investigation."

"No, there's nothing else. Just," my voice cracked, and I paused, collecting myself, "just find them. Please."

"We're going to find them, Mr. London," Knowles said, and I watched as the other officer slid the pen into his shirt pocket, followed by the notepad. "It's a small island, and we have a very limited amount of suspects. We're going to find out the truth about everything."

# CHAPTER THIRTY-FIVE

## ANDY

When the evening arrived, the sun lowering on the horizon, they finally released us from our huts. I'd told the police everything—every last horrible detail, and I knew what was coming.

I walked toward the water, wondering what it must've been like for Emily. How it must've felt as the water filled her lungs. It must've burned… Had she known it was the end? Given up early and let it happen? Or did she fight with everything she had to the bitter end?

Fresh tears filled my eyes at the thought. I missed her so much it hurt.

*I wish I'd been there.*

*I wish I could've saved you.*

When the water hit my bare toes, I sank down onto the sand, bending my knees up in front of me and wrapping my arms around them. I couldn't deny the guilt I felt, though the police assured me it was misplaced. I had done the right thing, told the truth, but it didn't make it any easier.

I'd broken a pact, betrayed a friend.

Still, Emily deserved justice for her death. Even if it meant doing something I'd never thought I'd do. I was a loyal friend—always had been. I'd never betrayed my friends, not in high school when it meant taking the blame for a note being passed I hadn't written, or in college when it meant being expelled for a fight I'd only been trying to break up.

But this was different.

It had to be.

I hadn't heard them approaching me over the sound of the ocean's roar and my own tears, so when a hand touched me, I jerked my arm back, ready to attack.

"Andy?" Natasha asked, hardly fazed, sinking down beside me in the sand. "You alright?"

Jaren sat down beside her, and Nick and Brad took the space on the opposite side of me. They wanted to be there for me. To comfort me. They had no idea what I'd done yet.

"It was just hard, you know?" They thought I was talking about losing her, about talking about it to the police. I let them keep thinking it.

"I know," Natasha said, resting her head on my shoulder. "But it's over now. The police will talk to Manu. They'll figure out what's going on and get us out of here safely."

"At least now Emily can be laid to rest," Jaren said, staring out at the ocean.

"And hopefully they'll find Laura and Megan," Brad said. He was fighting back tears, refusing to look at any of us, though I didn't know why it mattered. We were all a blubbering mess anymore. "I saw them unloading the dogs off the boat earlier. They asked for pieces of Laura's clothing and had the dogs walk around our hut to get a good feel for her scent."

"Yeah, they asked for a piece of Megan's clothing, too. I haven't heard them bark yet," Nick said. "That's got to be a good thing, right?"

I sniffed, wiping my cheek on my shoulder. "I'm sure they'll find them."

"Do you think we'll get to go home tonight?" Jaren asked. "I mean, when the police leave?"

"I don't want to leave until I know what happened to Laura," Brad said quickly.

"Me either," Nick agreed. "I won't leave until we know they've been found. Safe or…otherwise." He ran a finger over his nose, shaking his head. "I can't imagine going anywhere until we know the truth about what happened."

I nodded because none of it mattered. By the time we left, they'd all know the truth about everything.

Like I already did.

# CHAPTER THIRTY-SIX

## NICK

The dogs were called out of the woods after dinner, their officers behind them. There were no signs of Laura or Megan, and I couldn't decide if that was good or bad.

The overall feeling among the group had grown more grim, our hopeful tones at the arrival of the police shifting quickly. Nothing had been figured out. They were still missing. We had no answers.

As more time passed, the possibility of them no longer being on the island at all grew more and more worrisome and undeniable in my mind. Something was wrong.

More wrong than I'd realized.

Where were they?

The police showed no signs of leaving as the evening dragged on, their boats still rising and falling with the tide near the pier. They'd had their meals inside in the dining room, while we ate under the pavilion in silence. I didn't think it would take so long, if I were being honest. I thought they'd have us on the boats already, be moving us to safety, but it hadn't happened.

In fact, aside from the questioning, the officers hadn't spoken to us at all. Manu was treating them as if they were the guests, waiting on them hand and foot. The employees had practically forgotten we were still there. Our usual eight waiters had been reduced to two, and our stewards were nowhere in sight.

When night came, I half expected them to ask us to give up our huts for the officers, but I quickly remembered the extra huts past ours as the parade of men dressed all in black made their way down the shore. I could see them now, from where I was standing on the dark sand. Two officers had taken posts outside of the huts, walking across the sand with flashlights in hand.

I should've been sleeping, but it was no use. I wasn't sure how long I'd been awake, but the idea of sleep was enough to send my stomach spinning. I needed to be awake in case someone else needed help. Every time I began to doze off, I'd hear Emily's scream, hear the sounds of Laura tossing rocks at my window, and remember the far-off look in Megan's eyes when I'd seen her last. It was enough to drive me crazy.

I'd been walking across the shore. Pacing. Running. Trying anything and everything to wear myself out. I needed to sleep. I needed to get some rest before I started hallucinating, but it just wasn't an option.

As I moved across the sand, I looked up as a light flicked on in a hut up ahead. One of ours.

Who was awake at this time of night?

Relieved to have someone to talk to, I pushed forward. It was the second hut from the right. *Andy's.*

I jogged up the incline, hoping everything was all right and it was just a case of not being able to sleep, but as I drew closer, I froze. The light flicked off just seconds after it had come on, but I knew what I'd seen.

*No.*

My heart leapt, my feet moving faster through the sand. *Not fast enough.* I couldn't move fast enough. Sand dug in between my toes, my calves burning as I pushed, my lungs gasping for air, heart pounding in my chest.

It wasn't possible. It wasn't real. Could I be hallucinating after all?

I reached the stairs to his porch, grabbing the railing and hauling myself up. I grabbed the handle of the sliding glass door and stared inside, seeing the moonlit outline of what I thought I was seeing. What I, at the same time, *hoped* I was seeing and very much wished I wasn't. Andy held Laura in a tight embrace, the moon's glow casting a shadow across their faces.

*She is alive.*

*She is a liar.*

# CHAPTER THIRTY-SEVEN

## LAURA

The sliding glass door slid open in an instant, and we broke apart. I gasped when I heard it, saw the shadow of a man in the doorway. We'd been caught. Andy would be furious with me. I wasn't supposed to come. I wasn't supposed to have left the safety of my hiding spot, and I certainly wasn't supposed to turn on the lamp to give others a peek inside the hut.

"What the hell?" Nick asked, his voice way too loud. I couldn't totally see him, but I knew the voice. I'd know it anywhere.

"Nick, what are you doing here?" I asked, walking toward him, keeping my own voice low.

"What am I—" His mouth opened and closed as if he were forming words, but no sound came out. He blinked back fresh tears—I could see them glinting in the dim light—and leaned forward, pulling me into a hug. I breathed in the scent of him—warm. Safe. "Thank God you're okay." He kissed my cheek, pulling back, his hands still on my shoulders. "I thought you were dead. I pictured all of these horrible things..." He trailed off, dropping his hands from my shoulders and looking at Andy.

I saw the muscle in his jaw twitch. "This is why you were so interested in my feelings for Laura. You two were…" He pointed back and forth between us, and I flushed red, thankful he wouldn't see it in the darkness. Shadows couldn't reveal my embarrassment.

"God, Nick. No. No, Andy and I aren't together." I put a hand to his chest. "It's nothing like that."

"What, then?" he asked, shaking his head. "I don't understand. Where have you been? Did he tell you the police are here?" He pointed out the door. "They've been looking for you. We have to go tell them you're alive." He pulled me into another hug, and I inhaled his scent again. I wanted to savor it. Even without the usual aroma of his cologne, his scent was so familiar. It felt like home, a place I desperately wished I could be.

"They know, Nick." I patted his chest again. "The police know. Look, we have a lot to tell you and not a lot of time, okay? Let's just sit down, and I promise I'll explain everything. How did you—how did you find me anyway?"

"I was walking on the beach…looking for you. I haven't been able to sleep. I saw you through the window. I-I couldn't believe it." There were fresh tears in his eyes again, and he shook his head. "I can't believe it."

At Nick's words, Andy grumbled, glancing outside to see if anyone else was coming. "You shouldn't have turned on the lamp, Laura."

I didn't respond, though I knew he was right. It was why he'd turned it off immediately after jumping out of bed. I shouldn't have come, but I had to talk to him. I had to know what was happening. If we'd been seen, the plan would be ruined. I watched his expression, and only when he nodded and his shadowed face moving in the moonlight gave me the go-ahead, did I exhale with relief. I turned to Nick. "I'm sorry, Nick. I'm sorry I worried you. If I'd had any other choice, believe me, I would've told you."

"What are you talking about? Why couldn't you tell me? Where have you been?"

"I've been here. I've always been here." I paused, trying to study his face in the moonlight. "There's so much to tell you, and it starts with the fact that we know what happened to Emily."

"Oh, God," came the instant response. "You know who killed her? How? Who?"

From behind me, Andy touched my shoulder. "Laura, you really shouldn't be here. I can fill Nick in on what's going on, but you should go back. If anyone else saw him come here, it could ruin everything."

"Hang on a second," Nick said, pointing at Andy. "You've known where she was all along? All this time? We spent an entire day in the jungle looking for her, and you've known everything?"

"I had to keep it up, man. It was for her protection."

"For her protection? What does that even mean?"

I cleared my throat, trying to hide the tears that were coming no matter how hard I tried to fight them off. "If you'll let me talk, we'll explain everything. But, like I said, you should sit." He was never going to forgive me.

# CHAPTER THIRTY-EIGHT

## LAURA

**THREE DAYS EARLIER**

"I can't believe our drinks are empty again," Emily said, a brilliant, charming smile on her face. She leaned her head back in the chair. "They may as well leave a few refills next time they come."

"I don't have time to wait," Natasha said with a quick laugh. "I had mine finished before y'all even started." She started to lean up. "I'm going across the hall to get more. Everyone want the same as what they have?" She pointed at each of us. "This round's on me."

I laughed at her ridiculous joke, the wine aiding my good mood. "I can go this time, Tash," Emily said. Natasha hated nicknames, hated it even more when someone took it upon themselves to create one for her, but to my surprise, she smiled. "You went the round before last, and Megan went last time. It can be my turn. I need to stretch my legs anyway."

"Okay, you won't hear me complain about having to do less work. Go for it." Natasha sat back down, and Emily sauntered out of the room. After we heard her footsteps growing fainter, she smiled at me. "Little Miss Thang ain't so bad after all, I guess."

"She's sweet," Megan said, her head leaned back, cucumbers on her eyes.

"Young," Natasha agreed. "But sweet."

"What do you think the men are talking about?" I asked thoughtfully.

"Oh, honey, that ain't even a question. The question is, do you think they've ever stopped talking about *her*?"

I laughed. "Ah, I know. Brad denies it, but she *is* pretty."

"Unfairly pretty," Natasha agreed.

"Half our age," Megan said. "With skin that screams it."

"It's enough to make you sick, isn't it?" Natasha asked with a laugh. "But hey, if she's going to keep vacations like these coming, Jaren can keep right on staring for all I care."

I smiled, but it was less free than hers then. I didn't want Brad to stare at her. Not the way I'd seen him. Footsteps were headed back in our direction, and I looked up, the conversation cut short. "Hey, Laura, would you mind helping me?" Emily's head popped in the room. "Mina is right in the middle of something, and I told her we could bring our own drinks back, but I don't want to try to carry the drinks alone." Without a pause for my answer, she went on. "I figure since Megan and Natasha have already gone, it's our turn."

I nodded, attempting to dry my feet before standing up. It seemed silly that she'd made the trip to ask for my help when she could've brought half the drinks this time and half next. It was the same amount of trips either way, but it didn't matter. No point arguing. "Yeah, of course."

"Thanks." She waited for me to join her in the doorway before leading me across the hall. To my surprise, instead of heading into the dining room, she pointed toward the exit door. "Sorry, I just really needed to get you alone." She laughed, covering her mouth. "Wow, that sounded creepy. Um, do you mind if I talk to you for a minute?"

I hesitated. What did she need to talk to me about? Had she overheard us talking about her? A million thoughts swam in my mind, and I nodded silently. She pushed open the door, and the moment I stepped outside, sand began to cling to my still-damp feet. We stopped in front of the building, a few feet from the door, and she leaned back against the wall. Her expression was conflicted, a wrinkle forming between her brows.

"Is everything okay?" I asked when she didn't immediately begin to talk.

She wasn't meeting my eyes, her hands behind her back against the building as she stared out ahead of us. "I need to tell you something."

"Okay..." My mind went to the strange interactions I'd seen between her and Brad, and I knew what she was going to say before she even said it. My shoulders tensed, and I wondered instantly why I'd agreed to come with her. What was I going to say? How was I going to handle the news that my husband was cheating on me? It was going to destroy me. It was going to destroy Andy. What were we—

"I'm your daughter."

My body convulsed—my full body rolling like a wave at the news. *"What?"*

She met my eyes then. "You had a daughter twenty-two years ago that you put up for adoption."

It wasn't a question. She knew the one thing no one in my life did—not my parents, not my friends, not my husband. "What are you talking about?"

"You did, didn't you?"

I studied her face, her chin, her eyes. Did she look like me? Maybe, but it was faint. The dark hair wasn't mine, but the high cheekbones were familiar. The cleft in her chin, identical to my father's, couldn't be mistaken. "How could you possibly know that?"

"I was adopted by an amazing family, but I was always curious about my biological parents. Last year, my parents were killed in a car accident. I used some of their life insurance money to hire a private investigator. The adoption records were sealed, and my parents had never been able to tell me anything about you, but the investigator thought he might be able to find you anyway." She tilted her head to the side, playing with the end of her hair. "I don't blame you…or-or expect anything from you. I don't want to disrupt your life, and I'm sure you had your reasons for giving me up." She paused, and the tears in her eyes matched my own. "I had a really great life. Two parents who loved me so much. I don't need anything from you, but I just… I want to know you. I want to know where I came from."

I couldn't speak. I stared at her, shock overwhelming me. *How could this have happened?* The records were sealed by the adoption agency. I was never supposed to have been able to be found. I felt as though I was going to be sick. The world around me began to spin as I tried to piece together my thoughts. It felt like I'd been placed on one of those rides at the fair that suck you to their walls because of the speed of their rotations—so quickly shifting from anger over a nonexistent affair to confusion and sadness over finding out the truth.

She let out a loud, obnoxious sigh. "Anyway, I know you weren't expecting this. Obviously, it's shocking. But I wanted to get to know you. I was kind of…stalking you a bit, I guess. Not in a threatening way. I just followed you around to get to know you and figure out how to approach you." She laughed under her breath, twisting a strand of hair around her finger. "This sounds terrible. I've rehearsed it a million times, and it's still coming out a jumbled mess." She tossed the hair over her shoulders, inhaling deeply. "One of the times I followed you, I met Andy. He thought I was just a girl in a bar, and he asked for my number. And…it was my *in*, I guess. I realized that was the perfect way to get to know you, to get closer to you… I wanted to feel like your friend. And now I do, but it feels dishonest. I don't want to keep lying or let this go on for much longer. I've wanted to talk to you and Brad about this so many—"

*"No."* Her words hit me, shocking me back to reality. "No, Emily. You can't say anything. Not to anyone."

The crease between her brows deepened. "I just want to know my parents, Laura. My real parents. I don't need an explanation. I hold no grudges." She held her hands up to show she was sincere.

"Emily, listen to me, I need to break this news to Brad myself. When you were put up for adoption…" My voice broke. "It was the hardest thing I've ever had to do. Can you just give me some time to process everything?" Panic filled me. Had she mentioned this to Andy? Would he mention it to Brad? "You haven't told anyone, have you?"

Her mouth twisted, and she glanced away. "No. I wanted to tell you first. You were the easiest to approach." She reached for my hand, and I recoiled from her without thinking. "You've been so nice to me."

I reached forward, pulling her into a hug. I didn't know how to feel, how to react. Was this really my daughter standing in front of me? The daughter I'd given up? The daughter I never thought I'd see again when I placed her into the arms of strangers while I sat crying alone in a hospital bed? I rubbed her back, releasing a sob. "I can't believe it's you."

Emily started to cry, too, and I felt her shoulders shaking in my arms. "I've dreamed about you my whole life. I want to know so much."

I pulled back. In the distance, a door shut, a seagull cawed overhead, and the ocean waves continued to roar. Nothing else mattered. I couldn't focus on anything except my own panic. This would change everything. "I want to tell you everything," I swore, wiping my eyes. "And I promise I will. But can you do me one favor?"

She nodded, swiping a finger across both her cheeks as she laughed through her tears. "Anything."

"Can you wait until we get back home before you mention this to anyone? I want to break the news to Brad gently. He's… he's not good with surprises."

"Imagine that, neither am I. It runs in the family, I guess," she said, a bright smile on her face. She pulled me into another hug, and I gave in, waiting for a response.

"So, we'll just talk to him once we're back home, okay?"

She nodded, her chin bumping my shoulder. "I just can't believe it's you."

I couldn't believe it was her, either. I couldn't believe everything was going to fall apart. "Emily, I need you to tell me you understand." I pulled away from her, gripping her shoulders. "I need you to promise me you won't tell anyone anything. You have to keep pretending nothing's changed between us until I can tell Brad when we get back home."

Her glowing expression began to fade, and she nodded, her chin quivering. "I understand."

"No one can know until I'm ready to deal with this." I shook my head, anger swelling in my belly at being forced to face the truth of what I'd done.

"I'm sorry, Laura—"

"You don't need to apologize. I understand why you did what you did, but you need to realize I had my reasons, and this wasn't planned. I have to process this… It's a lot, Emily. And what about Andy? What are you going to tell him?"

"Wh-what about him?" She blinked.

"This is going to break his heart. He's in love with you, don't you see that? To find out you've used him to get to us? How do you think he's going to react to that?"

"I guess I didn't think—"

"Well, you need to," I said. I wasn't being fair to her, I knew. But my privacy had been violated. And I felt trapped here on the island with no choice but to face it. It was unfair. I'd made the decision. I hadn't wanted to know Emily, but she hadn't respected that. "You need to think things through. What you do matters. Your choices hurt people." I sighed. "I'm sorry for being so harsh, but you have to think…" I trailed off. "I need to go back inside. I can't do this right now."

"Laura, wait—"

"Please just…please give me some time, okay?" I looked back at her as I pulled the door open. "It's really good to meet you, and I'm glad you had a good life, but I need a minute." I walked through the door, my heart breaking at what I'd said. It wasn't fair. Not to her. Not to me.

My words echoed in my head. *What you do matters. Your choices hurt people.* Was I talking to Emily? Or myself?

# CHAPTER THIRTY-NINE

## NICK

### PRESENT DAY

As she told the story, the room was eerily quiet. When she finished, I shook my head. "So…when you came to me because you said Emily was dangerous? That you thought she knew secrets about us…"

She nodded. "It was because I already knew that she did, but I had no idea how to tell you."

"So…" I looked to Andy, who was watching me closely, then back to Laura. I'd been right all along. How was Andy okay with this? "Now you're hiding from the police? You can't plan to stay here, what, forever?"

"What? No, I'm not hiding from the police—"

"That's what you're saying, isn't it? You killed Emily because of what she knew?" I looked at Andy again, trying to read the expression on his face. "Because she was threatening to tell Brad about the baby?"

Laura shook her head, swiping a hand across the back of her neck and wiping the sweat on her shorts. "No. You have it all wrong. I *didn't* kill Emily. I didn't know she was dead until we all woke up. I would've never... She was our daughter, Nick." She put her hands over her face, and I wanted to comfort her, but I couldn't move. I couldn't do anything but watch. "She was our daughter, and she was going to tell Brad. She thought Brad was her father. I was so scared. I didn't know what to do, but I would've never done that."

"Had you told him about..." I trailed off, wondering what exactly Andy knew.

"No," she said quickly. "No. Everything we did that summer, our relationship, the baby, the adoption... I put it all behind me just like I said I would. Brad was gone to Haiti for two years, and when he came home, I just moved on from what we'd gone through. We both agreed to never talk about it again..."

She was right. We had agreed, but that didn't mean it wasn't a mistake. It didn't mean I hadn't wondered if it was the right decision. She was still dating Brad when the affair had happened between us, but the start-up of his company—bringing clean water to Haiti—had sent him overseas for two years. He promised he'd come home whenever he could, but he didn't return a single time. I'd never thought of Laura as being someone I could develop feelings for in that way, but as Brad's absence weighed on her, we spent more and more time together. We ended up moving in together for one of the last semesters of college when my roommate's fiancée moved in and I needed a place to crash, and the relationship went from there. I never knew what it was, or what it meant—she'd always been my best friend, but those feelings were new and unexplored. All I knew was that I didn't want it to end.

And the feelings didn't. But when we found out she was pregnant, I was ready to propose. I'd bought the ring. I didn't care that she was still technically in a relationship. I loved her, and I thought she felt the same.

Instead of a proposal, the night I'd taken her out for dinner, she asked me if I would sign over my rights in an adoption. She didn't want the baby. She said what we'd done had been a mistake. She said I should move out.

It was then I realized that what had felt so real to me was never more than something to pass the time for her until Brad returned. So, I moved out the next month, signed over my rights, and never looked back.

The year that followed, we were the most distant we'd ever been. When she married Brad, she asked that I come. That I serve as her man of honor. Like the dutiful best friend I'd always been, I did as I was told, fighting back heartbreak every step of the way.

I never knew anything about the baby, except that it existed somewhere. Somewhere in an alternate reality where Laura loved me back, I imagined our life from time to time.

But in this time, in this reality, she was just my best friend, and I had to accept that.

"So, you didn't kill her?"

"Of course not."

"But...but did you tell her about me?" I looked at Andy. "Did you know?"

Andy shook his head. "I didn't know any of this until Laura told me who Emily was. I knew you had feelings for Laura, but I never knew you'd had an affair, let alone a child."

"So," I blinked, trying to process. "She really was our daughter?"

Laura nodded, and I caught the reflection of the moonlight on a tear as it cascaded down her cheek.

I put a hand over my mouth, anger, confusion, and outright sadness filling me. I had to know the answer, no matter how much it pained me. "But if you didn't kill her, who did?"

# CHAPTER FORTY

## ANDY

"I saw you two together the night that Emily died. I was walking along the beach, looking for her, and I saw something move in the clump of palm trees not far from our huts. When I got closer, I realized it was you. Both of you." I spoke the words, letting them wash over Nick. He'd lied to me about his feelings for Laura, about so much, but I wanted him to know I knew the truth. All of it. "When I realized what was happening, I ran away. I was shocked, to say the least. I planned to ask you about it, to confront you. I wanted Brad to know the truth about what his friend was doing, about what his wife had done. But I wanted to talk to you first. I made it down to the shoreline, still trying to process what I'd seen, and that was when I saw him." I paused, wishing it had been anyone but him. Anyone but my best friend. "I thought I'd seen him in the same cluster of trees where I'd seen you two, but I convinced myself it was just you, Nick. But when I walked away, I saw him again. Up near the huts. Brad was walking back from the same direction I'd been. He had to have seen you; I knew it right away. But it was right at that time I saw Emily's body. I forgot about everything else."

"Hang on—*Brad?*"

"When I got back to the hut, he was in bed. I had no idea he'd been awake," Laura said. "But then Andy showed me the footage—"

"Footage?" Nick asked.

"After everything had happened, when they brought Emily's body back here, Manu began looking through footage. They have cameras around the pavilion and in between the clusters of huts, but they can't see everything. Manu showed me a glimpse, just about a two second shot of Brad walking near where you and Nick were. There's no way he would've missed you. About ten minutes before that, Emily was walking in the opposite direction from down past the huts. It looked like she was coming back home from down the beach. They were the only ones awake and on the beach that night besides the three of us. They must've run into each other at some point. But, even knowing all of that, at the time, it didn't make sense. Brad would have no reason to want to hurt Emily."

"At least, that was what he thought," Laura said, and I could hear the pain in her voice.

"When Brad and I went out drinking, I told him about you two. I had to. I asked him if he'd seen it, and he said yes. He was bitter about it, obviously, but he said that he'd suspected for a long time."

*"What?"* Nick asked.

"When I asked him why he hadn't done something about it, he said sometimes you just have to get the timing exactly right. He said he was going to take care of it. I didn't know what he meant, but then he said that I was better off without Emily. He said whoever had killed her had probably done me a favor because women do nothing but cause problems." Andy wiped a stray tear. "I've never seen him so cold. It was like I was talking to someone I didn't even know."

"What the hell?" Nick asked.

"I ran into Laura the morning of her jog and confronted her about the two of you. I was mad. Mad about Emily, mad that you'd hurt Brad. But when I told her that Brad knew, and that he'd seen you that night, she argued. She said he was asleep that night and he couldn't have seen."

"I didn't believe him. I thought he was lying to get me to tell Brad the truth," Laura confirmed.

"When I took her to show her the tape Manu had shown me, he asked me not to tell anyone else. Not until the police came. He didn't want anyone to think he was suspicious of them. Especially if Brad was guilty. But when we watched the tapes again, we noticed that Emily never made it down to the pavilion, but we knew Brad made it back to the hut, because he was there when Laura got home. So, her path was intercepted somehow, or by someone."

"Brad had to have run into Emily when we were together," Laura said, her head hung down. "It was just a matter of minutes after Brad was caught on tape that Andy found her body."

"What?" Nick stood, shaking his head. "But that still doesn't make sense. He wouldn't—you can't honestly think—*why?* Why would he..."

"We think Emily must've said something to him then, despite Laura's request that she wait. She was upset, he was upset. We think Emily must've told Brad that he was her father, and because he didn't know anything about Laura giving up a child that belonged to him, and because he could've done the math to realize she couldn't have been his, he must've put it all together."

"He killed her to keep our secret?" Nick spun back around, staring at Laura.

"To keep his own. He had to have known that it coming out would ruin our marriage. Maybe he was never planning to say anything about our affair. Maybe he was happy not knowing. Not *confirming*," she said.

"Once we realized that, I worried Laura wasn't safe. So, Manu offered to give her a place to hide in his office until the police could get here," I said. "I was trying to do the right thing and keep her safe. I'm sorry I worried you, but if I told you, it was a risk that Brad would find out. The safest thing for all of us was to keep pretending like I didn't know anything."

"You thought Brad would...do the same to you?" Nick asked, the question directed at Laura.

"I had no idea what he would do. What he was capable of. I never thought he could hurt anyone, but he has. It's the only thing that makes sense. It was just the five of us on the beach that night. We know neither of us hurt her. Andy was on the camera walking that direction after Brad. That only leaves the possibility that Emily jumped in the water herself, or Brad hurt her. Given what we know, and based on what Brad said to Andy, only one of those options sounds likely."

"I didn't tell you about the bracelet," I said. "I hadn't had the chance." Laura looked over at me, frowning.

"Bracelet?"

"They searched your hut today, said that they needed clothes of yours to complete the canine search, and Brad gave them permission." I looked out the window, feeling sick to my stomach. "They found Emily's bracelet under Brad's side of the bed. A gold one her mother gave her. She never took it off. It must've slipped off when—" I couldn't finish the sentence. "I meant to tell you when I saw you, but we were interrupted."

"Oh, my God," Laura said, shaking her head with both hands over her mouth and nose.

"I'm just glad we know the truth. It takes some of the guilt away, you know? We did the right thing."

"Oh my God," Nick repeated, covering his mouth. "This is insane."

Laura breathed out a sob. "I can't believe he really did it. I'd held out hope that we were wrong."

I nodded, unable to move. "Me too," I said stiffly.

Laura sighed. "So, you see, I had to make a choice when I realized what happened. One of us had to make it back for our girls, and if he was going to jail, I just couldn't risk him hurting me first." She breathed heavily. "Maybe I sound ridiculous."

Nick moved beside her, pulling her to him. He kissed her head, and I turned away, giving them a moment's privacy. "You don't sound ridiculous. I'm so glad you're okay."

After a bit, I heard him speak again. "But what about Megan? Did Brad hurt her? Could he have?"

I spun back around. "Megan's safe, too. She's been hiding out with Laura. I went back to my hut to put on sunscreen, and I saw her running away from your place and confronted her. I was worried something had happened. When she told me you were worried she'd done something to Laura, I had to tell her Laura was okay. She was so upset. She asked if I could help her hide, too."

"But why?" Nick asked.

"She said she couldn't face you without being able to tell you the truth about Laura, and she didn't want anyone to be in danger," I said. "So I told her to find Manu, and he put her with Laura. I'm sorry, man. I hated that you had to worry about them both."

"I'm just glad they're okay," he said, rubbing Laura's back rhythmically. "Thank you for keeping them safe."

"No problem," I whispered, the power gone from my voice. *I should've been able to keep Emily safe, too, but I failed.*

"So, what are you doing here?" Nick asked Laura. "Why did you come out of hiding?"

"I needed to ask Andy for an update. Manu has been giving them to me. We knew the police were coming, and we knew they were going to tell him about Brad. They met with us earlier today, too, but they didn't tell us anything, and Manu has been with the police all day. I was going stir crazy waiting for answers."

"I told her she shouldn't have come," I said.

"But what are the police waiting for?" Nick asked. "If they know Brad did it, why are they waiting?"

"They're waiting for an arrest warrant," I told him. "Brad will be arrested tomorrow." The words sent chills down my spine. I hated having to betray my best friend. Despite everything he'd done, he was still the best friend I'd ever had. We'd been through so much together. He'd lent me money and couch space more times than I could count. He'd been with me the day we'd buried my baby brother. I'd been with him the day he got married, the day he brought his daughters into the world.

It felt like the biggest betrayal of my life, and I knew the guilt would eat at me for the rest of my days.

I glanced out the window, to the dark hut just a few yards away, where Brad would be sleeping peacefully, as a lump rose in my throat.

"So, what now?" Nick asked. "What do we do until they arrest him?"

"We wait," I answered, not taking my eyes off Brad's hut. "We all just wait."

# CHAPTER FORTY-ONE

## NICK

It was the first night's sleep I'd gotten in so long. It felt like years, but it had only been days. Andy, Laura, and I curled up in the king bed where my daughter should've been sleeping.

I had wild, vivid, painful dreams of a baby ripped from my arms, thrown into the ocean. Again and again I cried out for her, but she never surfaced. The dream repeated on a loop for most of the night. I was always searching for a different outcome, but it never came.

When I awoke, Laura was curled into my chest, Andy's back against hers. Even in the most tense and heartbreaking situations, she brought me peace like I'd never known.

Realizing it was starting to get light outside, and remembering all that I'd discovered the night before, I sat up abruptly. Beside me, Laura and Andy stirred. When her eyes popped open, she sat up quickly, too. Her face was ashen, her lips drawn in.

Today was the day.

Today, everything would change.

I slid out of bed as I saw a group of officers walking past our hut, wondering if that was what had woken me, or if on some level, I just knew to wake up.

Andy was up then, too, and together, the three of us made our way toward the door. We watched quietly, my thoughts racing as the officers, led by Knowles, made their way up Brad's porch. Without warning, they opened the door. Laura took my hand, wrapping her free arm around mine. She was shaking, despite the heat. This was going to destroy her.

It was too much.

I wanted so badly to shield and protect her from everything, to keep her safe, but how could I? I couldn't do anything.

I heard Brad screaming then, yelling at the officers, his voice sleepy and angry.

*"What the hell?"* he demanded, and the officers must've responded because his next response was much louder. "What does that mean? Why? No! No, I have rights. I'm an American citizen. You can't just—you can't—"

Laura stepped through the door, pushing past me on her way toward the hut.

"Laura, wait!" Andy and I hurried after her. We reached the porch at the same time, watching as the officers led Brad out. His eyes grew wide when he saw Laura. *"Laura?* What are you doing? Where have you—" The officer jerked him, and he turned to look at him. "Laura," he called over his shoulder, "you have to call our lawyer. They think I did something to Emily."

She was crying then, and I touched her arm gently, causing Brad to look at me. "Did you have something to do with this? Andy," he looked at Andy, "tell them I wouldn't do this. I'm your best friend. I'd never—"

Andy put his hand on Laura's shoulder, too, and I saw his own shoulders shaking with sobs. All the commotion led Natasha and Jaren to wake from their hut behind us, and they walked in our direction.

"What the hell?" Natasha asked, her fingers looped through

Jaren's. She pulled him to stand next to us, watching it unfold. "What's going on?" It took her a moment to process that Laura was standing between Andy and me, and when she did, she squealed, throwing her arms around her friend. "Oh my God. It's really you? You're okay? Where have you been? Are you hurt? Are you okay? *Oh my God.*"

Laura hugged her back, squeezing her eyes shut as tears poured down her cheeks. "I'm okay," she lied.

Truth was, none of us were okay, and as they led Brad away from us, his cries still carrying across the beach, I didn't know if we'd ever be okay again.

# CHAPTER FORTY-TWO

## LAURA

"Okay, do you have everything packed, then?" Natasha asked, her face still shiny and raw from the many tears we'd cried this afternoon. They'd taken Brad to shore on one of the boats, where he would be flown back to the States in police custody.

Manu had let me use the island phone to call my parents and let them know we were on our way home early. I didn't tell them what had happened—couldn't make myself form the words just yet.

One of the police boats remained outside, waiting for the rest of us to board. We'd been given the option of staying for the remainder of our trip, but I don't think any of us considered it. Truth be told, Manu looked rather relieved to be rid of us.

"Yes, I think so," I said, looking around the room. I'd been in an odd state of confusion, denial, and grief, bouncing back and forth between the emotions nearly to the minute. I'd been crying non-stop, then feeling angry and confused. Now, I was just trying to focus on getting off the island. I would deal with everything else as it came. I just wanted to get home to the daughters that I could still hold. We'd packed Brad's and my stuff into their respective suitcases and moved everything near the door. Since Megan and I had returned, it had become an unspoken rule that neither of us were to be left alone. I think they were worried we'd disappear again.

"Oh, don't forget Brad's phone charger," Megan said, pulling it from the wall on his side of the bed. As she handed it to me, I started to cry again. Why had he done this? Why had he ruined everything? So much could've been fixed, but not this.

Natasha hugged me without asking what was wrong. She always just seemed to understand. Sliding the charger from my hand, she put it in our luggage and turned back to face me. "Okay, I'm going to go over and help Jaren, Nick, and Andy, then," Natasha said. "Do you want to come with me? Get out of here for a bit? Manu said if we just set our bags outside the huts, the stewards will load them for us."

"Actually, I'm just going to stay here for a while, if that's okay?" I said, running my fingers across the edge of the freshly made bed. I just needed a minute to process all that had happened, and I couldn't do that with Natasha and Nick breathing down my neck. They had good intentions, I knew, but the bottom line was that I'd be dealing with most of this alone. I needed to start that now. I wanted to say goodbye to Emily. To the life I'd led before I came to the island. Leaving here was like leaving my old life behind, the last memories I'd have of my daughter. The last memories I'd have of my marriage.

"Oh, okay," Natasha said hesitantly. "Well, that's fine. I'm sure the men are capable of packing their bags. We can just hang out here." Her smile was forced but sincere all at once. She would do whatever I needed her to, and that meant so much to me.

She brushed away my tears, hugging me again. "You sure you're okay? What can I do?"

"I'm fine," I lied, sniffling as I hugged her again. "I will be."

"Natasha?" I heard Jaren call from Andy's hut.

"I can wait with her, if you want to go check on them," Megan offered.

"Don't you want to go check on Nick?" Natasha looked at her, then me, trying to decide what to do.

"He ran back up to the relaxation center to grab some of our dry cleaning," she said. "He'll know where to find me when he's done."

Natasha still looked hesitant, despite the assurances.

"I'll be fine here, I swear," I said with a small smile. "You go check on them. I won't disappear again."

She started to cross the room, but in one swift motion turned back to me, her arms going around my neck as she nuzzled her face into my hair. "You'd better not." She squeezed me tightly for good measure and pulled away, her arms stiff as she held my shoulders. "I'll be back in, like, half an hour. Don't go anywhere."

I nodded. "I'll be here. Swear."

When she left, Megan glanced at me from where she sat near the window. "It feels weird, doesn't it? Being back when we never really left."

She was right. It felt like we'd returned from something catastrophic, when, in reality, the devastation was happening here, without us. We'd been the safe ones. "It does."

"What will you do?" she asked quietly, not looking at me.

"About Brad?"

She nodded, but I had no answer. I had no idea what to do. About any of it. I was struggling to deal with the loss of my daughter, the devastating realization that I'd never really known her, and now I'd never have the chance. The guilt of what I'd said to her, of pushing her away when she'd told me who she was, ate away at me. If I'd behaved differently, perhaps she'd still be here. If I'd come clean right away, maybe I could've saved her life. Saved Brad's life, too.

I wasn't sure how I'd ever live with that simple truth. And

the only person I truly wanted to talk to about it had given Megan the ring on her finger. He wasn't mine to discuss things with anymore. He'd chosen Megan. He loved her.

And I was alone.

All those years ago, I'd chosen wrong, and now I'd have to live with those consequences. I pulled at the covers, adjusting them though they couldn't get much straighter. I just wanted to keep my hands busy.

"I don't know," I whispered, after a moment. "I guess I just really want to talk to him. To…to understand. I wish things could've happened differently so I could've talked to him first." I couldn't decide who to be more upset about—Emily or Brad. Though Brad had done unspeakable things, I couldn't deny the love I still felt for him. The guilt at the pain I'd caused him. Maybe things would've been different if he would've told me what he'd done. Maybe I would've protected him. I could've convinced Andy if I'd tried. He would've listened. But it didn't feel right. Emily deserved justice. Her death was a tragedy. She'd been stolen from me. Her future had been stolen from her.

Andy deserved justice for what happened.

I was so torn, but at the end of the day, I felt loyal to him. To his loss. His pain. That was the deciding factor. We were both stuck choosing between a person we'd loved most of our lives and a person we could've loved if given enough time. A person who was wronged. If anyone understood my pain, I felt it was Andy.

"Did they say why they think he did it?" she asked, interrupting my thoughts. It was a question she hadn't asked before. During our day in Manu's office, we'd hardly spoken, despite being in such close proximity. Manu brought us books to read and movies to watch, kept us fed and updated on what was going on, and we'd mostly just existed in silence. Breathing the same air, eating from the same spread, but not really talking.

In part, it was because I felt guilty over what had happened between Nick and me. In part because I was still upset over Brad. But also, and maybe mostly, because I was growing to resent Megan. Her overly positive presence made it hard to hate her like I wanted to. On top of that, I had no idea what she did or didn't know about what had happened, and it wasn't my place to tell her. Nick would have that conversation whenever he was ready, or maybe he wouldn't at all. I had no right to demand that it happen. And, to be honest, I had too much on my mind to worry about it.

A week ago, I hadn't thought about Nick in such a way for years. But discovering Emily, meeting her and seeing his dark hair and dark eyes in our daughter, brought all the memories rushing back. And now, flooded with emotion and memories from so long ago, I was struggling to deal with processing them amidst such chaos.

But I could never tell Megan any of that. Nor could I tell her why Brad had killed Emily.

So, instead, I said, "I have no idea. I'm sure the police know more."

"I'm just so sorry, Laura," she whispered, her voice cracking, and when I looked up, she had tears in her eyes.

"You were close, weren't you?" I asked, resisting the urge to hug her. "I forgot how close you seemed to Emily."

"Oh, we hardly knew each other," she said, waving me off. But that wasn't exactly true. Megan and Emily had bonded, thrown together as the newbies of the group, and growing closer as time went on. They'd sat next to each other on the plane, giggling the whole way. "All that talk about secrets…" she whispered. "Whoever's secret she knew, at least it's theirs to keep now."

I looked up at her, her tear-filled eyes locked on me with a knowing stare. "What do you mean?"

"Nick said that you mentioned you thought she may have been dangerous because she knew someone's secret… I just thought, well, whoever's secret it was, it went with her…didn't it? In a way, maybe Brad did us all a favor."

I winced, surprised by her harsh words. "I wouldn't say that. She was a person. She didn't deserve to die over a secret…"

Megan adjusted in her seat. "Of course not. I'm sorry. I didn't mean it to come out the way it did." She glanced back out the window, and a memory rushed back to me.

"Hey," I said quickly. "Did…she say anything to you at the spa? After we went to get drinks, you talked to her after, didn't you?" Yes, it was coming back to me then. I'd returned to the room without drinks, leaving Emily to calm down after we'd talked. When Megan asked where our drinks were, I realized I'd completely forgotten them.

Instead of going back, Megan said I looked like I was upset. She offered to go for me, and because I *was* upset, I sat down next to Natasha, trying to pretend everything was fine.

When Emily and Megan returned with our drinks awhile later, I'd mustered my best *everything's-fine* smile, pretending my life wasn't unraveling at the seams.

"I just went to get the drinks," Megan said. "I could tell you were upset."

"But you were gone a really long time…" Wasn't she? Or had I imagined it? I was so upset and distracted, I hadn't paid any attention. But there was something Natasha had said that meant nothing to me then, but was striking a chord now.

*"Either it's my birthday and y'all are planning a surprise party or I stink, 'cause I just can't seem to keep anyone in here with me,"* she'd said when Megan walked from the room that day.

I looked up at Megan, remembering her words. I'd been so distracted, why hadn't I asked more questions?

"You went to the bathroom when Emily and I had gone outside… I remember hearing the door shut." The memory was there, completely overshadowed by what Emily was telling me, but there nonetheless. And Natasha had confirmed it, though I'd only been half listening when I'd returned.

"Yeah, I went to the bathroom. Why does that matter?"

"Because when we were talking to Andy, you said she seemed fine, but that wasn't true. You were gone with Emily right after I'd left her upset. She couldn't have been fine. Were you just protecting her or…" I shook my head, trying to understand. "I didn't think anything of it because I was so upset, except…you were gone for twice as long as I was. Why did you go out there?" I met her eyes, the challenge there. "You overheard what we were talking about. That was the door I heard, wasn't it? You knew Emily's secret all along, same as me, even though you pretended not to, didn't you?"

She looked as though she were going to deny it at first, but eventually, the indignant look faded from her face. "I couldn't let her do it, Laura. I couldn't let her tell anyone. And I can't let you tell anyone now."

# CHAPTER FORTY-THREE

## MEGAN

**FOUR DAYS EARLIER**

"I'm going to run to the restroom while they're getting our drinks, okay?" I removed the cucumbers from my eyes as I sat up. Alcohol had always run straight through me.

"Okay, sure," Natasha said, waving a casual hand at me as I stood up and hobbled across the room, my feet still wet.

I walked out into the hallway and toward the bathrooms near the exterior doors. I glanced into the dining room as I passed it, surprised to see that Laura and Emily weren't there. *Strange.*

When I neared the door, I heard their voices. Hushed. Whispered. But unmistakably theirs. I stopped in front of the bathroom door, knowing I shouldn't eavesdrop, but unable to deny my curiosity.

*"No."* Laura was speaking. She sounded distressed. "No, Emily. You can't say anything. Not to anyone." I'd definitely stumbled onto a private conversation. I should've walked away, but I couldn't. Not yet.

"I just want to know my parents, Laura. My real parents. I

don't need an explanation. I hold no grudges." It was Emily now. What was she talking about?

"Emily, listen to me, I need to break this news to Brad myself. When you were put up for adoption..." *What?* She paused, and I put a hand on the bathroom door, hoping if they opened it, I could pretend I'd been going inside. "It was the hardest thing I've ever had to do. Can you just give me some time to process everything?" I couldn't believe what I was hearing... Had Brad and Laura really given up a baby for adoption? Then, Laura asked, "You haven't told anyone, have you?" Why did she sound so panicked?

"No. I wanted to tell you first. You were the easiest to approach. You've been so nice to me."

I heard one of them sob, and I put a hand over my mouth. Was this truly happening? *Emily is Laura's child?* "I can't believe it's you."

Emily spoke again. "I've dreamed about you my whole life. I want to know so much."

With that, I pushed open the bathroom door and disappeared inside, my bladder screaming for relief. I couldn't believe it. Couldn't believe it had happened, couldn't believe I'd overheard it. Why had they given her up for adoption? They had such adorable little girls. *No wonder Emily had seemed so obsessed with Brad.* It was all starting to make sense then. I'd thought she'd had a crush on him, but in reality he was her father. *What in the world?*

My eyes bugged out as I processed all I'd learned. But why had Laura seemed so upset? Not happy...not merely shocked, but genuinely upset. When I was done using the restroom, I washed my hands and made my way back into the spa. Laura and Emily still hadn't returned.

I tried to act calmer than I felt, but when Laura returned, she was alone. I bit down my smile, looking away. *Please tell us before I burst.*

Why was she alone? Where was Emily?

After a moment's silence, I asked about the drinks, and when I realized something was very wrong, I offered to go get them. In truth, I wanted to find Emily. Of all the girls, she was the one I felt closest to. If anyone could explain what was going on, it was her.

I walked out the door, leaving Laura and Natasha behind, and made my way outside. When I found Emily, she was kneeling down in the sand, her face pressed into her hands.

"Come here," I said, putting my hands around the poor girl. "What's going on?" I pretended not to have overheard anything.

"It's nothing," she said, though she couldn't even pretend to hope I'd believe her.

"Did something happen?"

She sighed, standing up. "I'm an idiot. I made a mistake."

"What are you talking about? You aren't an idiot. Come on, tell me what's going on."

She shook her head. "I shouldn't talk about it. I need to… there are others involved who I should tell first. I'm sorry. It's complicated."

"Is it about Laura?" I asked, and she pulled her hands from her face to look at me finally. When she didn't speak right away, I went on. "I overheard you talking."

"You did?"

"I swear I won't tell a soul." I wrapped my arms around her neck, pulling her in for a hug.

"I just thought she'd be happy to see me. To meet me. I'm so embarrassed. I never thought it would go like that. I've been rehearsing what to say for years, and I never thought I'd find one of my parents, let alone both."

"Don't be embarrassed. I'm sure she's happy to see you, sweetheart. It's just a lot to process. There are a lot of really intense emotions for you both right now. You have to give her some space, okay?"

"But why? Shouldn't she be happy? I'm not asking for anything. I just want to talk to her. To know her. To know where I came from."

"I know," I said, rubbing her back and whispering in her ear. "Just give her time, okay?"

"Maybe I should just talk to Brad. If I tell him everything, maybe he can get her to agree. Maybe he'll be excited. From all Andy's said, he's such a good dad."

I rubbed her back. "Brad and Laura are both excellent parents, but you know, this is such a sensitive thing." I paused, preparing to tell her something I'd sworn to always keep to myself. "One of my closest friends gave their baby up for adoption in college. I'm sure it still weighs on Laura and Brad as much as it does N— *Nicole.*" I started to say his name but changed my mind. I'd promised Nick I'd never reveal his secret, but Emily needed to hear this.

"Really?"

When she pulled away, I nodded, but something in my chest tightened as I stared at her. I'd never noticed the familiar way her skin crinkled between her brows. Or the fact that her eyes were such a soft cognac shade of brown. Almost identical to eyes I'd spent so much time looking into. *No.* I was seeing things. Imagining them. It wasn't possible.

Nick's baby hadn't been Laura's.

They hadn't had a child together.

But what were the odds?

"How old are you, Emily? When were you born?"

"June thirteenth, nineteen ninety-seven," she recited, staring at me strangely. "Why?"

I did some quick mental math, trying to keep my expression still. *No.* "You've had so long to wonder about your parents, and I'm sure they've done the same." In fact, I knew at least one had. "So, maybe just do what Laura has asked and give her some time. Maybe telling Brad is a bad idea. She knows him best, after all." If she told Brad, he'd tell her the truth. That he wasn't her father. If that came out, there was too great a chance that he'd leave Laura. If that happened, could I be sure Nick would stay with me? Especially at the reappearance of their daughter? My hands were shaking, and I shoved them into the pockets of my robe.

"Don't you think he wants to know about me?" I looked behind me, panic settling in as I tried to figure out what to say. No matter what, I couldn't let her tell Brad.

"I'm positive he does. Positive. But why don't we give Laura a bit of time to decide how to proceed, okay? Tell you what, do you want to talk about this later? When we can have a little more privacy? You can vent all you'd like." I looked over my shoulder. "Right now, there's too much of a chance someone will overhear. We can talk more after dinner. What do you say? The girls are going to be wondering why we haven't come back and, for right now, I think the best thing is for you to abide by Laura's wishes and keep her secret." I put an arm around her, forcing a smile. "We're going to get this all worked out, okay?"

"You really think so?" Emily asked.

"I know so. We just have to do it the right way."

Emily smiled then, an eerily familiar smile that had bile rising in my throat. "Thanks, Megan. I really appreciate you."

"Don't mention it," I said. *Please, don't.*

---

THAT NIGHT, I lay awake, worrying about Emily. Where was she? What had she told Andy? Why hadn't she stuck to the plan to meet me after dinner instead of bailing in the middle of the meal? My thoughts were interrupted by a noise at the window.

*Tick, tick, tick.*

I stood up, wondering if it was her, but was shocked to see

Laura standing outside the window. I jumped back in the darkness as Nick began to rouse from sleep.

I moved quickly. What was she doing? Did she know I knew? Did she know I'd seen her?

Without thinking, I hopped back into bed. I didn't want to face her. I couldn't. I threw the covers over me and closed my eyes just as Nick sat up, looking around the room. He stood up as the noise came again.

*Tick, tick, tick.*

She was throwing either sand or rocks at the window. I couldn't be sure which. Within a few moments, he'd pulled his pants on and walked out the door. I could hear them whispering, but I couldn't make out what they were saying. Was she going to tell him? My heart plummeted at the thought.

As their voices grew fainter, the pounding of my heart drowning them out, I opened my eyes. They were no longer in the doorway. I looked to the window, watching them walk out across the sand. Away from the hut.

I slipped out of bed again, making my way out the door and down the stairs cautiously. I didn't want him to see me. If Laura was going to tell him, I wanted to hear what he thought. I wanted to know what he would tell her. Was he going to choose me? Or would he say one thing to her and another to me? My heart breaking was worth the risk to know the truth.

I followed them as they made their way toward a clump of palm trees, hiding behind one myself as they finally stopped. I breathed heavily, holding my skirt back as the wind picked up. *Please don't see me.* If they caught me, there'd be no denying what I was doing. I put a hand on my chest, willing myself to hear their quiet voices as they began to speak.

"It's about Emily." Oh, God. So I was right. She was going to tell him.

"What about her?" Nick asked.

"Something's...*off* about her. Have you noticed? I'm worried she's up to something." I sucked in a breath, listening carefully. What was she doing? This wasn't how I expected the conversation to go.

"What do you mean?" he asked.

"I just...I don't think she invited us here for the reasons she said she did." I put a hand over my lips as I felt a drop of rain hit my scalp. If it started to rain, they'd make a run for it and find me here. Listening.

"What reason could there be?" he asked. *Please don't tell him the reason. Please.*

"I don't... I don't know. I just have a strange feeling about her. I don't think we can trust her." What was she doing? Out of the corner of my eye, I caught a movement down by the water. *Emily.* Off in the distance. She couldn't see us, wasn't looking our way, but if she looked up and saw Laura, I knew she wouldn't heed my advice to give her space. And if Nick was there, would he put it all together? I had to stop her. But how?

"Is this about her and Brad?"

I peeked around the tree, looking to where Laura and Nick stood, completely lost in each other. The way he was staring at her caused my chest to tighten. There was no denying he'd choose her if ever given the chance. "What about her and Brad?"

"What did Brad say when you told him?" *Told him what?* Had she already told Nick about Emily?

"I haven't told him... I wanted to talk to you first." She looked down, and my heart sank. I felt tears prick my eyes.

"Why me?"

"You're my best friend, Nick..." She reached for his arm, and he didn't shy away. To the left, Emily was getting closer. I heard another noise to my right, and looked up. Brad was creeping around the back of the huts. I froze, remaining completely still. If he saw me, it was game over. "And you never act like I'm crazy for telling you things that might be crazy," I heard Laura say. To my great relief, Brad continued walking, darting from my hut to a tree, and then another. He didn't step foot inside the close cluster of trees, choosing to dart around the outside. He couldn't hear what was being said yet, but he was determined to try.

"It's not crazy," Nick said. "I just—I'm not quite sure what you're talking about. Do you think she's dangerous? Or do you think she's not serious about Andy?"

"I don't—" The wind picked up, and I looked back at them. I couldn't stay much longer. Emily was getting too close, the wind whipping her hair in every direction. How had they not noticed her? Laura laid her head on Nick's chest and he wrapped his arms around her, and I had my answer. They would never notice anyone when they were with each other. They were lost in a world entirely their own.

Eventually, the wind died down, and she stepped back, but not before my vision had blurred with tears. I'd lost sight of Brad, but Emily was drawing nearer. "It's probably nothing," Laura said finally. "I shouldn't have woken you up." I pushed away from the tree, darting away from the trees and behind the huts where Brad had just left from, and rushed as fast as I could in the sand until I reached the last one. I closed my eyes, taking a deep breath and moving forward, praying no one would see me. I glanced over at the clump of trees once, but from where I was, I couldn't see them. They were camouflaged, hidden away from the world like they'd hidden the truth from all of us.

Every one of us was bound to be hurt by their lies—Brad, Emily, me.

"Emily!" I called quietly as I made my way toward the water. She looked back, surprised to see me.

"What are you doing?" she asked, stumbling as she tried to turn around.

"Keep your voice down," I whispered as the wind whipped again. I waved her over toward me, and when I could reach her arm, I took hold of it. "Come this way so we don't wake anyone up."

"I'm sorry about dinner," she said. "I was just upset. I should've never told Laura. Not like I did. I don't want anyone to know anymore. It was stupid. I don't need them." She was drunk, a wine bottle in her hand, her words slurred and too loud.

Relief flooded me as she said it. "Oh, sweetheart, it wasn't stupid. And you don't have to apologize. I understand why you did it."

"I just think, you know, if they didn't want to be around me... If they didn't want me in their lives, maybe I don't want to be in theirs."

"That's really brave of you." It would break Andy's heart, but it would save so many others. With Emily gone, Laura could keep the secret to herself. Nick would never have to know. I fiddled with the ring on my finger.

"So you think it's the right decision, then?" She swayed in place.

"I do," I confirmed, patting her arm.

"It's just," Emily went on. "Well, I think Brad should have the right to make that decision, right? I mean, he should be able to tell me if he wants to know me or not. Laura doesn't? Fine. But she can't speak for Brad." She was rambling then, through sudden, loud sobs. "But he is his own person. She doesn't control him. For all I know, he's like your friend. Maybe he's always wondered about me. Maybe he didn't even want to give me up. I'll bet she made him." She poked at her chest, her voice raising. *"Well, here I am, Brad—"* I launched forward, putting a hand over her lips.

"Shhh, you're being too loud."

*"Get your hands off me!"* she screamed, pulling my hand away from her.

"Emily, it's the middle of the night. You're just tired. You're drunk. You need to sleep, to think this through." I needed to think it through. Make a plan. Decide the best course of action. "You'll have more clarity in the morning."

"I don't want clarity," she sobbed. "I want a dad. I wanted this to go differently. I wanted them to want me."

I shook my head, glancing over my shoulder. She was too loud. Much too loud. Soon, Nick and Laura and Brad would come to investigate, and then the truth would be out. It would be too late.

"You just have to calm down," I said, grabbing her shoulders as she started to sob louder. "Please, Emily. They're going to hear you."

"Let them hear me!" she screamed as the wind whipped through her hair again, her arms out wide at her sides, raindrops falling quick and heavy. "So what if they do? Maybe that's what should happen, you know?"

"No, no. I don't think it should."

"What do you know, anyway?" she cried, shoving back against me. "I'm going to tell him. I'm going to wake him up and tell him, and then if he doesn't want to be in my life, I'm going to get Manu to take me back home. You all can stay on this stupid island if you want, but I hate—" She froze. "Brad!" She jumped up, waving her arms, and when I looked down the coast, I could see Brad walking up near the huts again. We were hidden in the shadow of a clump of trees separating our huts from the empty ones, but if he got much closer, I knew he would hear her. *"Brad!"*

*"Shut up!"* I cried, slapping my hand over her mouth and shoving her down without thought. I pushed her under the water, watching the wine bottle fall from her grasp as she went under. I was on top of her, panic filling me. I knew what I was doing, but I wasn't actively aware. It was just what I had to do. It felt like survival-mode, and the only way for me to survive was to stop her screams. She fought back, pushing herself up, but I

pushed back down. I heard her gasp for breath as she resurfaced momentarily, felt her shaking under my arms as I pushed her out farther, down deeper. She fought for so long—I'd always imagined it would be much quicker, much less strenuous, but it wasn't. It took every ounce of my strength to keep fighting, to keep her held down, to keep myself above the crashing waves as rain poured down around me.

When she finally quit fighting, quit struggling, quit living, I let go of her body as if it were on fire. My forearms burned, my body shook. I looked at my hands as if I expected them to bear proof of what I had done. The life I had taken. In my palm was a golden bracelet with a small heart charm. It must've slipped off her wrist in the struggle. For some reason, that bracelet broke me more than anything. What had I done?

Her body floated up, and I pushed it away, crying and shaking as realization overwhelmed me. Was this worse than her truth? What if her truth came out anyway? What had I done?

The body floated back to me, and I turned around, rushing away and back toward the sand. By the time I made it back to the hut, my legs were covered in sand up to my knees. I rushed inside, relieved that Nick hadn't returned. I didn't have the strength to worry about what that meant. I hurried upstairs and pulled off my wet clothes, my entire body trembling beyond my control. I threw them in a bag with the bracelet and carried them back downstairs, my bare body exposed in the moonlight from the windows as I tossed the bag into my suitcase. I'd have it washed tomorrow with the dirty clothes. I pulled on dry clothes and ran a brush through my hair. It was wet on the ends, so I tied it back into a bun. Would Nick notice? I didn't have time to worry about it. I moved toward the door, squeezing my hands in front of my chest as I willed them to stop shaking.

When I glanced out the door, I saw Nick headed up the walk. He'd seen me. He must've. I sucked in a breath, darting toward the bed. My chest rose and fell wildly, and I squeezed my eyes shut despite the tears.

I was sure I'd been caught. I would've bet anything he caught a glimpse of me at the door, but to my relief, he walked inside and climbed in bed without a word. I cried in silence, my back to him, until I heard the undeniable screams through the storm outside.

*They've found her.*

# CHAPTER FORTY-FOUR

## LAURA

**PRESENT DAY**

"Don't you see? I did what I had to do to protect you. To protect all of us," Megan said, her eyes wild with fear. I backed away from her, taking careful steps. I couldn't believe it.

"She was…just a child," I whispered, shaking my head in horror. "You were protecting yourself."

"Maybe," Megan said, her lips thin as she pressed them together. "But I was also protecting Brad. Your children."

*"My children's father was just arrested for a murder you committed!"* I cried.

"I didn't want that. I wanted them to think she'd drowned. She'd been drinking. It was plausible. But you and Andy wouldn't stop pushing, stop digging. If you'd stopped asking questions, no one would've been arrested," she reasoned.

"You killed her so Nick wouldn't leave you, but now you've just pushed us closer together. How did you plan to keep us apart once Brad was in jail? Because if you didn't, Emily died for nothing at all!" I put a hand to my stomach, sure I was going to get sick. My knees began to tremble under my weight.

"Nick will never be with you. I don't want to hurt you, Laura. I'm going to tell Nick after this that we need to leave. He shouldn't allow himself to be hurt by you anymore. Not after this."

I shook my head furiously, the idea of losing Nick causing me to grab hold of the bed to keep myself standing. "Nick will never go for that."

"He won't have a choice," she said firmly, crossing her arms. "Either we leave, you drop all contact with him and we all live out the rest of our lives safely and peacefully, or..." She glanced behind her. "Well, now that I've gotten the hang of this *shutting someone up for good* thing, I guess I could probably figure out how to do it again."

"You're *threatening* me?" I demanded, stepping backward. I looked to my left, then right, searching for a weapon. We were so incredibly alone.

"I don't want that. I don't want to hurt you, Laura. Honestly, I don't. I never meant for this to happen. I didn't want anyone to get in trouble. I just wanted Emily to keep the secret to herself. That was it. I didn't mean for Brad to get arrested. I only planted the bracelet because you kept pushing for answers. You wanted someone to pin your guilt on for what you'd done to Emily—the way you'd treated her. I gave you that. You told me the police were coming. You said they'd search the huts for proof, and I had the proof they needed. I helped you!"

"No, Megan, you didn't. I didn't want your help. I wanted the guilty person to go to prison. Brad's innocent," I said, shaking my head. "I can't let you do this."

"Do you have any idea how hard it was to sneak away and plant that bracelet? Do you have any idea how much it hurts that no matter how good I was to Nick, deep down I knew he'd still choose you? Do you know how much it must've broken your husband's heart to know you were with Nick that night? The way he was looking at you...it must've destroyed Brad. And don't even get me started on Nick. Do you know how much you've hurt him? So many times, over and over. You just hurt people, Laura. It's what you do. You're the guilty one. You're the one who deserves to pay for your crimes. We're all victims of your crimes!"

I shook my head, the sting of her words undeniable. "No. No. I didn't do this. I'm not perfect, but I didn't do *this.* You have to tell the police the truth."

"I can't," she said, taking a step toward me. She was still trying to reason with me, but there was an assertiveness now that hadn't been there before. I imagined this was how Emily had seen her. My daughter's last sight on Earth.

I thought then of how selfish I'd been. How right Megan was. How my secret had caused so much devastation. I wouldn't let Brad go down for something I'd caused. I wouldn't let anyone else suffer for my selfishness.

"Megan, you have to tell the cops. You can't let this go on—"

"I didn't mean to do it—"

*"But you did it!"*

"Because of you!" she screamed, taking another aggressive step toward me. "Because of your lies and because you couldn't just be happy with one amazing man. You had to lead them both on. Do you have any idea how much Nick loves you? How much damage you've done to him? I'm the only one trying to fix it—"

"That's not true—"

"You have no idea what is or isn't true. You've only managed to bring him pain for years, and he puts on a brave face and pretends it's all fine in order to protect you, but who's protecting him? If you truly cared about him, you wouldn't do this. I'm all he has."

"That's not true. He has me. He's always had me. He had a daughter, but you killed her—"

"After you took her away. He was going to propose to you, and you asked to put her up for adoption—"

Tears blurred my vision. "That's not true. We weren't ready for a child! He agreed!"

"He didn't. He never has. He never told me it was you, but he told me how much giving that baby up broke his heart. He told me how much he wanted to marry its mother."

I shook my head. It wasn't true. It couldn't be.

"He's always gone with whatever you said because he loves you blindly, and you've been so selfish you never saw it."

I moved to shove past her, trying to dart out of the room, but she grabbed hold of my hair, jerking me backward. I threw a hand to my scalp as I fell to the ground, my head connecting with the floor with a loud *THWACK*. "Let me go!"

She slapped a hand over my mouth, just as she had Emily's, and I saw her eyes go dark as her hand slid up to cover my nose, too. She was going to kill me.

I fought back with all my strength, an even match for her as we struggled. I inhaled, my lungs screaming for air, but her hand blocked all chance of getting any. I twisted, freeing myself from her grasp and moved to crawl away. She grabbed hold of me again, sitting on my back as her hands wrapped around my neck. She planted them firmly over my nose and mouth again, pulling back. I heard my neck pop, and I froze. Was this how it ended?

"I don't want to do this," she whispered. "Please don't make me." Pleading. "It wasn't supposed to go this way. I don't want to hurt you."

I wiggled, but she pulled back further. "You need to listen to me. You're giving me no choice," she warned.

I was trying, but the edges of my vision were growing dark and fuzzy. I tasted the salt of her skin. I felt my head growing heavy as I heard the door behind us closing. No. *Opening.*

A commotion.

Footsteps.

Oxygen.

Breathe.

*Breathe.*

"Let her go."

The hand was off my lips. I gasped for air, my hands at my throat as I sucked in a breath and spun around, scooting away from my assailant with wild eyes.

Natasha was there. And Nick. Andy. Jaren. Manu. The police. An officer was pulling Megan backward. The sound in the room seemed to fade. Screaming. Crying. Breathing. So many people. I fought for air, so amazed at how easily it came, yet my head was still fuzzy.

I lay back against the wall, trying to breathe. Trying to understand.

"You're okay," Nick whispered, moving past Megan and toward me. An officer was on my other side, but I didn't remember him approaching me.

"Get the doctor," Manu called behind him. I couldn't see to whom.

Natasha kneeled down beside me, her eyes full of tears. "Just breathe. We're here."

*Just breathe.*

I nodded.

I could do that.

I could breathe.

# CHAPTER FORTY-FIVE

## LAURA

**ONE WEEK LATER**

It was just Nick, Andy, and me. Walking alone along the shore. There was so much weight between us. So much we should've been saying. Instead, we moved in silence.

In the week since we returned from the island, Brad was released from police custody and Megan had been charged. From the hut next door, Natasha had heard the screams, gotten the police's attention, and ultimately, saved my life.

Once in jail, Megan had revealed to them, as she had to me, how everything had gone so wrong. Her trial was still months away, but I didn't see how she'd manage to get away with any of it.

Brad and I had agreed to separate. He could forgive me for cheating, for lying about so much, but he said he could never forgive me for believing he was capable of murder. For allowing him to be arrested.

I couldn't say that I blamed him.

Still to this day, I wondered...did I really believe it? Or was it convenient for me? Was it easier for me to hope he had done such an awful thing than to consider coming clean, disrupting my life, and admitting what I never had to anyone, myself included? That I was, and always had been, in love with Nick.

Megan had been wrong about so much, but she'd pointed out something so crucial. I had let my selfishness hurt the people I cared about. The secrets I'd asked Natasha to keep, the pain I'd caused my husband, the rift in our relationship that had hurt my daughters, the pain of abandonment I'd caused Emily when she'd come to me looking for acceptance. For love. I'd been a selfish person, as we all are from time to time, but my selfishness came at the expense of so much. It was a flaw I was now completely aware of.

One I was working to change.

One I *would* change.

Brad was keeping the girls for the week while the three of us had flown down to Florida to say goodbye. The ocean made us feel closer to Emily.

To my daughter.

As her only living relatives, Nick and I were able to claim her ashes and, though we didn't know her that well, I had to believe she'd want her final resting place to be at sea. Her life had been spent traveling, her love had been soaking up the world. Andy said she'd always wanted to retire somewhere warm.

We stopped at the water's edge of our private beach access, all dressed in black. Against the bright and sunny backdrop, I'd guess we looked out of place. Something told me none of us would ever see the ocean as a happy place again.

I twisted the lid off the urn, pausing. I would've given anything to go back. To make a different decision. Any different decision along the path of horrible decisions I'd made. But I couldn't. I could only go forward. Only make better choices from there. I turned the urn over, watching as some of the ashes began to fall away, dancing on the wind and carrying her out to sea. "Goodbye, Emily."

I stopped, passing the urn to Nick, who did the same. "Goodbye," he whispered before passing it to Andy.

Andy wore dark sunglasses to hide the tears that had been falling. He held on to the urn tightly, unable to turn it over as he continued to cry. We stood in silence. I would've stood there for a week if that was what it took. Andy had to be the final one to say goodbye, Nick and I had agreed on that.

After a while, he scooped his hand in the urn, pulling out the last handful and holding his fist in the air. I watched the last of her ashes blow into the air and then out over the vast blue.

"She would've liked this," Andy said, sniffling. "All of this."

"Yeah, she would've. She would've been glad you could come."

Nick nodded, patting him on the back gently.

When we got home and every bit of truth had come out, Andy asked me if Emily really cared about him or if she'd been using him. I'd told him how much she cared about him. How much she hoped Nick and I would be okay with their relationship continuing. It brought him peace I could never give him in any other way and, because of that, it was the one secret I was content to keep the rest of my life. But as for the others, I was done. Over the past week, I'd revealed every secret I'd kept from anyone.

I told Brad the truth about everything. Told the girls about their sister. Told Nick that I loved him. That I was in love with him.

I had no idea what the future held. I was taking it a day at a time, but what I did know was that it would be filled with honesty.

Selflessness.

Friendships.

Appreciation.

I would take my life one beautiful day, one amazing second, at a time.

I would breathe each breath like it was my last. As we turned to walk away, Nick wrapped an arm around my waist, pulling me close.

When I'd told him I loved him, he'd said it back. Without a moment's hesitation. As if he'd been waiting to say it his whole life. That was when I knew Megan had been right about Nick's feelings, too.

With him by my side, I felt peace like I'd never known. It wouldn't be perfect. We hadn't even defined what *it* was yet. I was still married. We still had so much to figure out, but the one thing I knew—the one thing we'd agreed on was this: we would take each day as it came, each breath as we were given.

Unlike our daughter, we could still breathe. We could still feel pain and loss and love.

We'd been lucky in that way. Lucky enough to suffer. Lucky enough to live.

And, no matter what life threw at us, we'd never take it for granted again.

# CHAPTER FORTY-SIX

**TELL US ABOUT YOUR EXPERIENCE:**

*ISLA DEL AMOR* changed our lives last summer. It gave us perspective where we desperately needed it. The owner, Manu, took amazing care of us, going above and beyond despite a few troublesome situations during our stay. We'd especially like to thank him for naming the spa after our late daughter, in her loving memory. When you go, be sure to visit *Emily's Isle,* and know you'll be taken great care of. We were. Thank you for everything, Manu.

*-Nick and Laura London, ISLA DEL AMOR guests*

## DON'T MISS THE NEXT PSYCHOLOGICAL THRILLER FROM KIERSTEN MODGLIN!

It was the perfect plan...
until everything went wrong.

Read *The Arrangement* today:
mybook.to/arrangement

# ENJOYED THE PERFECT GETAWAY?

If you enjoyed this story, please consider leaving me a quick review. It doesn't have to be long—just a few words will do. Who knows? Your review might be the thing that encourages a future reader to take a chance on my work!
To leave a review, please visit:
mybook.to/theperfectgetaway

Let everyone know how much you loved
*The Perfect Getaway* on Goodreads:
https://bit.ly/3mNfmr5

# DON'T MISS THE NEXT KIERSTEN MODGLIN RELEASE!

Thank you so much for reading this story. I'd love to invite you to sign up for my mailing list and text alerts so we can be sure you don't miss my next release.

Sign up for my mailing list here:
http://eepurl.com/dhiRRv
Sign up for my text alerts here:
www.kierstenmodglinauthor.com/textalerts.html

# ACKNOWLEDGMENTS

As always, I could fill an *island* with the gratitude I have for everyone who helped to make this book a reality.

First and foremost, to my amazing husband and beautiful little girl, thank you for being my biggest cheerleaders every step of the way. This journey would be a lot less fun without being able to celebrate each success with you.

To my beta reader, Emerald O'Brien, thank you for being the first set of eyes on this story. Thank you for helping me fine-tune what worked and clean up what didn't. Special thanks for loving our favorite character as much as I do. ;)

To my immensely talented editor, Sarah West, thank you for your ability to find the story through the fog. I am so grateful for your insights and ideas.

To the proofreading team at My Brother's Editor, thank you for your eagle eyes and for never failing to add value to my stories. I'm forever thankful to work with you.

To my loyal readers—thank you to each and every one of you who take the time to review my books, help spread the word, send me emails, contact me via Facebook, Instagram, or my website, and cheer me on from wherever you are—on the days when I doubt whether I'm good enough to do this, it's your words of encouragement that keep me going. I could **never** do this without you. My success is your success—we have built this together. I am so grateful and humbled to have you reading my stories.

To Joy Westerfield, Sarah DeLong, and Shelly Reynolds,

thank you for your constant support of my books. I could never say thank you enough for all that you do to help get new eyes on my stories. Please just know that I see you and I'll never forget it.

Last but certainly not least, to you—the person reading this book. Thank you for supporting this crazy dreamer. Thank you for supporting literature. Thank you for being a reader. Whether this is your first Kiersten Modglin novel or your twenty-second, I hope that it kept you guessing and entertained every step of the way.

# ABOUT THE AUTHOR

KIERSTEN MODGLIN is an Amazon Top 10 bestselling author of psychological thrillers and a member of International Thriller Writers, Novelists, Inc., and the Alliance of Independent Authors. Kiersten is a KDP Select All-Star and a recipient of *ThrillerFix*'s Best Psychological Thriller Award and *Suspense Magazine*'s Best Book of 2021 Award. She grew up in rural western Kentucky and later relocated to Nashville, Tennessee, where she now lives with her husband, daughter, and their two Boston terriers: Cedric and Georgie. Kiersten's work is currently being translated into multiple languages and readers across the world refer to her as 'The Queen of Twists.' A Netflix addict, Shonda Rhimes superfan, psychology fanatic, and *indoor* enthusiast, Kiersten enjoys rainy days spent with her nose in a book.

Sign up for Kiersten's newsletter here:
kierstenmodglinauthor.com/nlsignup

Sign up for text alerts from Kiersten here:
kierstenmodglinauthor.com/textalerts

kierstenmodglinauthor.com
www.facebook.com/kierstenmodglinauthor
www.facebook.com/groups/kmodsquad
www.twitter.com/kmodglinauthor
www.instagram.com/kierstenmodglinauthor
www.tiktok.com/@kierstenmodglinauthor
www.goodreads.com/kierstenmodglinauthor
www.bookbub.com/authors/kiersten-modglin
www.amazon.com/author/kierstenmodglin

# ALSO BY KIERSTEN MODGLIN

## STANDALONE NOVELS

Becoming Mrs. Abbott

The List

The Missing Piece

Playing Jenna

The Beginning After

The Better Choice

The Good Neighbors

The Lucky Ones

I Said Yes

The Mother-in-Law

The Dream Job

The Liar's Wife

My Husband's Secret

The Roommate

The Missing

Just Married

Our Little Secret

Widow Falls

Missing Daughter

The Reunion

Tell Me the Truth

The Dinner Guests

## ARRANGEMENT NOVELS

The Arrangement (Book 1)

The Amendment (Book 2)

The Atonement (Book 3)

**THE MESSES SERIES**

The Cleaner (The Messes, #1)

The Healer (The Messes, #2)

The Liar (The Messes, #3)

The Prisoner (The Messes, #4)

**NOVELLAS**

The Long Route: A Lover's Landing Novella

The Stranger in the Woods: A Crimson Falls Novella

**THE LOCKE INDUSTRIES SERIES**

The Nanny's Secret

www.ingramcontent.com/pod-product-compliance
Lightning Source LLC
Chambersburg PA
CBHW030607310726
48979CB00003B/602

* 9 7 8 1 9 5 6 5 3 8 0 8 3 *